LEAF'D

LEAF'D

Joseph Charles Sisk

To order additional copies of this book, contact:
Xlibris
1-888-795-4274
www.Xlibris.com
Orders@Xlibris.com
801872

Contents

In loving memory of Madge Bean,

the first beta reader and editor of the Chronicles of the Vanquished trilogy,

and

to my best friend, Allon;

love you, my best pal and confidant always.

Also by Joseph Charles Sisk

Chronicles of the Vanquished Book I
The Crystal of Light

Chronicles of the Vanquished Book II
The Tablet of Dreams

Chronicles of the Vanquished Book III
The Gold of Youth

ACKNOWLEDGMENTS

I'D LIKE TO thank all who made this novel possible: Xlibris for their fantastic support and publication, and my readers–you are amazing.

–Joseph Charles Sisk

INTRODUCTION

WITH ALMOST EVERY writer, there is a dream of publication. For me, this was no different. I chose a rewarding yet challenging endeavor. Even though I am physically handicapped, I have a mind and the willpower to succeed in almost everything I set out to do.

At the first start of my publishing journey, I was unsure where to start. For the Chronicles of the Vanquished trilogy, I knew I wanted to publish. I have been fortunate enough to have the honor of working with the talented people at Xlibris, who make my dreams of writing a reality.

As a child, there was some inkling inside me that told me I should be a writer. My life's ambition was—and still is to this day—to be a writer and later become an author. I have accomplished this and more.

There is always one person in life who helps you succeed along your way—one who believes in all you set out to accomplish. For me, that was my grandmother. She was my rock and strength. If I were having a terrible day, she would help me work through it. I am forever grateful for my family, also, who help me with moral support and mold me as the person I am today.

    Leaf'd is my fourth novel. While I am excited to be finally releasing something after the Chronicles of the Vanquished trilogy. I am nervous to see how it the public receives it. I hope my readers find *Leaf'd* surprising as it describes the heroism of friendship, and finally of triumph as the final page is turned.

LEAF'D

PROLOGUE

THE POSITION OF leaf'd prince was a noble one for any prince willing to face the dangers that came with the profession. It was not for those princes who were faint-hearted. (The threats included foreign foes who deemed to have their way with the Irish people.) At birth, a prince needed to have magic born into him. In his latter years as a teenager, he needed to have been taught to be a noble leader by elders who were gracious elects in their time. As an active and gentle leader, a prince needed to be on the lookout for those who desired to challenge him. He therefore had to defend his beliefs no matter what—even if it meant laying down his life for them. To become a noble leader (or the leaf'd prince, as some Ireland natives remember), one needed to compete in a tournament to prove his loyalty and bravery among the Irish people.

And so princes across the land would rouse their horses from their sleep and venture off in search for an empty field in which to practice their skills, alongside their opponent, each hoping he had what it took to become the leaf'd prince.

The Three-Leaf'd Tournament was greatly prized, and it was this very tournament that made every Ireland native come out and cheer for his or her favorite participant. It had three leaves (more commonly known as rounds) for the potential applicants to get through: the first, a physical round; the second, a mental round; and the third, an endurance round. Each leaf of the tournament was harder than the last, and each one challenged a contestant to be better than his opponent.

For the physical round, a prince had to test his physical strength by combating a two-headed dragon (preferably Irish) with magic. A sword made of steel and encrusted with red rubies would appear on behalf of a prince's magic to aid him. He was given a choice to either kill the beast or injure it, but he had to choose quickly and wisely, as its fiery breath would harm him.

A prince also had to joust a potential opponent, either on a horse of his own (provided by the tournament caretaker) or on foot. The tournament caretaker, a king and queen's squire who was short in stature but had a loud, commanding voice, would start the tournament with a whistle.

The contender would be on horseback, riding like the wind, as his opponent would do the same. Moments would pass, and as soon as their jousting lances would touch, and roars and cheers from the bleachers would ring out across the arena.

Clanks of jousting poles would ring out, silencing the roars and cheers from the bleachers. The second clank of jousting poles and an opponent would be lying–somewhat lifeless and disoriented–on the grass of the arena. It would not keep his opponent down, however. He would get up stronger than ever, ready to fight back with equal strength.

When at last the jousting competition was over and one contender was left standing, he could continue to the next round of the tournament: the maze.

A dense and thick hedge would have popped up in a prince's path, generally ten feet to twenty feet tall, to prevent him from seeing the crowd momentarily. But he'd eventually get to view the crowd's reactions as traveled undetected with other princes and, if he was lucky, attack certain foes. A fire pit would obscure the prince's powers and vision for a moment, but if he had the right training and collective consciousness, he would be able to cross it easily.

Once the prince thwarted a swarm of tricky leprechauns, a door would have grown to the size of each prince's height so he could go through it without trouble.

A tower out in the distance would pique the prince's curiosity, and he'd venture forth to it, wanting to save a damsel in distress. Using all the strength he had left in him, he'd scale the smooth stone walls of the tower, hoping he'd get a kiss from the beautiful damsel. After a kiss, he'd take her with him quickly through the dangerous and timed maze.

Deep within the heart of the maze, the prince and damsel would meet evil magical gnomes brought on by the maze itself. They would not take pity on the travelers. They would have long, thin putters. At their feet were golf balls, and with one stroke, they'd explode at the travelers' feet.

A prince would not be intimidated by the evil gnomes at all. He'd use his inherited powers to take them out. As a thank you and a good gesture, the damsel—whether it be a princess or duchess of a foreign dignitary—would offer her loyalty and nuptials in exchange for her safety. He'd accept, and they'd marry.

Once the tournament was over and a winning participant was chosen, he and his new wife would go in front of the tournament's judges. They'd look on the merit of the prince's accomplishments throughout his arduous journey, and if they liked what they saw, he would be noted as the leaf'd prince and the sole protector of Ireland and its inhabitants. These were the rules of the Three-Leaf'd Tournament and will forever be so.

CHAPTER I

Prince William

Medieval times. After 1720.

WILLIAM DID NOT want to be a prince. As a child, he often wondered what it would be like to play with the commoners' children outside his tower window instead of being confined to his parents' castle. To keep their son occupied, Queen Kathrynne and King Diamond had arranged for William to receive piano and Latin lessons from dignified teachers who, according to Prince William, were boring in their teaching styles.

Prince William had reluctantly agreed to the lessons because he did not want to upset his parents, but he regretted his decision almost at once. His piano teacher had a long, thin nose with small nostrils, which made it difficult for her to breathe. Her voice sounded as if she had a clothespin permanently upon her bony nose.

"Play the second line of the composer Bach again," she said.

Prince William drummed on the piano, hardly caring if he had played the right notes. She sighed heavily, knowing that she had wasted her time on yet another student who did not care for the carefully crafted pieces of Bach. She soon quit, frustrated at Prince William's lack of appreciation for the musical arts.

"You will never find another piano teacher for your ignorant son," were the last words Prince William remembered as he recalled the incident. "At least not one with patience to teach him."

His Latin teacher had a particularly dull personality, which made it hard for Prince William to understand Latin, much less care for its romance-themed literature. His voice droned as Prince William heard Latin tales of heroes rescuing their beloved damsels in distress.

Prince William sighed. He did not care for such stories. He had other things on his mind.

Prince William longed to see what was beyond his castle's walls. He wanted to see the greenery of the fields, the small woodcutters' cottages at the edge of his castle's boundaries, and people in the bustling village square. For years his parents had confined him, unaware that his real desire—his only hope—was to be with the people his parents governed. He vowed that one day he'd venture beyond his castle's walls to see what the countryside offered.

***

Whoosh!

An arrow split the air as Prince William pulled back a thin string. He pulled back another arrow and cut the air again; this one sailed a little farther than the first.

"Wow! Your agility has surely grown. Your mother will be pleased that you are so diligent about practicing for the Three-Leaf'd Tournament," observed Lance, the Rowzand Family servant.

"Not by choice, I'm not," said Prince William. "I'm only doing this because I don't want to upset my mother."

"But the fact you're good doesn't hurt either. I think you'll have a good chance of winning this tournament."

"If it were up to my mother, I would. But please know I'm mad at her for signing me up for the Three-Leaf'd Tournament in the first place."

"I know you are," said Lance. "I don't blame you."

"And I know you are on my mother's side," said Prince William. "It's only natural you'd be on her side. You're her primary servant."

"I assure you I'm not on anyone's *side* here," said Lance. "I was only commenting on how your agility has grown; that's all."

Queen Kathrynne approached her son just as he pulled back a third arrow. It whooshed past her ear and hit a target yards away.

"I'm glad you're so diligent about practicing for this tournament," said Queen Kathrynne. "Your father has met a girl at the village square. A princess."

"Yeah?"

"He told me she's smitten with you. Your father and I think it's a good idea for you to go on a date with her—to see how it goes. And perhaps you could marry Princess Lexis if it turns into a strong relationship."

Princess Lexis had been excited for weeks about finally getting a date with Prince William. In her youth at the village square, she saw him buying produce from a local merchant and fell hopelessly and desperately in love with him. King Diamond had later promised her that she would get a date with his son and soon marry him.

"I will not go on a date with Princess Lexis," said Prince William. "And I will not marry someone I don't know."

He desired to marry someone he loved.

But against his wishes, Prince William had agreed to go on a date with Princess Lexis to please his parents.

***

The Green Leprechaun was packed to the brim as Princess Lexis and Prince William entered through a side door. The restaurant was Irish themed, and it surely made every Ireland native feel at home with its leprechaun memorabilia. The tables were pots of gold. Pictures of dignified leprechauns littered the Green Leprechaun's walls.

A flowing fountain in the center of the restaurant glowed magnificently as gold coins poured into a silver basin below the spout. Precautionary measures were considered for the coins, because leprechauns would otherwise have been tempted to steal them.

Prince William and Princess Lexis were seated at a table shaped like a pot of gold that lay just beyond the fountain's silver basin.

"So have you been to the Green Leprechaun before?" asked Princess Lexis awkwardly.

"I have, as a child," said Prince William. He took a sip of his root beer a waitress had brought him.

"So when do you want to get married?" she asked.

Her question caught Prince William off guard. He stared blankly, unable to fathom what had just happened. He had known Princess Lexis was likely to ask the question at some point during their date, but hadn't thought it would come so quickly.

"Excuse me?" was Prince William's reply.

"When do you want to get married?"

"I … I don't know. The truth is, Princess Lexis, I've never thought about the topic of marriage before. I've got plans–"

"Oh, we can do these plans together," said Princess Lexis excitedly. "What type of plans were you thinking?"

Another princess suddenly entered the Green Leprechaun. Leprechauns seated at the restaurant's bar stopped eating their greasy meals and craned their heads to glimpse this unknown princess. They had come to the Green Leprechaun several nights a week before, but never once had they seen anyone like her. Her red dress sparkled, drawing the attention of more leprechauns seated at the back of the restaurant who had been drinking root beer and talking in hushed tones. Her black high heels clanked on the wood floor as she strode past the restaurant's bar.

"A root beer, please."

The Green Leprechaun's bartender looked at her for a few seconds as if he were lost in thought, and he then proceeded to pour a root beer into a tall mug.

Prince William, who had been silent for a few moments, trying not to engage in conversation with Princess Lexis, looked at the new princess too. The restaurant became silent.

"Ah, Prince William," said Princess Taylor, who had spotted him from the bar. "I didn't know you liked coming to the Green Leprechaun."

"I haven't been here in years, but occasionally I like coming, yes."

Princess Taylor strolled over to where Prince William and Princess Lexis were seated, just beyond the fountain's silver basin. The entire restaurant began to make noise again, as if Princess Taylor had not entered.

As soon as Princess Taylor sat down next to Prince William, an invisible force knocked her to the floor. Stunned, she gazed at Princess Lexis, seeing out of the corner of her eye a wand on the edge of the table.

"You did that on purpose," she said. "You used that wand to knock me to the floor."

"I don't know what you mean. My hand didn't move."

"Oh, don't lie to me. I know you used the wand to knock me to the ground because you were jealous."

"Why would I be jealous of you?" said Princess Lexis. "I don't know you."

"But you were certainly jealous of me. Why else would you use your wand to knock me to the floor?" Princess Taylor insisted.

"I don't know. Maybe one of the leprechauns knocked you to the floor. I surely didn't," said Princess Lexis.

"Then how come you have a wand just lying about?" asked Princess Taylor, keeping her eye on the wand.

"Can't I have a wand? It doesn't mean I used it to knock you to the floor, does it?"

Prince William had been listening carefully to the two princesses, and he decided to speak up. "You did knock her to the floor," he said. "I saw you do it."

"Oh, so you did do it. I knew you couldn't help yourself. I knew you knocked me to the floor," said Princess Taylor, still gazing at Princess Lexis.

"So what if I did?" said Princess Lexis, her glare unchanging. "I just couldn't bear you taking away my fiancé."

"I'm not your fiancé. I never agreed to be your fiancé," said Prince William, aghast.

Green light burst from Princess Lexis's wand, bouncing off the Green Leprechaun's walls. Customers, including the leprechauns, stopped eating their meals and gazed in horror at the sight before them: a beet-red Princess Lexis was now on top of Princess Taylor on the floor, her wand inches from Princess Taylor's perspiring face.

"Please don't blast me," she begged, her voice shaking. "What have I ever done to deserve such a thing as this?"

"You've flirted with the man I love and the man I plan to marry. For that you must be punished." Her hand remained motionless.

Princess Lexis flicked her wand, but before the spark could cause severe damage, Princess Taylor managed to break free of Princess Lexis's firm hold on her, and she got up. Princess Taylor held a wand of her own directly in Princess Lexis's face, ready to defend herself if necessary.

"I will defend myself. And if I must injure you, so be it," she said.

Princess Taylor's threat did not intimidate Princess Lexis. She held her wand directly in Princess Taylor's face, her hand unmoving.

"Your threat doesn't faze me! I'd have a better match with tricky leprechauns."

Everyone continued to stare at the scene before them, their gazes inert.

Princess Lexis flicked her wand again, and a bright green light illuminated the entire restaurant; light bounced off every corner, making a noise like thunder.

Before Princess Taylor had time to react or defend herself, light from Princess Lexis's wand hit her, making her fall to the floor. When this happened, Princess Taylor dropped her wand, and it landed just inches from Prince William's feet.

Using her full strength, Princess Taylor–despite having been injured and disoriented–tried to reach for her wand, but she couldn't. It was out of her reach.

She was then able to reach for her wand, just in time for a jet of light from Princess Lexis's wand to illuminate the air. She stood, stumbling, looking at Princess Lexis's angry face.

"Just know that I'm not taking away Prince William from you. I don't intend to do that," she said, her voice still shaking.

"Yes, you are. That was your intention all along," said Princess Lexis.

"No, it wasn't. And for you to think that is truly and utterly pathetic."

Despite herself, Princess Lexis flicked her wand again, and a jet of light hit a waitress who was serving food to customers in the back of the head. She stumbled from the blast almost at once, making the food on a server's tray spill onto the table and the floor.

It did not faze Princess Lexis in the slightest. She held her wand at Princess Taylor. Her eyes showed so much fury in them that Princess Taylor was sure Princess Lexis would kill her with just a flick of her wrist.

"Please don't hurt me," Princess Taylor begged.

Princess Taylor, to defend herself, flicked her wand; light illuminated the whole restaurant again, bouncing off chairs and tables. Frightened customers backed away from their seats as the chaos from the two wands continued for several seconds more.

Upon his embarrassment by the scene Princess Lexis and Princess Taylor were creating with their wands, Prince William fled the restaurant, hoping the awful experience he had endured just a few moments before would soon be erased from his mind.

CHAPTER II

Bridgette Greenhouse

BRIDGETTE GREENHOUSE WAS small in physique, which made it easy for her to pull weeds growing in her garden. As she knelt to pick the last of the weeds, a foot appeared.

"Your sheep have pooed on my lawn."

Bridgette recognized the voice at once. Her neighbor, Don Saint James, stood in the weeds by her plants, his angry expression evident.

"I'm sorry," said Bridgette. "It won't happen again."

"You're darn right it won't happen again. I'll make sure it won't," said Don Saint James.

Bridgette stood up from the ground, looking intently at her neighbor. "What do you mean?"

"I've talked to King Diamond about your little sheep problem, and he said he would take care of it."

"Meaning ...?"

"Your sheep will be taken away from you if the problem persists," said Don Saint James, matter-of-factly. "And I'm positive it will happen again, because unlike all the other peasants I know, you are the only one in the countryside who still lets her sheep poo all over the place."

Bridgette lived on a farm, where her father had grown up. It was here, as a child, that she had learned to tend to her father's sheep. Her father had been a shepherd, and he had loved his work. He had loved animals of all kinds: horses, pigs, goats, cats, dogs, and, of course, sheep. He had loved his sheep most of all. Maybe this was because when he called them—as he usually did on cold nights—they'd come. They had loved him, and they loved Bridgette too. She was kind and gentle to them, and they could sense her gentle spirit.

Upon her father's unexpected death from smallpox, Bridgette had taken the responsibility of tending his farm, his garden, and his sheep. It was a devastating loss for Bridgette, but she pressed on, keeping the memory of her father with her always.

Don Saint James had been upset for weeks because he thought Bridgette should have done something about her late father's sheep pooing on his lawn. Bridgette believed the opposite. She felt her father's sheep could never be trained not to relieve themselves on lawns. It was ridiculous, in Bridgette's point of view, to think anyone would want to teach undomesticated sheep. Don believed Bridgette's sheep she had inherited from her father were simple-minded creatures, and that their humans should have dominion over them.

When King Diamond did nothing to appease Don for his issues with Bridgette's sheep, he took it upon himself to sue Bridgette for allowing her undomesticated sheep to roam free–something he hated most of all. When his case was dismissed by the judge who dealt with small civil suits for being too unreasonable, Don was distraught. Soon his anger dwindled and disappeared, but the passion he had before still lingered whenever sheep lifted their legs on his lawn.

***

Prince William stood in a forest clearing, wondering where he'd go next. Panting and tired from running, he looked through the trees and saw a faint path. The sun was setting, and he knew he needed to venture forth through the forest clearing before dark.

"*Oi.* Watch it."

Prince William stopped and looked around. The voice he had heard seemed to have faded.

He continued to stroll down the path, unfazed by the tiny voice. Then he heard it again:

"Watch it, watch it! You're hurting me!"

He stopped again. He looked around but saw only a few trees next to the path, blowing in the breeze.

Was he imagining things?

On closer inspection, Prince William saw a tiny leprechaun sitting on a tree stump, breathing heavily.

"You stomped on my foot! How could you do that?" said the leprechaun.

"I'm sorry. I didn't mean–"

Prince William stopped himself to look at the leprechaun a little closer. "What's your name?"

"What's it to you if I tell you my name," said the leprechaun, slightly offended by Prince William's question. "Everyone seems to hate me because I do bad things to them."

Prince William's curiosity grew. "What kind of bad things?"

"None of your business!"

Prince William had always had a knack of wearing down creatures who did not want to tell him things he wanted to know. And stubborn leprechauns were no exception.

"Please tell me what type of bad things you do to other creatures. I promise I won't be mad at you or be offended."

The leprechaun looked at Prince William suspiciously. "Why should I tell you? You'll go and tell someone else who is aroused by the story you tell them."

"No, I won't," Prince William insisted. "If you first tell me your name and then tell me what type of bad things you do to other creatures, I won't tell anyone; I promise."

The leprechaun looked at Prince William; his doubt was evident. "How can I be sure you're not trying to trick me now?"

"I guess you can't," said Prince William, sighing. "But I would like to know your name, at least."

"Hamish. Hamish Greentines."

"Well, nice to meet you, Hamish Greentines. My name is–"

"Prince William, I know," said Hamish. "Everybody who's anybody knows you … Well, at least across Ireland they do."

"How do they know me?"

"You're famous. Well, at least across Ireland you are."

"How, then, did I get so famous?"

"We leprechauns know everything about royal families throughout the centuries," said Hamish. "We have to know for … for personal knowledge."

"Then you know I'm in the Three-Leaf'd Tournament, then, right?"

"Oh, yes, I do know that," said Hamish. "That's why you're famous. No other prince of this side of Ireland dares to enter such a large and dangerous tournament as the Three-Leaf'd Tournament is and is becoming."

"Just know I didn't enter by choice," said Prince William. "If I had my choice, I wouldn't have entered it."

"I know," said Hamish. "Your mom, Queen Kathrynne, entered you into the tournament, did she not?"

"Yes. Do leprechauns have to know that, too?" asked Prince William, annoyed.

"No. I saw your mother enter the registration tent at the village square."

"Were you spying on me?" said Prince William, his eyes narrowing, his suspicion growing.

"No. No, I wasn't," said Hamish. "I just happened to be there at the registration tent at the time."

"Well, I'm going to leave before it gets dark."

Prince William began to stroll down the path toward the forest clearing. He had not gone far when Hamish stopped him.

"Wait!"

Prince William looked at Hamish, wondering if he was to be trusted. Every leprechaun he knew had a hidden agenda, but Hamish, just looking at him now, seemed innocent enough—too naive for his own good.

"What is it?" Prince William asked.

"I need some gold."

"Why?"

"I just need it."

Prince William's suspicion was growing even more. "For …?"

"To help me out," said Hamish. "I lost my home to some evil magical wolves. They ransacked my home and set fire to my house, and because of it, I have nowhere to go."

"Really?" said Prince William.

He had hoped Hamish was not lying to him about gold, but he was not about to leave a creature homeless. "How many pieces of gold do you need?"

"A few pieces. Not much," said Hamish.

Prince William knew there was gold at the village square. Merchants always had spare gold coins, and if a creature was in need, they were happy to give a few away.

But not Hert McGawn.

A merchant by trade, Hert lived on the borders of Ireland in a tiny one-bedroom house, just beyond the village square. His only source of income was selling fruit and preservatives to Ireland natives who would come by his cart. Hert hated Hamish Greentines. He hated him with a passion. Perhaps it was simply because Hamish would steal all his coins from his wagon, leaving his money basket empty.

As Prince William and Hamish strolled through the village square, they saw a bustling parish filled with creatures buying goods and other items from carts. Hamish glanced at the carts, mesmerized by all the things displayed on them. Bonnets, dresses, and bags of all sorts–big and small–were some of the things that were shown. Peasant children were playing in the center of the village square, near an old fountain, just as Prince William and Hamish strolled by Hert McGawn's produce cart.

"What'll it be?"

Hert, at first, did not recognize Prince William or Hamish. He had been groggy for most of the morning because he had gotten up to ready his cart for the early morning rush of creatures who would pass by his cart.

"Oh, it's you," Hert grumbled, looking at Hamish. "What d' you want?"

"Hamish needs some gold," said Prince William.

"I'm not going to give him gold," said Hert sternly. "He's taken most of my source of income already, and what I do have is not much."

"Please, sir," said Prince William. "Hamish just needs a few pieces of gold coins to help him get by."

"Look here, Prince," said Hert, glancing at Prince William crossly, "I will not give up the last of my gold coins to this thief who thinks he can rob me."

"But he needs them."

"He doesn't need them! Did Hamish tell you a sob story of how his house was burned down by evil magical wolves?"

Prince William nodded.

Hamish grumbled.

"Well, I'm not surprised," said Hert. "He tells the same story two or three times a week to unexpected strangers who have a heart. The story's details may change from time to time, but the basic concept is there. He tells them he's homeless, that he needs gold. He then lures them to the village square, where he goes by my cart. Last week he lured an old peasant woman here at the square, and she was forced to give him some of her gold coins because I said I wouldn't give up any of mine."

"Is this true?"

Hamish did not respond to Prince William's question. Instead he eyed some coins lying in a basket near the edge of Hert's cart. Before Hert could utter a single word, Hamish disappeared in a green puff of smoke, taking with him the coins from Hert's basket.

***

Bridgette entered the village square. She was there because she had hoped to buy produce from Hert McGawn for a party she was having later that evening. As she strolled through the village square, she noticed something particularly odd about the scene before her. The village square wasn't bustling with creatures buying items, and peasant children weren't playing in the center of the village square. Thinking it was an off day, Bridgette continued to stroll through the village square. Just as she got to Hert's cart, someone grabbed her, pulling her behind an empty cart.

"Are they gone?"

"Who's gone?"

"The princesses who were chasing me."

"I don't know," said Bridgette. "I really should be going."

Prince William could not help himself. "Wait!"

Bridgette turned from walking away to glimpse at Prince William. He stood there, drenched in sweat. He looked as if his whole body would collapse at any moment.

"Why were you running?" Bridgette asked.

"I needed to get away from the princesses who were chasing me," said Prince William. "I told you that already."

Prince William glimpsed from behind the cart and saw that Princess Lexis and Princess Taylor were looking among the carts. He could scarcely breathe, afraid that he would be discovered. He crouched behind the empty cart, trying not to move.

Princess Lexis and Princess Taylor continued to glimpse among the carts. Prince William peeked from beyond the unoccupied cart again and saw that the two princesses had disappeared from the village square.

"May I hide at your place?" asked Prince William quickly.

Bridgette glanced at Prince William. "Excuse me?"

"May I hide at your place?" Prince William repeated. "Just until I know for sure the two princesses aren't still out there looking for me."

"Are you nuts? No! I've got a party to plan for tonight, and if the guests see you, well–"

"Please."

"No. If the guests see you–"

"Your guests won't even recognize I'm there. I'm desperate for a place to hide. I'll pay you."

"Oh, I don't need any of your gold coins," said Bridgette, throwing up her hands.

"Please … I'm desperate. If there were any other way, don't you think I'd do that first instead of asking you?"

Bridgette had guessed Prince William would have had explored other alternatives to getting away from the two princesses. What could it hurt having a prince stay at her house? Her neighbor, Don Saint James, would not be around to complain about her sheep relieving themselves anytime soon, and she did not know when he'd be back. But she did not care.

"Sure," said Bridgette, sighing. "You may hide at my house."

"Oh, thank you," said Prince William. "You will never know how much this means to me."

"Oh, I think I do," said Bridgette. "I think I do."

***

Bridgette's house, built out of logs from the surrounding forest, looked like a small house compared to what Prince William was used to. The windows were tiny, letting through just enough light to warm the two-bedroom cabin. The front door appeared old and worn from age, its hinges lose from use. Bridgette put her key into the front door and turned it. Instantly Prince William was greeted by the warmth of a glowing fireplace and the smell of tea boiling in a chamber pot, hanging aloft from a swinging arm attached to the stove.

"Did you make the tea yourself?" asked Prince William as he stepped further into the room, smelling the intense aroma of tea boiling in the fireplace.

"Well, yes, I did," said Bridgette. "Peasants, as you know, must provide for themselves, and what I do best is make tea."

Prince William had never witnessed a peasant say such a thing. Peasants, as far as he knew, were simple people who needed the upper class's assistance to get by. Bridgette was more than a simple peasant. Prince William assumed she knew how to boil tea, cook, clean, and mop. In his castle, Prince William had never witnessed any of his servants make tea before or even do chores. There was something about Bridgette that he could not easily forget–something he liked.

"Do you want some tea?" asked Bridgette. She grabbed a wooden spoon from a hook attached to a fireplace, and she began to stir the tea. It bubbled and popped, making the aroma of the tea even stronger.

"I don't know," said Prince William warily. "The tea does smell heavenly, but–"

"C'mon, my tea is good," Bridgette insisted. "Even the creatures who meet here once a week can never turn down a glass of my tea. You're the first one who has ever turned down an offer of tea."

"Okay, all right," he said. "I'm a little thirsty from running from manic princesses."

Bridgette poured a swig of tea into a tin cup and then handed it to Prince William.

He drank. The taste was surprising; it was a mixture of lemon, honey, and fig.

He smiled. "Oh, this is good."

"Oh, you want more tea?"

"Yes, please."

Bridgette poured more tea into the tin cup and then handed it back to Prince William.

"Thanks," he said.

"Sure," said Bridgette.

Prince William drank. "So what type of party are you having?"

Bridgette didn't expect the question. "A dinner party."

"Anyone I know who's coming? More peasants, maybe?"

The question under any other circumstances would have caused Bridgette to be angry, but she just ignored it. It was not worth arguing with a prince who had a higher authority than she.

"No."

"Oh, okay," said Prince William awkwardly.

"You might want to hide now," said Bridgette, who had checked the old, oak clock on the wall by the fireplace, which said six o'clock. "My dinner party starts in less than twenty minutes. Hide in this closet here." Bridgette pointed to a closet located by the front door.

Prince William glanced at the closet warily. "Are you sure I can't hide anywhere else? A back bedroom, perhaps?"

"No, unfortunately I can't let you hide in one of the two bedrooms," said Bridgette, "because the guests are women creatures, and they like to be spread out in my house. The bedrooms are their favorite meeting places."

Prince William heard female voices outside the cabin. They became louder and more distinct as they approached.

"Inside here," said Bridgette quickly, pointing to the closet. "Before the women creatures know you're here."

Prince William was about to object, but he thought better of it. Bridgette swiftly opened the closet door, and Prince William hurried inside.

A loud, brash Irish voice echoed from outside Bridgette's cabin.

"Ugh! The cabin's still here."

Bridgette recognized the Irish accent almost at once and dreaded opening the door of her cabin. The accent was that of a woman who hated nearly everyone except her deceased husband. Her husband was a log maker. A kind man, he loved to help those who were in dire need of log cabins. He would gather logs from the surrounding forest and begin his work, constructing a cabin that suited a person's needs.

And so, when Bridgette asked the log maker if he would build her a cabin, he gladly accepted, knowing the massive task that lay ahead for him in constructing Bridgette's cabin.

The log maker had never once complained about his duties as the log maker. Although he did not get paid much money, his heart and compassion for his job made up the difference.

When the log maker died unexpectedly (the cause was still unknown), the log maker's wife had taken sole responsibility for the duties as a log maker, and she hated it.

"Still have the cabin, I see," said the log maker's wife as she stepped through the threshold of Bridgette's cabin.

"Yeah, I do," said Bridgette warily. She did not like this woman at all.

The log maker's wife was huge. Her neck held large green gemstones, carefully crafted from unique and costly stones that were imported from foreign countries. They clanked together loudly as she moved further into the cabin's small living space.

"'Course, if it were up to me," she said quickly, "I would've gutted your cabin years ago." She looked at Bridgette intently, making her feel uncomfortable. "But as it is, I made a promise to my husband that I wouldn't gut your monstrosity of a cabin."

"That's very kind of you," said Bridgette awkwardly, not knowing if the log maker's wife's comment was a compliment or a complaint.

"I know it is kind of me. It was my late husband's wish not to tear down your cabin. He loved it. I sincerely don't know why. It's filthy and disgusting in here."

"So do you want anything to eat? A piece of pumpernickel bread, perhaps?"

"Oh, no thank you," said the log maker's wife, putting up her hand in protest. "I already ate."

The log maker's wife glanced around the cabin, inspecting all the knickknacks and souvenirs, finally spotting Bridgette's old china cabinet that her father had given her in his will.

"So how long have you had the china cabinet?"

Bridgette was not listening to the log maker's wife. Instead, her attention was on the closet where Prince William was hiding.

"So how long have you had this china cabinet?" repeated the log maker's wife, this time a little louder.

Bridgette glanced at the log maker's wife. "Oh, a year now."

"Huh." The log maker's wife eyed Bridgette's china cabinet carefully. "And I suppose your father gave it to you in his will?"

Bridgette nodded. "He did."

"Well, I notice you haven't used any china since your father passed. Any particular reason?"

"No reason. I haven't used it yet."

"Don't you think this dinner party would be the perfect opportunity to use some of the china?" asked the log maker's wife, her gaze still on the china cabinet.

"I guess."

"You don't seem sure of yourself," said the log maker's wife. "I'd expect your father would want you to use his china."

Before Bridgette had time to stop the log maker's wife, she started to pull out some of the china and place it on Bridgette's wood dining room table. "Where are your utensils?"

"In the second drawer to the right, near the fireplace."

The log maker's wife opened a wooden drawer near the fireplace and saw many metal knives, spoons, and forks. They had dust on them, and the log maker's wife immediately went to a metal sink and washed them thoroughly.

"Your silverware is filthy. When was the last time you used this silverware?"

"I don't know. A few weeks ago."

The log maker's wife shook her head. She placed the silverware next to each glass plate and sat down quietly.

She was silent, and by her silence, Bridgette knew that the log maker's wife did not like the disarray of her kitchen.

After the women had their fill of conversation and food and went home, Bridgette opened the closet door, letting Prince William out.

"Wow!" he said. "I almost fell asleep."

"I'm sorry about that," said Bridgette. "The log maker's wife is surely a character, isn't she?"

"Then why do you put up with her?" The question seemed to fall out of Prince William's mouth.

"Her husband built my cabin," said Bridgette. "He's the village's log maker. I put up with her because it is the nice and courteous thing to do."

"But you shouldn't have to."

"Oh, but I do."

"Your father wouldn't want you to put up with Ireland natives who are rude in nature."

"How would you know what my father would have wanted?" Bridgette said sternly. "He has always told me to be courteous to those people who aren't kind."

"But this situation is different," Prince William insisted. "No creature of any kind should be treated like dirt–less than dirt."

"That's very kind of you," said Bridgette, "but I think I can handle the log maker's wife just fine." She sighed. "Besides, she's only here once every few years, and every few years, it is the same routine: she comes in, says how filthy my cabin is, says if she had it her way, it would been gutted."

"Well, I'd better go," said Prince William. "I think I overstayed my welcome."

Bridgette glanced out of her kitchen window and saw that rain was falling hard. "You might want to wait until the rain stops," she said.

"Okay. I guess I can stay for a while–just until the rain stops."

"By the way, I'm eating dinner in a few minutes. Would you like some?"

Prince William shook his head. "I don't want to impose."

"No, you wouldn't impose on me," Bridgette insisted. "Besides, I've already made it." She scooped a large helping of soup into a brass bowl and then handed it to Prince William.

"Thanks," he said.

"Sure."

***

Days passed, and Prince William and Bridgette began to get closer. Despite their closeness, Bridgette started to wonder why Prince William had never desired to leave the forest and go back to the familiarly of his castle and his life as a prince. And so she gave up the courage and asked him.

"Why aren't you returning to your castle?"

Prince William didn't expect the question. "To put it simply, I'm sick of being royal."

"But aren't you supposed to go back to your castle? Don't you think your mother and father would be worried about you should you not return?" said Bridgette.

"Possibly."

"Then you should go back to your castle–for the sanity of your mother and father."

"They'll be okay."

"But you should," Bridgette insisted. "The kingdom needs a future king to lead them. If you're here, you can't lead the Irish people."

"Do you know why I ran away?" Prince William asked Bridgette.

"No. I honestly don't know why. Why?"

"I ran away partly because I was forced to marry a snobbish princess named Lexis. She was obsessed with me," said Prince William. "We went to the Green Leprechaun. It was there that Princess Lexis began flirting with me. I didn't return the flirting, as I was only there to please my parents.

"I never agreed to the date with Princess Lexis. Then another princess entered the Green Leprechaun, and to be honest, I was glad, because the date was becoming a bit awkward. The other princess, Princess Taylor, seemed to know me. She came over, and before she had a chance to sit next to me, Princess Lexis discretely used her wand to knock Princess Lexis to the floor.

"The next moment is a blur. Before I knew what was happening, Princess Lexis had Princess Taylor pinned to the floor. Wand sparks flew everywhere. I had to get out of there before things could get more out of hand. I quickly left the Green Leprechaun."

"I'm sorry you had to deal with that," said Bridgette, taking in the story as best as she could.

"And that's not the worst part," said Prince William, "I have to compete in the Three-Leaf'd Tournament. I don't think I'm qualified to be competing in such a hard tournament."

"Why is that?" said Bridgette.

"Because a lot of other princes have been training for weeks–months, even–to prepare for the dangerous tasks that lay ahead for them. I've only been training for weeks."

"So? I'm sure many of these princes are more nervous than you are about competing."

"But my mother expects a lot more of me than of most princes my age," said Prince William. "I don't think I'll live up to her expectations."

"Mothers expect a lot from their children," said Bridgette. "That doesn't mean they don't care about them. It's quite the contrary; they want their children to succeed in all they do. I'm sure your mother wants the same for you."

"I suppose you're right," said Prince William, sighing. "But I still refuse to go back to my castle and pretend to be someone I'm not."

"But you know you're going to have to go back," said Bridgette. "People of the small island of Ireland expect you to govern them; I expect you to govern them—and me. Your mother knows you can be a great ruler. She would never put you in a position as important as the rulership of Ireland if you weren't ready for it."

Silence developed between Bridgette and Prince William for a few seconds. Then Bridgette glanced out of her kitchen window and said, "Oh, the rain has stopped. You may need to go back to your castle before it starts again."

"I told you, I'm not going back to my castle and my life as a prince," said Prince William sternly.

"Then get out," said Bridgette, opening the kitchen's back door. "If you're not going to take responsibility as a great, noble leader, then leave. I don't want a coward here at my house."

"I'm not a coward."

"Really? So refusing to go back to the place you are most familiar with and where people love you and miss you and expect you to be a great, noble leader doesn't make you a coward? I must've missed something. I think it does. I don't trust cowards."

"Please let me stay. At least until I know for sure the two princesses are long gone."

"I think they're long gone now. No, leave."

"Well okay," said Prince William. He got up from the wicker dining room chair and reluctantly made his way to the door. He looked back at Bridgette. Her expression was not at all empathetic. As soon as he stepped out onto Bridgette's porch, Bridgette slammed the door closed.

The rain began again. Prince William could feel the water dripping from the roof's edge.

"Marry me."

The words seemed to fall out of Prince William's mouth.

Bridgette opened the door. "Excuse me?"

"Marry me," Prince William repeated. "Please?"

Bridgette considered her options: marry a prince who had no interest of ruling an Irish civilization, or refuse his proposal and find someone else— someone with whom she shared the same ideals and beliefs, though there would be a risk of the other person not loving her in the same way as one loves another. Her father often told her to follow her heart. It was not every day that a prince, wet from the rain, proposed to her. True, she loved him. And the fact that Prince William was willing to leave his sacred life as a prince and be with her—a peasant who had no sacred royal blood in her veins—said something about his character. He truly loved her.

"Yes," was all Bridgette could muster. "Yes, I will."

***

Bridgette and Prince William married in secret, as it was not customary for a commoner to marry a royal. If either his mother or father had known of the marriage with Bridgette, they would have disowned Prince William. They believed a commoner had no place in the royal bloodline. Such behavior was unacceptable for those involved.

Despite this, Bridgette became pregnant. Prince William soon feared that his parents would find out about his marriage with Bridgette and her pregnancy. But weeks went by, and then months, and there were no indications that his parents knew anything about his marriage or Bridgette's pregnancy.

A few months later, Bridgette went into labor. She had a boy. Bridgette and Prince William named him Benjamin. He had the same features as Prince William: brown hair and brown eyes.

Sarah, Bridgette's maid, was small in stature. Despite her small size, she had an unusual power of command. Bridgette did not like her, but she was her father's friend, and it was his wish that if Bridgette became pregnant, she would help Bridgette in her pregnancy through the birth of her child. And so she complied with her father's wish.

***

Crackle. Hiss.

Bridgette's bedroom door shook violently. Heat from a hooded figure's wand slowly melted the knob of Bridgette's bedroom door. Fear struck Bridgette at that instant. Was her baby boy going to be all right?

Bang.

The force from the figure's wand knocked Bridgette's bedroom door off its hinges. Amid dust and debris, a body lay lifeless, just inches from the door. Later Bridgette realized it was Sarah, her nursemaid.

The shock of her death was heart-wrenching. No person she knew had died other than her father. Memories started to flood back to Bridgette—memories of hope, love, friendship, and death. She instantly tried to erase the memory of her father's departure for the time being. There was no use in worrying about things she could not do anything about. At least, that was what Bridgette thought as she saw Sarah's body, cold and lifeless.

The figure's wand remained lit, illuminating Bridgette's bedroom.

"Drop out of the Three-Leaf'd Tournament," echoed a voice.

"No," said Prince William bravely. "I won't. The people of Ireland expect me to compete; I want to compete."

"Believe me; you won't make it past the first round if I have anything to do with it." The figure pulled back its hood, fully showing its hideous features.

A seemingly unattractive wizard stood before Prince William and Bridgette.

Lyon, a wizard, stood, his wand stretched out, motionless. He glanced at the newborn baby in Bridgette's arms.

"What a lovely baby," he said, giving Prince William a smirk. "It'd be a shame if it died before it was acknowledged it is in this world."

"You'd better not hurt my child," said Prince William, "or I'll—"

"Oh, calm down," said Lyon. "I'm not going to hurt your child. I was only bluffing." Lyon laughed a wicked laugh.

"I doubt you were bluffing," said Prince William, his voice calm but serious. "You have already hurt many Irish people, according to my mother and father. I can't—I won't let you hurt anyone—especially my son."

Before Lyon could say a word or react, Prince William took out a thin wand made of oak and, without hesitation, flicked it. A burst of green sparks lit

Bridgette's bedroom, which was dimly lit only by candles. There was a crackle and hiss as the sparks from Lyon's wand met those from Prince William's.

"No!"

Prince William quickly craned his head and saw that Bridgette was in a cold sweat, as pale as a ghost. Terror flooded Prince William's face as he realized at that precise moment that his new baby had magically disappeared from his wife's arms.

"*Where is he?* What happened to my son?"

"I don't know what you're talking about," said Lyon, his wand still raised to defend himself.

"You know what you did," said Prince William, his voice stern. "You know where my son is, because you made my son disappear by your evil magic."

"I'm sorry to disappoint you, but I did not make your son disappear," said Lyon. "Another magical being did. As much as I wanted to, I did not."

"Oh, sure. I don't believe you."

Lyon and Prince William stood still. Neither one moved. Then there was a noise like thunder and a bright light from a wand's tip; Lyon's wand shook from his spell. Prince William was pushed back, struggling, as he tried to remain on foot.

Bridgette was horrified as her husband fought with all the strength he had in him to ward off Lyon's spell.

Then there was a pop.

Prince William then gazed down at his wand and realized it had snapped in half.

Lyon was pleased with himself.

It did not faze Prince William, however. He waved his hand over the broken pieces of his wand, and it instantly repaired itself. Its tip was brighter than ever before, giving off a dull, warm glow. Prince William and Lyon continued to stand their ground. There was another hiss and crackle as wand sparks exploded. Lyon flicked his wand again, this time injuring Prince William in the chest.

"Why are you doing this?" asked Prince William, coughing from his injuries. "Why do you want to kill me?"

"You know that question isn't worth answering." Lyon flicked his wand, and Prince William could feel his feet buckle beneath him. Then everything went dark.

***

Lyon desired to become the three-leaf'd prince because the position held power. He wanted to wield that power. If he were to enter the Three-Leaf'd Tournament and win, he would be able to manipulate the citizens of Ireland and their reliance on the three-leaf'd prince. It was this kind of power that made every villain stark raving mad. But Lyon didn't care. He wanted that power, and he wanted it now. And he would do anything to wield that power—even kill the most precious baby to get it: the future protector of the Irish people.

***

The countryside of Lyon's castle had less vegetation than Prince William and Bridgette had seen. A swinging bridge lay just inches from a cobblestone pathway that led to Lyon's front door. The air seemed denser as Prince William and Bridgette made their way across the cobblestone bridge.

"I hope our son is all right," said Bridgette, covering her head with the hood of her burgundy silk cloak.

"Me, too," said Prince William.

The castle had a dark and ghoulish atmosphere as they stepped inside. Spiderwebs littered the walls and paintings. Prince William and Bridgette walked down a narrow hallway, staying close to avoid uncertain danger.

Then–

"*No! Get away!*"

Prince William then turned a corner of the narrow hallway and stopped. Amid the dull light by lanterns on the stone walls, Lyon, the Wizard stood at the edge of the hall, dressed in a green silk cloak, holding Bridgette in his long, dead-looking fingers.

"Let Bridgette go!" said Prince William boldly.

"I will not," said Lyon, pressing his wand upon Bridgette's perspiring neck like a dagger. "Now I would, perhaps, let her go if you'd do something for me in return."

"Do whatever Lyon is asking you so we can find our son!" said Bridgette wearily, her voice strained.

"Shut up," warned Lyon, and he pushed harder upon Bridgette's neck, making an ugly purple bruise.

"And that would be …?" said Prince William, and he turned his attention away from Bridgette for a second to Lyon, longing to hear more.

"Drop out of the Three-Leaf'd Tournament and I will free your precious Bridgette."

"You know I can't do that," said Prince William. "I have a duty and obligation to the people of Ireland to protect them from enemies who threaten their way of life."

"Then I'll have to hurt your precious one," said Lyon, and with a flick of his wrist, Bridgette was uprooted from her spot. She landed against a stone wall, just inches from where Lyon was standing.

Prince William noticed at once that Bridgette had a small gash on her forehead and that it was bleeding. She appeared unconscious from Lyon's rough treatment.

"See? I told you I'd hurt your precious Bridgette. She's not dead, of course— at least not yet, anyway," said Lyon with a sneer. "Of course, if you have a change of heart and decide to drop out of the tournament willingly, I promise I won't kill you both."

"And if I refuse?"

"If you refuse, I will kill you both."

"I can't do that," said Prince William. "I can't drop out of the tournament. Too many people count on me to compete. If I drop out, I will disappoint them; I would disappoint myself."

"Then expect your precious one to die," said Lyon.

A light flickered in the dim hallway. Lyon's wand hit Bridgette immediately, and she lay lifeless, nearly unconscious. Tears flooded Prince William's face. The girl he loved—the girl who didn't care whether he was a prince—had died. Or at least he thought she had died.

"You killed her! You killed my wife!" shouted Prince William, his voice shaking from disbelief. "How could you?"

"I only did what was necessary," said Lyon. "And now you."

"You won't."

A rush of adrenaline filled Prince William's blood and he cleared his mind. He lifted his wand and pointed it into Lyon's smirking expression.

"You will not kill me here," he said boldly. "You've managed to kill Bridgette, but you certainly won't kill me." With a flick of his wand, Lyon was lifted into the air, and he landed flat on his face. Prince William glimpsed at Lyon now lying on the marble floor of his castle, his expression stricken with sudden fear. "You may be able to swindle more people who come across you, but you don't swindle me."

Prince William turned to his wife and gently guided her out of sight of Lyon. He took Bridgette outside the castle, hoping they would not be followed. They were halfway across the castle's swinging bridge when a red spark from a wand flashed above their heads. Prince William, holding Bridgette tightly, turned his head to see another red spark fly in his direction. He fought intensely, blasting Lyon with his free hand while still holding Bridgette so she would not collapse.

But Lyon's strength was too much for him; he collapsed, breathless, still holding Bridgette gently, embracing her.

Lyon stepped onto the swinging bridge and knelt, looking intensely into Prince William's frightened expression. "If you stay in the tournament, you won't win," he said. "I assure you, Prince; I will find your son and kill him. And now, so you don't find me, I'll kill you here so there's no doubt of who won the fight."

Too weak to fight back, Prince William accepted his fate, hoping in his heart that his son would escape Lyon's wrath.

And so Lyon lifted his wand; red sparks ignited the night sky.

***

Meanwhile, near a bush, a figure dressed in a dark green cloak was astonished at all it had seen. Picking up what seemed to be a wicker basket concealed in the bushes, it turned away from Lyon's castle, made its way across the swinging drawbridge, and disappeared.

CHAPTER III

Lyon, the Wizard

1890.

L YON SOON RETURNED to his castle, which was secluded from the Irish community. It was here that he vented about the Irish people. He hated their Celtic skirts, their funny-looking hats, and their long, messy, untamed beards. As he looked out of his dungeon tower window, Lyon saw a few Irish children playing at the barrier of his castle's grounds. He hated these Irish children. He hated how happy they were, gladly playing at the boundary, not even thinking of the dangers that might be lurking beyond the wall and forest clearing a few feet away.

Seeing these children playing, Lyon was reminded of his childhood and how awful it had been. He remembered how, at the age of five, he wasn't invited to any of the slumber parties.

At that time, he didn't have powers yet; all the other children his age had developed their skills early. He was, however, invited to one slumber party at the age of nine. But the party proved to be more than just a disappointment.

Lyon clearly remembered how several children forced him to stay magically tied up and mocked him. He committed to memory how they—the children—had magically turned him into a monkey with no tail. They laughed and taped a tail on his bum. From that time onward, he hated children because they were crude and cynical to him.

"Oh, look at monkey-boy," said a little girl. "His tail is longer than his body. Let's pin his ears back and mock him some more."

And so they did.

Now a teenager, the memory of the event of several slumber parties slowly faded into Lyon's memory. He had forcefully tried to forget the humiliation he had felt as they made fun of him.

At seventeen, a girl named Suzette came into Lyon's life. She was pretty in Lyon's eyes. At first sight, Lyon could sense that Suzette was freaked out by his rough appearance. Then, as time progressed, Suzette came to see that Lyon was growing generous.

***

The night was chilly as Lyon and Suzette strolled through a carnival's grounds. An array of carnival stands stood side by side, a few inches apart in the damp, sticky grass.

"This is nice," said Suzette, "to be with you."

Lyon smiled wearily. "Yeah. It is," he said.

"Do you know where the Ferris wheel is?"

A girl, almost the size of a toddler, was standing before Lyon and Suzette. Her hair, which was pinned back by a bobby pin, hung loosely around her short sleeve silk dress. Her brown eyes, as big as saucers, gazed intently at Lyon and Suzette.

"Oh, are you lost?"

"Don't bother this little girl," said Lyon. "I'm sure the girl's mother will be able to find her."

"Nonsense," said Suzette, and she turned her attention to the girl. "Do you know where your mother is? Maybe I can take you to her."

"I don't know," the girl said, starting to cry. "The last thing I remember is that my mom was at the Ferris wheel."

"Oh, is this necessary?" asked Lyon.

"Oh, of course, it is," said Suzette.

Lyon gave Suzette a piercing look. "You can't solve the world's problems. Let the world solve its problems."

"But we have to find this little girl's mother. Don't you think this girl deserves to find her mother?" said Suzette.

"Well ..."

"I can't believe you're heartless. I thought you were kind, but you're not."

"I am kind," said Lyon, "to you."

"Yes, to me, but what about the rest of the creatures–and to this little girl?" Suzette asked.

"Forget them. These creatures are of no use to me since I have you," said Lyon.

The little girl couldn't stand it anymore; she had to say something. "Are you ever going to help me find my mother?"

Bothered by Lyon's words, Suzette choked back her disgust and instead turned her attention to the little girl. "Of course, we'll find your mother. Let's go find her."

Suzette had just reached the Ferris wheel when a jet of green light entered the air. Suzette craned her head and saw that Lyon was holding his wand, motionless, in the direction of the little girl.

A second jet of green light entered the air, and the little girl's feet buckled beneath her. She lay unresponsive on the grass in front of Suzette, who was wearing a horrified expression.

"Lyon—how could you?"

The adrenaline rush of killing the little girl had quickly worn off for Lyon. He stared blankly at the scene before him. He had killed an innocent little girl all because of his jealousy.

"I'm ... sorry. I didn't mean—"

"Oh, of course you meant it," said Suzette. "I don't think we should be together if your jealous rage explodes every time I help those in need."

"What are you saying?"

"I'm saying we're done."

***

Suzette's words lingered even as Lyon left the carnival alone. Years passed, but the memory of what happened on that cold night never left Lyon's mind. He became nastier than ever before; because of this, he began to study black magic, growing better at conjuring magic spells.

One night, while going back to his castle high above a hill, secluded from the Irish community, Lyon had learned of the Three-Leaf'd Tournament from a woman at the town's farmers' market. He crouched down near a food cart, carefully listening to the woman's conversation. Lyon could see other creatures with the woman, but he could see only their cloaked silhouettes.

"… Yes, that's what I heard … a tournament for the elite princes …"

"What about wizards? Aren't they banned from entering the tournament?"

"Yes, of course," said the woman. "King Diamond and Queen Kathrynne made sure it was protected from–"

"From Lyon, the wizard," said an unknown figure in a pale blue cloak. "Didn't he attempt to steal a baby from Prince William?"

"I don't know. Isn't that Prince William's baby, though?" said the woman.

"I think it is," said a third unknown figure in a silver cloak.

"What happened to Prince William's baby?" asked the figure in the blue cloak.

"I honestly don't know. No one knows," answered the woman.

Lyon was intrigued by what he had heard. He wanted to be the three-leaf'd prince because he figured the position held power, and he wanted to wield that power.

And so he continued forth toward his castle, confident in the knowledge that he would one day find Prince William's son and kill him.

CHAPTER IV

Ben McNealy

Present day

THE CARNIVAL WAS beginning to get crowded as Ben McNealy hurried his way through a crowd of people. Elizabeth stood at the snack bar, waiting patiently for Ben. Less than thirty-six hours ago, Ben had asked her to be his girlfriend, and it was the most crucial moment of her life. She loved Ben, and he loved her, too. And when Ben had asked Elizabeth to a carnival, she accepted.

Evan must have overheard Ben's conversation with Elizabeth, and he told Ben he wanted to go. He was sitting on the fence about Evan going, but he didn't want to hurt his best friend's feelings. He and Evan had grown up together and had been incredibly close since they were little.

But this was his first date with Elizabeth, and he wanted it to be perfect. Having Evan there with them would have been awkward.

For half of the night since they arrived at the carnival, Ben had concentrated on his date with Elizabeth. This bothered Evan, because he had thought it was to be a night of hanging out–just the three of them. He bottled his feelings in and said he was fine, even though he pretended otherwise.

***

A figure in a silver cloak appeared. It was wearing a tall top hat; a gold belt buckle was barely visible underneath its long cloak. It pulled back its hood; a man was visible. He was very tall and thin and had a long, bushy beard. None of the people saw him because he had been crouching low in a tall bush. All that was visible was an inch of his face.

Two girls were seated at the edge of the Ferris wheel, on the grass, when they spotted Saint Patrick in the bushes.

"Look what we have here–a tall freak," said one of the girls, gawking at Saint Patrick's colonial-style clothing. "You know, Halloween is not for another eight months."

The girls snickered.

"I know," said Saint Patrick. "I just wanted to try out this costume early." He was sarcastic, but the girls hardly noticed. "So do you know where Evan is?"

A red-headed girl gazed at Saint Patrick. "Who?"

"Evan," Saint Patrick repeated. "Do either of you know where he is?"

"Uh, no, I don't," said the red-headed girl crossly, "and even if I did know him, I wouldn't tell you."

"Well, thanks," said Saint Patrick. He turned toward the direction of the crowd and saw a hazy image of a teenage boy and girl. They were sitting on a bench near the snack bar.

Saint Patrick weaved in and out of the crowd, toward the direction of Ben and Elizabeth.

***

"I'm sorry I'm late. The crowd's heavy tonight."

"That's okay," said Elizabeth, hugging Ben.

"I got you something."

"What is it?"

"Mini corndogs," said Ben. "I thought we could share them."

Elizabeth smiled. "Okay. But you didn't get mustard, did you? You know mustard stains my clothes."

"All taken care of; don't worry."

Ben took out a mini corndog and ate it and offered one to Elizabeth.

Elizabeth took the mini corndog and ate it. "Thanks."

"Sure," said Ben, smiling.

Ben and Elizabeth sat down at a picnic table and divided the mini corndogs between them.

"I saw a tall, mysterious man."

Evan stopped in front of Ben and Elizabeth, almost stumbling over his feet. His breathing was fast and shallow.

"Evan, what is it?" Ben asked midbite.

"There's a man … following you two."

"Oh, Evan, don't you think you've had enough funnel cakes for one night?" Elizabeth asked. "Isn't that your eighth one?"

"This is my first one," said Evan, slightly offended. "I swear I saw a man following you two."

"Then what does 'this man' look like?" Ben asked. "Describe him to me."

"That," said Evan, "is what I don't know. He was very tall–of that I'm certain."

"Okay, tall. Anything else?"

"No."

"What was he wearing?"

"I don't remember what he was wearing," said Evan. "He was moving quickly among the crowd; I didn't get a chance to look at him."

"Well, do you remember anything else about this man?"

"No. I don't remember a thing."

"Don't pester your friends," said a voice behind Ben. "It's rude. Besides, Evan wasn't lying. He saw me."

Ben jumped. Elizabeth jumped too, and she dropped the greasy bag of mini corndogs to the ground.

A tall, cloaked man was standing before Ben and Elizabeth, his pale emerald eyes shining brilliantly in the sun's dim light.

"I'm sorry I startled you," said Saint Patrick. He turned to Ben. "You must go back with me to Ireland. There's a great peril unfolding, and you are the only one who can help me."

Ben laughed. "Really? You can't be serious. Is this a joke?"

"This isn't a joke. Why would I joke?"

"Look," said Ben, "I'm sorry about the imminent peril in Ireland, but I don't see what this has to do with me–or my friends, either."

"Look, Ben; an evil wizard named Lyon has already killed and tortured innocent creatures. You are the only one who can stop him."

"Me?" said Ben. "Why me?"

"You are the key to Ireland's peace and harmony," said Saint Patrick. "Your father was being trained in a tournament to protect Ireland's luscious landscapes and its civilizations, but he died. It will be up to you to finish your father's mission. I can't make that decision for you."

"I still don't get what you mean."

"I want you to compete in the Three-Leaf'd Tournament–a game of sorts," said Saint Patrick.

"No. Absolutely not," said Ben. "I can't compete. I don't have the agility or strength to compete."

"Yes, I admit agility plays a small part of the tournament," said Saint Patrick. "However, I believe you have something that's above everyone else who has ever competed in the Three-Leaf'd Tournament–something that sets you apart."

"And what's that?" said Ben, longing to hear more.

"You dare to stand up to those who challenge you in your beliefs."

"You don't know me."

"You're right. I don't know you. However, what I do know is you are like your father," said Saint Patrick. "He had the courage and a strong sense of will to fight those who, he believed, put him down. And I know you do, too. That's why I want you to come with me to Ireland. You are the only one left to save those creatures. I certainly cannot. I don't have the agility and the stamina I once did to save those in peril. You do."

"No. I won't."

"No?"

"Yes, no. I won't go with you," said Ben.

Elizabeth had been quiet for some time now, but then she spoke. "Why should Ben trust a man in colonial-style clothing? Isn't there anyone else who could take Ben's place as 'protector of Ireland?'"

"Unfortunately, no," said Saint Patrick, sighing. "Ben must go with me to Ireland to train and to compete in a tournament—a tournament that changes his life ... changes all of your lives."

"I won't go with you," repeated Ben. "Elizabeth is right. Why should I trust you, a man in colonial-style clothing?"

"I don't blame you for doubting me and what I've told you," said Saint Patrick. "What I've told you is far-fetched; believe me, I know. But please keep an open mind. I wouldn't say these things only to lie to you. Your life is too precious for me to do that. Now listen to me. Your mother and father were Irish. Your mother was a peasant while your father was a prince. Lyon killed them both."

Ben was struck with intense pain in his stomach. Never in this life had he felt a feeling of emptiness, a sense of wanting a family.

Saint Patrick pressed his palms together, and a three-leaved locket appeared. "Here. In case you change your mind."

Ben glanced at the locket and then at Saint Patrick. "What's this?"

"A locket." Saint Patrick placed the locket on the picnic table. "It will help you to defeat Lyon. It gives you the magic that you wouldn't have otherwise. For instance, it gives you the ability to travel undetected. But if I were you, I wouldn't reveal the locket's true purpose; it would cause serious consequences if misused."

Saint Patrick placed his top hat on the ground and, waving his hand over its brim, became the size of a figurine. Then he jumped into the top hat. It disappeared, leaving a trace of green smoke.

Ben was stunned.

Elizabeth was speechless.

Evan stared at the spot where Saint Patrick once stood and did not look away.

"I don't know what to think," Ben finally said, "or what to believe."

"I think Saint Patrick was sincere," said Elizabeth. "I mean, at first I didn't want to believe it, but the more I thought about it, the more I realized that what Saint Patrick said about going to Ireland makes sense."

"What do you mean?"

"I want you to go to Ireland to train with Saint Patrick," said Elizabeth. "He seems sincere, and I think this is a great opportunity for you to train."

"Train with him? A stranger? No thank you."

"Please think about what you'd be giving up."

Ben looked at Elizabeth. "What would I be giving up? I doubt I'd be giving up much."

"You'd be training with a historical figure—one highly respected in the Christian communities."

"I'll pass."

"Okay," said Elizabeth, sighing. "I'm just saying you should give Saint Patrick a chance."

"What made you change your mind so quickly?" Ben asked. "Just a few moments ago, you doubted whether we should trust Saint Patrick. Now you're saying I should trust him? What's up with that?"

"I have a right to change my mind, don't I?"

"Yeah. I guess so."

"Well, I think this Saint Patrick mess is stupid," said Evan. "I'm going to go."

Evan was about to leave, but Elizabeth stopped him. "Stop. Remember what Saint Patrick said? He talked about a tournament and said it would affect all our lives. Saint Patrick must want us to go with Ben for moral support."

"I doubt Saint Patrick wants us to go with Ben," said Evan. "Besides, if there is any danger involved, which I'm sure it will be, I refuse to go."

"Well, I haven't decided to go back to Ireland or not," said Ben. "I'm not saying I'll go, but it sure seems that the Irish people need a hero."

"Then are you saying you'll be their hero?" Elizabeth asked eagerly.

"I guess I have no choice, do I?"

"I guess not," said Elizabeth.

"I guess I'll go too," said Evan.

Ben grabbed the locket off the picnic table and placed it in his pocket.

Then he, Elizabeth, and Evan walked through the grass toward the bike racks, still pondering what Saint Patrick had told them.

CHAPTER V

Ben McNealy

A HOUSE BECAME visible in the distance as Ben, Elizabeth, and Evan rode through the trees upon a narrow path. Leaves crunched between their feet as they approached the house. Windowpanes lit from Halloween candles illuminated their way.

"Oh, it's good to see you, Elizabeth, Evan."

A woman was standing before them in a nightdress, holding the front door wide, smiling. Her hair was wrapped in a bun. Her face was free of makeup, and she appeared to be drained of everything.

"It's good to see you too, Mrs. McNealy," said Elizabeth. She smiled.

"Yeah. You too, Mrs. McNealy," said Evan awkwardly.

"I see you're already decorating for Halloween," Elizabeth observed as she, Evan, and Ben entered the house.

"Yeah. Well, it's not much," said Mrs. McNealy. "Our neighbors always go out for Halloween, and I thought I'd put up a few decorations."

"Oh, well, it's very nice," said Elizabeth.

Mrs. McNealy grinned. "Thank you. Do you want some cookies? There are some in the kitchen. I made some fresh this morning."

Elizabeth took a cookie. "Thanks."

"Sure," said Mrs. McNealy. She turned to Ben. "How did the carnival go? Did you have fun?"

"Yeah, it went fine."

"Were there a lot of people there?"

"Yeah."

"Did you ride any rides?"

"No. We just walked around."

"Did you eat?"

"Yeah. Elizabeth and I split mini corndogs. Evan had funnel cakes."

"Oh, I think it's time for Elizabeth and Evan to go home," said Mrs. McNealy.

"But can Elizabeth and Evan spend the night?" Ben asked.

"No. You guys have school in the morning, and I want you all rested."

Mrs. McNealy tried to rush Elizabeth and Evan out the door, but a green mist entered the house through a cracked window.

"Wait. Elizabeth and Evan may spend the night after all," said McNealy through hazy speech. The mist must have affected her.

Through an open window, Ben sensed a familiar presence, and he suspected it was Saint Patrick.

Moments later, Ben and his friends looked and saw that Mrs. McNealy had collapsed in a nearby chair and was dozily sleeping.

"Ben."

Ben glanced toward the window but couldn't see who had spoken. Moments later, he heard the voice again.

"Ben, over here."

Ben glanced toward the window again, and just beyond its sill, Saint Patrick's silhouette was visible through the tall bushes.

Ben walked over to the windowsill.

"Have you decided to go back to Ireland?" he said. "I don't want to alarm you, but if you don't go, chaos and destruction will continue to erupt across Ireland and beyond. So I advise you to choose wisely."

"Yeah, I have decided to go," said Ben, "on the condition that Elizabeth and Evan go with me for support."

"Okay, that's fine," said Saint Patrick, turning his back from the windowsill and dropping his tall hat in the grass. "Shall we go, then?"

"I guess so," said Ben.

Elizabeth and Evan looked toward the window and saw that Ben was on the edge of the windowsill, debating whether to jump.

Ben took a deep breath and jumped.

Elizabeth and Evan followed suit.

***

A castle came into view. In the distance, Ben and his friends saw the greenest hills they had ever seen. Ireland was a very different scene than what Ben and his friends were used to. Small cottages were barely visible just beyond the horizon. Townspeople were going about their business, tending their livestock and tending their gardens.

Further along, Ben and his friends could make out children playing just beyond the cottages. At the river's edge, Ben saw some cabins that were once lively and homey feeling but were now desolate and destroyed.

Lyon must have damaged some cottages and left others, Ben thought.

"This is the countryside that borders Ireland," said Saint Patrick, who had immediately picked up his gray top hat. "This is where your parents met and fell in love. Your mother lived in a cabin just beyond the village square." Saint Patrick pointed to an old clock tower in the center of the square. "They say her cabin was built by the famed log maker just a little further past the clock tower, in the forest."

"Whatever happened to him?" Ben asked. "The log maker, I mean?"

"He died mysteriously," said Saint Patrick. "Although the townspeople still have their suspicions."

"Oh," said Ben. "I'm sorry."

"Don't be," said Saint Patrick. "Most of the townspeople have forgotten the incident. Now, let us forget about the log maker for a second and instead focus on the reason you're here in Ireland." He tapped the grass with his cane. Instantly a bow and arrow appeared by his feet. "This is what you will use in the archery portion of the tournament. Creatures and royalty alike love this portion of the tournament because it proves to them that the potential contender has what it takes to take down enemies who attack from far distances."

"I don't know how to shoot a bow and arrow," said Ben.

"That's okay," said Saint Patrick. "Many princes didn't know archery at first, but they had to start somewhere. And you will too."

"I don't know. Archery isn't my strong suit."

"Well, your father was skilled in archery," said Saint Patrick. "And besides, you should practice with diligence if you're ever going to defeat Lyon. He's ruthless and relentless. He won't stop attacking you until you're dead."

"*Oi*. That's terrifying to know."

"I know it is, but don't worry. If you're diligent about practicing, you should be fine. Here." Saint Patrick handed the bow and arrow to Ben.

Ben held the bow and arrow, his hands shaking. He put back on the delicate string, and its arrow flew into the bushes, just a few feet away.

"That's all right," said Saint Patrick. "Try again."

Ben pulled back another arrow and let it go. It flew past Saint Patrick's ear, past Elizabeth's and Evan's heads, and hit a target a few inches from Evan.

"Very good. I knew you had it in you. You are truly Prince William's son." Saint Patrick gazed above him and saw the sun appearing low in the sky. "We'd better go."

"Go where?" asked Ben.

"Home," said Saint Patrick. "To your century. It's not safe here."

"Oh, C'mon. You dragged my friends and me here to Ireland to save the Irish people, and now you're telling me I must go back to my century. What gives?"

"I know," said Saint Patrick. "I know. It's doesn't make any sense now, but you've got to understand that if you're in this century, without any training, Lyon has an advantage in finding you and killing you—and your friends."

"Well, okay," said Ben.

"If you trained here, you could stay here at the castle—at least for the night. I think you and your friends will be fine. From there, I'll think of somewhere else all of you should go," said Saint Patrick, thinking aloud.

"Okay," replied Ben with a sigh.

Ben and his friends silently walked down a wobbly bridge toward Ben's father's castle, letting the cool breeze lightly touch their skin.

CHAPTER VI

Christine and Jeremy

Medieval Times

"WAKE UP."

Ben heard Saint Patrick's voice through the door, rolled over, and groaned.

"Wake up, I said!"

Saint Patrick opened the iron door to Ben's room. Inside he saw that thick pale blue curtains covered the long, ornate windows. Barely any light seeped through the curtains.

"Get up, Ben!" repeated Saint Patrick. "We've got a long journey ahead of us. I've decided we must go to the peasants' house just beyond the castle's boundaries."

"Go where, again?"

"The peasants'. Just beyond the castle's boundaries."

"Why go there?" Ben asked sleepily.

"They have a house that's hidden by dense bushes, trees, and underbrush," said Saint Patrick. "We need to hurry. There's no telling when Lyon will show up."

Ben got out of a king-sized bed. "Okay."

"And by the way, your friends are already down in the foyer, waiting."

"All right. I'll hurry."

Ben and Saint Patrick were soon making their way to the castle's foyer.

***

Grasslands and underbrush surrounded the perimeter of the peasants' property. The house was merely a small dot as Ben and his friends made their way through a grassy field. As soon as they reached their destination, Saint Patrick used his cane as a door-knocker, and the door immediately swung open.

A woman dressed in dirty clothing stood in the threshold of her home; she was hesitant, as if she had not seen visitors in years.

"Yes, may I help you folks?" she said. Her voice seemed crackly.

"Christine, it's me, Maewyn Succat. Don't you remember me?"

Christine wavered, looking at Saint Patrick with childlike wonderment. As she looked at Saint Patrick a bit longer, her confused expression turned into a bright smile.

"Yes, of course, I do," she said. "What are you doing here? And who do you have with you?"

"This is Ben and his two best friends, Elizabeth and Evan," said Saint Patrick.

"Excuse me; I'm Ben's girlfriend–not his best friend," said Elizabeth.

"Oh, sorry. This is Elizabeth, Ben's girlfriend."

"Well, it's nice to meet all of you," said Christine. "Won't you come in? It's cold out there."

Ben and his friends passed through the threshold, and immediately they smelled the aroma of warm bread baking in a dutch oven.

Christine and Jeremy's house was in disarray. There were items scattered all over the room. Some of their things were burnt, and some were not.

"It's good to be back at your house, Christine," said Saint Patrick. "It's been awhile."

"I wish my house were in better shape than it is now," said Christine. "If I had known you were coming earlier, I would've straightened up a bit." She sighed. "But as it is, there is nothing I can do."

"Oh, it's okay," said Saint Patrick. "It's understandable that you didn't have time to clean. You shouldn't be embarrassed about a messy home. You were worried about Lyon's wolves."

"Lyon's wolves?" said Ben. "Did they do all this damage?"

"Yes, certainly," said Saint Patrick. "Lyon created them with his evil magic to do his bidding. They ransacked and burned Christine and Jeremy's house and left it in shambles. I helped as best I could with the ashes and debris.

"The thing you have to know about Lyon's wolves is that they'll stop at nothing to obey Lyon's command. They might even kill you and your friends. So I suggest you use the locket I gave you to ward them off, should you encounter them."

"Yes, of course, I will," said Ben. He was unsure how an ordinary locket could aid him with Lyon's wolves, but he trusted Saint Patrick's judgment.

"Yeah, it was awful," said Christine, recalling the incident. She sighed again. "Now, would any of you like some bread?" Christine pointed to Ben, Elizabeth, and Evan. "I made it this morning."

"Oh, no thank you," said Ben. "I'm good."

"Yeah, I'm good also," said Elizabeth.

"I agree. I'm not hungry," said Evan.

Christine was slightly insulted. "Well, okay."

"I'll have some bread, Christine," said Saint Patrick. "Your bread is so crispy and warm. I enjoy it vastly."

"Well, all right," said Christine, smiling. "Hold on."

Christine went over to the dutch oven. Taking two potholders shaped like flower petals, she carefully opened the oven and placed a steaming pan of bread on an old and worn kitchen table.

The smell tickled the visitors' noses.

"Oh, it smells heavenly," said Saint Patrick, instantly seeing the steam rising from the brown and crusty bread.

Christine poked the center of the bread with a large wooden fork and let the steam escape a bit more. Then she carefully cut a thin slice and placed it on a simple china plate and handed it to Saint Patrick.

"Thank you," he said.

"Sure." Christine turned to Ben and his friends. "You sure you don't want any bread? I've got plenty."

Ben shook his head. "Oh, no thank you. Thanks, though."

"No. I'm fine," said Evan.

"Maybe I'll have a slice later," said Elizabeth.

A man opened a back door that led to the kitchen. He was tall and broad-shouldered. He had ash on his face and on his clothing. From his attire, Ben assumed he was a peasant. In his hands were two large metal tongs.

"Oh, hi, honey," said Christine, who had spotted the man.

"Hi," said the man. "Long day. I spent most of it getting coal out of a large barrel for Mr. Loxcaster."

"Oh, honey, you do too much for that old man. Didn't he ask you to clean his gutters last week, too?"

"Yeah, he did."

"Then why don't you tell him you simply can't do any more chores."

"Christine, you know I can't do that. You know Mr. Loxcaster is old and frail."

"I know," said Christine. "You're just trying to do the right thing." She turned to Ben and his friends. "This is my husband, Jeremy."

"How do you do? I'm Elizabeth."

"Jeremy." They shook hands.

"And I'm Evan."

"Glad to meet you, Evan. I'm Jeremy." Jeremy's eyes locked on Ben's eyes, making Ben feel a bit awkward. Jeremy then turned to Saint Patrick. "Who's this, Maewyn?"

"Oh, call me Saint Patrick. Everyone else does."

"Oh, you're not a saint to me," said Jeremy quickly. "What have you done to prove your sainthood?"

"It shouldn't matter how he achieved his sainthood," said Christine hotly. "The people of Ireland believe he is a saint, and that is all that matters."

"Well … all right," said Jeremy. "I still think he isn't a saint." He turned his attention back to Saint Patrick. "Who is this again?"

"This is Ben," said Saint Patrick, "the son of Prince William and Bridgette Greenhouse."

"Ah, yes," said Jeremy. "Yes, you certainly have Prince William's dashing good looks, although you have a dirty countenance–like your mother. Her skin could never get clean. I guess it comes with living life as a peasant. I should know; I am one."

"Ben has traveled far to defeat the wizard Lyon," said Saint Patrick. "Of course, with my training, he won't have any trouble defeating him."

Jeremy looked over Ben and scoffed. "Him? You chose him?"

"Yes. I did. Ben's the most qualified to defeat Lyon."

"Maewyn, I would have chosen a far better candidate than a boy who may or may not be 'qualified' as you say. I would have chosen another prince–one more dignified and proper than *him*."

"Jeremy! Enough!" said Christine. "You said what you had to say; now leave it be!"

"Well … okay," said Jeremy.

There was a low growl. Christine looked around nervously.

"What was that?" she asked.

"I don't know," said Jeremy. "But I'm going to check it out. I think it came from one of our bedrooms."

"Be careful," Christine advised. "You never know what had made the noise. It could be dangerous."

"I will."

Jeremy crept toward the bedroom, where the noise had come from, his heart beating rapidly. He took a deep breath and stepped inside. For a moment, it was silent–dangerously silent. Then, as he strode toward his closet, a persistent low growl continued.

With his nerves shot, Jeremy stepped further toward his closet. He touched his hand to the closet's knob. Quickly turning it, he peered inside. There were only clothes and a few dirty socks scattered here or there.

Had he imagined the growl? Surely not. Christine would not have heard the noise in that case. He closed the closet in disbelief.

He sat on his bed, wondering what to do next. He made a conscious decision not to tell Christine the wolves were not there. Jeremy didn't want his wife to be diagnosed as a crazy peasant. His sister, Genova, had a similar situation. She had heard the growl too. No one in the village square believed her. Lyon's evil wolves eventually got her.

Remembering the incident made Jeremy lose focus on the task at hand. He must leave with his wife, never to return to his home. If Lyon's wolves were indeed inside his house and they intended to cause harm to them, he didn't want to be here to find out.

Jeremy got up from his bed and took another deep breath. He walked over to his bedroom door and was about to leave the room when he heard it–a growl. A low but distinctive growl.

He stopped in midstride. He turned slowly, afraid what he'd find behind him.

"Hello," he said. "Is someone there? Christine? Maewyn?"

The growl persisted.

Seconds later the door of Jeremy's closet was torn to shreds, leaving an animal-sized hole at the base of it.

Jeremy saw the silhouette of a wolf; its eyes shone a deep bloodred. It crept toward him, its eyes locked on its target.

"Get away, wolf," said Jeremy, slowly backing away.

But the wolf ignored Jeremy's plea. Instead it kept creeping forward, never losing sight of its target.

"Help!" Jeremy cried. "Help me, please!"

The bedroom door sprang open. There, in silhouette, were Saint Patrick,

Christine, Ben, and Ben's friends, standing in the threshold of Jeremy and Christine's bedroom, silent but shocked. Saint Patrick, however, remained calm as he said, "Don't move. Any sudden movements will provoke them."

"Well, that's reassuring," said Jeremy. "What'll I do?"

"Remain still as possible," repeated Saint Patrick, his eyes locked on the wolves.

"What'll you do?" Jeremy asked. Beads of sweat damped the bedroom floor.

"You'll see," said Saint Patrick. "Just remain calm."

Saint Patrick tapped his bejeweled cane on the carpet. The wolves stopped inching toward Jeremy. They collapsed on the carpet, panting.

"We'd better hurry," said Saint Patrick. "The spell will only last for only so long."

"But where will we go?" asked Christine.

"The tunnel," said Jeremy at once. "Remember, honey?"

Christine nodded.

"We'd better go, then," said Saint Patrick.

The tunnel in Jeremy and Christine's house was damp and dimly lit. Ben and his friends ventured forth through the tunnel, afraid that unexpected things might happen to them. Saint Patrick, however, remained calm as he strolled through the tunnel, not saying a word. His brown leather Irish-accent shoes clanked the tunnel's surface as he strode in long strides. Christine, looking behind her, was afraid that the wolves would follow them and indeed kill them.

"Jeremy, how much longer until we reach the end of this tunnel?" she asked. "My feet are starting to swell from walking so far."

"Not too far," said Jeremy, not looking back but keeping his attention on getting out of the tunnel alive.

"What's that noise?" Elizabeth asked. Everyone stopped. She turned to Ben. "Did you hear that?"

"Hear what?"

"That noise."

"What noise?"

"A low but distinctive growl."

"I didn't hear a growl," said Ben. "You must be imagining things."

"Oh, no, she didn't imagine the growl, Ben," said Saint Patrick. "Lyon's wolves have a low but distinctive growl. I'm almost positive it was the wolves Elizabeth heard."

"What do we do, then?" Ben asked, glancing at Saint Patrick for guidance.

"Let's see how many wolves are in this tunnel with us," said Saint Patrick. "Then we may judge whether we should use magic or not."

"Are you crazy?" said Elizabeth. "You don't know how many wolves are in this tunnel. There could be thousands."

"Not thousands," said Saint Patrick. "Maybe hundreds, but not thousands."

"Hundreds?" said Elizabeth. "*Oi*."

Whoosh.

A blinding light flashed above Ben's and his friends' heads. They ducked as another flash of light flickered.

Then there was another flash.

Then another.

And another.

Looking behind him, Ben saw several wolf shadows bouncing off the darkened tunnel, provided by lanterns giving off dull light.

"What do I do?" Ben asked Saint Patrick.

"Use your locket."

"Why?"

"Use your locket."

"How?"

"Open it and you'll see," said Saint Patrick.

Without question, Ben opened the locket around his neck. Instantly a wand appeared in his dominant hand.

Ben turned over his shoulder, and while running, he flicked the wand. The burst of illuminating light entered the tunnel, almost blinding. Moments later, Ben heard a horrendous sound of an animal in pain. He glanced further down the tunnel and saw a faint image of a wolf lying lifeless. The bursts from the wand must have been too much for the wolf to handle, he guessed.

Still running and out of breath, Ben continued to cascade bursts of light down the tunnel as more wolves, in silhouette, followed them. Then, abruptly, Ben and his friends stopped.

Thick smoke filled the tunnel.

"What shall we do now?" Christine asked.

"I honestly do not know," said Jeremy. "I'm sure Lyon's wolves have blocked the other entrance of the tunnel with smoke too."

"I'm scared," said Elizabeth. "You know I'm terrified of cramped places, and this smoke isn't helping me any."

"I know," said Ben.

"Ben, I admire your heroism," said Saint Patrick. "Your father would have been so proud of you. My advice for you would be to open your locket again, because your wand's magic lasts for only so long."

"What'll that do?" said Ben. "The tunnel's already filling up with smoke, and I don't think Elizabeth will last much longer."

"Ben, I advise you to take charge," said Saint Patrick. "Open your locket."

"Then you take the locket. I don't want it anymore." Ben handed it to Saint Patrick.

"Ben, I can't have it back," said Saint Patrick. "Your mother and father gave it to you when you were born. It only opens to your touch."

Saint Patrick handed the locket back to Ben. "I don't want to hear you've given up," he added. "I don't believe you will give up so easily. It's not in your father's nature to give up in a moment of crisis, and neither should you."

"Ben, please hurry," said Elizabeth. "The smoke is too thick for me to breathe."

"Me, too," said Evan, coughing.

Ben still had some doubts, but he did what Saint Patrick suggested. He put the locket around his neck. With a trembling hand, he opened it. Instantly a large leprechaun's hat appeared.

Ben looked back over his shoulder and realized that the smoke that was once visible had disappeared; all that was visible was the leprechaun's hat, heretofore unknown to Ben and his friends.

"What do we do?" Ben asked, glancing at the leprechaun's hat and then to Saint Patrick.

"What do you think? Jump inside the leprechaun hat," said Saint Patrick, urging Ben and his friends to jump into his hat. Without question, Ben and his friends jumped inside the leprechaun hat, disappearing from the tunnel.

CHAPTER VII

Karoline Brickswough

Green Leprechaun

A TEENAGE WAITRESS dressed in a cute leprechaun outfit made her way around the crowded tables shaped like pots of gold. She was holding several trays of steaming Irish food. She carefully placed the Irish food on a freestanding server's plate by one of the tables.

"Who had chicken?"

A man with a gruff beard raised his large hand. "I did," he said.

She handed a steaming plate of chicken to the man.

"Who had Irish beef?"

"Me."

A tall but old leprechaun seated at the edge of the table waved his hand.

He had tucked his cloth napkin inside his long silk cloak. He seriously was going to throw down some Irish beef or die trying, the teenage waitress assumed. She walked over to the edge of the table and cautiously placed the plate of meat in front of the old leprechaun.

"Thank you, sweetie," he said.

The teenage waitress nodded. "Sure."

"Karoline."

The teenage waitress spun around. A tall but old man was standing behind her, concerned.

"Yeah?"

"You know I don't want you to work tonight."

"I know. But if I don't work, I'll be stir-crazy. Father, you know that." Karoline placed a plate of corned beef in front of a woman who had ordered it.

"I know you would," said the man. "And I don't blame you. But if Kevin shows up—"

"I can handle him, okay?"

"I honestly don't think you can," said Raymond, Karoline's father, "because Kevin's been persistent on coming to the Green Leprechaun ever since you broke off your engagement a few weeks ago."

"Has he now?"

"Yes! He has!"

"It's no concern of mine how Kevin spends his free time, Father," said Karoline, refreshing a leprechaun's glass of root beer. "If he wants to pity himself here at the Green Leprechaun, that's just fine by me."

"But I don't think he's here to pity himself, honey," said Raymond. "I think he's here to rekindle your romance and continue your engagement and perhaps marry you."

Karoline scoffed. "Kevin knows it's over between us."

"I don't know if he knows that, Karoline," said Raymond. "Besides, I don't want my daughter to marry a scumbag. He'll only break your heart again."

"Oh, believe me; that's the last thing I'm going to do," said Karoline, walking over to the kitchen's open bar counter and placing an empty tray on its surface. "The farther away I am from Kevin, the better."

"Oh, good," said Raymond. "As long as we're under an agreement that you'll never go back to Kevin, we're good."

Karoline gave her father a dirty look. "Father …"

"I know. I know. You won't go back to Kevin." Raymond kissed his daughter on the forehead. "Thank you."

"Sure."

Karoline continued serving customers.

***

Ben and his friends entered the Green Leprechaun, for lunch. Ben immediately noticed it was Irish themed, with many Irish antiques scattered across the restaurant.

"How many are in your party?" Karoline asked, taking several menus from inside a thin wooden stand and placing them under her arm.

"Five, including me," said Saint Patrick.

Grabbing an extra menu, Karoline said, "Follow me."

Ben and his friends followed Karoline to a table shaped like a pot of gold, just beyond a flowing fountain. Heaps of gold coins fell into a silver basin.

"What would each of you like to drink?" asked Karoline.

"Water with lemon," said Ben, glancing at his menu.

"Coke–no ice," said Elizabeth.

"I'll have a Sprite," said Evan.

"Tea with lemon," said Jeremy.

"The tea has mint in it. Is that all right?" Karoline asked Jeremy.

"Yeah, that's fine."

Scribbling the drink order on a small piece of parchment paper, Karoline turned to Christine. "And you?"

"Tea with lemon."

"I'll have your special green-colored ginger ale," said Saint Patrick, glancing at his menu with round gold-colored spectacles.

Karoline scribbled the rest of the drink orders on the piece of parchment paper and said, "Coke—no ice, water with lemon, two teas with lemon, a Sprite, and our special ginger ale—green colored. Correct?"

Everyone nodded.

"Great. I'll be back when you're ready to order," said Karoline. She turned her attention to other customers, all of them seated at tables shaped like pots of gold.

She helped a woman refresh her drink and cleared a plate or two.

***

Kevin Shooter entered the Green Leprechaun, his mind on his task at hand. Somehow or someway, he was going to persuade Karoline to give him another chance. He was stupid to let her go, and he was still grappling with the reasons he'd dumped her.

He walked to the bar, aware that drinking wasn't the best decision, but he needed a quick pick-me-up.

"A green-colored leprechaun beer," said Kevin.

A small leprechaun bartender quickly turned around and looked deeply into Kevin's face. "Are you Kevin? Kevin Shooter?"

"Yeah," said Kevin.

"You're not supposed to be in here," said the bartender. "I believe you were banned from coming here. I must tell Mr. Brickswough. Excuse me."

"Kevin, what are you doing here?" asked Raymond Brickswough. "I thought I told you a couple of weeks ago to get out of my restaurant because you caused a scene and frightened the customers."

"Yeah. You did, but I came to see Karoline."

"She doesn't wish to see you."

"But I want to see her. Is she busy?"

"Yes," said Raymond. "Extremely. You may want to leave before you cause embarrassment to yourself, to Karoline, and to the customers here."

"I'm not leaving until I get to see Karoline," said Kevin. "And have my leprechaun beer."

"No, it's time for you to leave," said Raymond.

"Please, sir," said Kevin, "all I want is to see your daughter. If I could see her for a moment or two, I'd–"

"No, you can't see her," said Raymond at once. "I already told you she's swamped serving customers."

"Please, sir … I'm desperate."

"No, you're not desperate," said Raymond. "You'll live without seeing her."

"With all due respect, I know you love your daughter, as do I," said Kevin. "I want to see her to apologize to her for the way I acted toward her. It wasn't right. I want to make amends."

"Well, did you love her when you cheated on her with a much older woman—a leprechaun woman?"

Kevin was speechless. "I'm sorry," he finally said.

"Don't apologize to me, because I don't accept your apology," said Raymond. "What you did was disgraceful, dishonorable, and wrong. What you did really hurt Karoline."

"I know. I realize that now."

"Really? I have a hard time believing your sudden change of heart."

"I know. I know I've been flaky in the past, but I've changed."

"No. No, you haven't," said Raymond, "because if you had changed, you and Karoline would still be planning a traditional Irish wedding. But you're not. The reality is, Kevin, you cheated on my only daughter. Karoline loved you; she worshipped the ground you walked on. Gosh knows I seriously don't know why."

"Kevin?"

Kevin turned his attention to Karoline, who was holding a large server's tray of Irish burgers. "Hi, Karoline."

"Don't be friends with me, Kevin," said Karoline, "I don't trust you; I don't trust cheaters. I don't want to see you. Go."

"Please, Karoline," said Kevin, "give me another chance."

Karoline scoffed. "No, I'm not going to give you another chance. I gave you many chances, and you blew every single one."

Kevin stepped forward. "Karoline ... please ..."

"No, get away from me," said Karoline.

Karoline turned her attention to customers who ordered the Irish burgers. She placed the tray on the edge of the table. "Want extra ketchup, mustard?"

"Karoline."

She glared at Kevin. "What?"

"Please be civil."

"I'm civil," said Karoline. "It's you that isn't civil."

"Karoline, look, I came here to apologize. Doesn't that count for something?"

Karoline wavered at Kevin's statement. "No," she finally said. "Cheaters don't apologize—not when they'll do it over again."

"Karoline, do you love me?" said Kevin quickly.

"No," said Karoline after hesitating.

"You do love me," said Kevin. "I know you still do, because otherwise there wouldn't be hesitation in your voice."

"I know you think I can forget the incident that happened between us and start anew, but as much as I desire for us to get back together, we can't. We just can't," said Karoline. "You cheated on me. No one can forget something so disgraceful, so dishonorable, as cheating. I certainly can't. I'm sorry. Now go."

"Karoline."

She quickly glanced at Kevin before returning to waiting tables.

"You heard my daughter," said Raymond, who had heard the conversation between Kevin and his daughter. "Leave."

Kevin's temper reached its boiling point. He swiped a bowl of greasy nachos off the restaurant's bar in one motion, breaking the ceramic bowl in the process.

Karoline, hearing the ceramic bowl crash to the floor, turned to pick up the excess pieces. But as she did so, Kevin stepped forward.

"Let me help," he said.

"No, you've helped enough," she said.

"Karoline, don't be silly. Let me help."

"No. Please get out of here."

"You heard my daughter," said Raymond. "Leave, before you make it worse."

"Karoline."

She looked up from picking up the excess pieces of the bowl.

"Answer me this: why do you allow your father to guide your choices?"

"He doesn't guide my choices," said Karoline.

"He does. He's doing it now. If you love me as you say, then we should be together."

"No."

"No?"

"Yes. No. You cheated on me," said Karoline. "I can't be in love with a cheater."

"But you're still in love with me, then?" Kevin asked.

"No, I'm not."

"Is this your decision or your father's?"

"Kevin …"

"Please answer me."

"Mine," said Karoline. "It is my decision."

"Oh, I see," said Kevin. "You'd rather choose your father, who has always told you what to do all your life–even now–than choose me, the one who loves you and will always respect your choices. I'll go, then."

Kevin stepped back from Karoline, but as he went, he knocked over another bowl of greasy nachos; the ceramic bowl they were in broke.

A man eating the nachos, asked Karoline, "May I have another bowl of nachos?"

Karoline gazed at Kevin, who had disappeared from the restaurant.

"Karoline."

It was Raymond, her father.

"Yes?"

"This man wants some more nachos. Are you going to get him some more?"

"Yes, of course."

She grabbed the bowl of nachos that was on the edge of a large counter. "Here you go."

"Thanks," said the man quietly.

"Sure," said Karoline.

A few tables down, Ben and his friends were in shock at the scene that had taken place a few moments before.

"I'm sorry about him," said Ben, who gazed at the bar and the greasy nachos on the floor, looking at Karoline.

"It's okay," she said. "Keven comes by here at least twice a week, but that's the first time he has caused such a scene." She placed a tray of drinks on the table and passed out them out to the correct person. "You ready to order?"

"Yes." Saint Patrick glanced at a large menu placed at the edge of the table. "What's in the Irish philly cheesesteak?"

"It's just a regular cheesesteak, but we put in it our famous Irish spices," said Karoline. "We make it fresh."

"Okay, I'll have that," said Saint Patrick.

"I'll just have a cheeseburger," said Evan, glancing at his menu.

"I'll have your specialty salad with green peppers and your Irish spices," said Elizabeth.

"Okay." Karoline scribbled the order on the parchment paper. "The salad is pretty spicy." She looked at Elizabeth, still writing on her roll of parchment paper. "Is that all right?"

"Yes. It is."

"Okay great." Karoline looked at Ben. "And you?"

"I'll have a hamburger."

"All right."

Karoline finished writing down the orders and retreated to the kitchen.

Meanwhile, Princess Lexis Tanglewood and Princess Taylor Flanking had entered the Green Leprechaun. As soon as their eyes became accustomed to the lack of light, they spotted Ben and his friends sitting at a round table.

"Isn't that Prince William?"

Princess Taylor glanced at Princess Lexis. "Where?"

"By the flowing fountain, there," said Princess Lexis, pointing.

"I think so."

"Well, since my previous date did not pan out, I get first dibs on dating him," said Princess Lexis.

"Why do you get another chance with Prince William?" said Princess Taylor. "You were the one who ruined my date with him, not me."

"Well, if my memory serves me right, your date was already a disaster before I came along," said Princess Taylor. "Prince William knew that, and he was too nice to tell you so, but I'm not that nice, and I just told you."

"Let's see what Prince William thinks and have him decide which one of us was a better date," said Princess Lexis. "Just know he'll pick me; it was arranged for the two of us to marry after our date."

Princess Taylor was slightly offended. "And who decided that?"

"Prince William's mother and father, Queen Kathrynne and King Diamond," said Princess Lexis.

"And Princess William went along with this prearranged marriage?" Princess Taylor asked.

"Well, not exactly," said Princess Lexis. "But he will once he realizes he can't live without me."

"In your dreams! What makes you so confident he will agree to marriage if he didn't want it in the first place?"

"He will. I'll charm him with my sexy figure and beautiful soul."

Princess Taylor laughed. "Beautiful soul? You?" she said. "Ha, well, I don't have to impress Prince William. He already knows me."

"Yeah, he seemed to know you already," Princess Lexis said sarcastically, not believing a word she was saying. "Didn't you notice at all what he was doing? He was dismissing your flirtations."

"Well, we'll see who Prince William dismisses once he sees the both of us," said Princess Taylor. "I think once he sees me, you'll be a fool."

"Oh, you'll be the one who's a fool once he recognizes me," said Princess Lexis.

"Okay … whatever."

"Hey, Prince William. Remember me?" said Princess Lexis, looking in the direction of Ben.

"Ben, do you recognize this princess?" Elizabeth whispered.

"No, I honestly do not," Ben whispered back.

"That is Princess Lexis, whom your father briefly dated," said Saint Patrick in Ben's ear. "Please be nice to her, as she doesn't know that your father has passed away."

"Hi."

"Hello," said Ben awkwardly.

"So I see you're back in the Green Leprechaun."

"Yeah. I am."

"Sorry about our previous date," said Princess Lexis. "Things got in the way before … anyhow, would you mind giving our date another chance?"

Ben was at a loss for words. He stood there, unable to fathom the entirety of what Princess Lexis was asking.

"Excuse me?"

"I am asking you out again," said Princess Lexis.

"He doesn't want another date with you," Princess Taylor interjected. "Besides, your date ended up in disaster."

"It only ended up in disaster because you showed up and ruined everything."

"I did not ruin anything," said Princess Taylor. "You did that all on your own."

"How did I do that?" Princess Lexis asked. "Tell me; I want to know."

"Well, first off, Prince William never did want a date with you. Isn't that right?" She glanced at Ben.

"Well … uh …"

"See? He agrees with me," said Princess Taylor. "And second, he doesn't want to marry you."

"But"–Princess Taylor gently touched Ben's quivering hand–"he does want to marry me."

Elizabeth was heated. She got up from the table and disappeared behind a lace curtain.

Ben followed her, scared that the two princesses might have jeopardized his relationship.

"Elizabeth," he said, "where are you going?"

"Away from here," she said.

"Why?" he asked.

"Why?"

Ben nodded. "Yes, why."

"Didn't you see those two princesses flirting with you? I can't be in the same room with you when that is happening."

"Eliza, you know I'm not my dad, right?"

Elizabeth crossed her arms and gave Ben a piercing look.

"And besides, these two princesses might've been confused about who I am," said Ben. "My dad must've had a horrible date between the two princesses, and they must've thought I was my father by mistake."

"But you didn't correct the princesses, did you?" said Elizabeth.

"Eliza …"

"Did you?"

"No," said Ben. "No, I didn't."

"Exactly my point," said Elizabeth. "Now, I just want to be by myself for a while."

She turned away, and Ben could instantly smell a sweet aroma of perfume. Ben remembered how fresh and clean it smelled–like cotton.

"Elizabeth," Ben began.

"I told you, I just want to be by myself."

Ben sighed. "Okay."

He returned to his seat by the flowing fountain, feeling a sense of despair and loneliness. Elizabeth had never retreated from him before, and he didn't know what he'd do.

"Are you all right?" said Evan. His tone was that of a sincere friend.

"I'm all right," said Ben softly.

"But you're not all right," said Evan. "You're confused, just as I am, about Elizabeth's response to the princesses, aren't you?"

"Evan, I appreciate your sincerity ... I do ... but–"

"You just want to be left alone about this, don't you?"

"Yeah."

"Well, we're going to go," said Princess Lexis. "You're not Prince William."

"Yeah," Princess Taylor agreed. "Sorry."

The two princesses left the Green Leprechaun without saying another word.

"Ben."

Ben looked at Saint Patrick.

"If it makes you feel any better, you can alter the situation with the two princesses–and Elizabeth."

"I thought the leaf'd prince was all about honesty and would not use his powers for personal gain," said Ben. "At least, that was the impression I got from you."

"Well, I can see you're confused and hurt by what has happened here in the Green Leprechaun tonight," said Saint Patrick. "True, your impression of always doing the honest thing as the leaf'd prince is on point, but I can sense your brokenness and despair. Use your locket. I promise you won't regret it."

"But what about honesty?"

"Please, Ben. I can sense you're hurting. Use your locket."

Ben, unsure whether his locket would work in the present situation, opened it. A slip of paper appeared on the edge of the table.

"What's this?" Ben murmured.

"Read it," said Saint Patrick.

Ben opened the folded note.

It read one word: "sorry."

"Ben."

Ben peeked behind him and saw that Elizabeth was standing there.

"Hi," he said.

"Hi," she said.

Ben got up from the table and hugged Elizabeth, feeling a rush of warmth in his fingertips.

"Sorry about everything," said Elizabeth. "I was a bit jealous of the two princesses flirting with you."

Ben laughed. "A bit?"

"Okay, I was jealous. I admit it."

"Shall we finish our meal?" said Ben, sitting down.

"Yes," said Elizabeth. "We shall."

Ben and his friends continued finishing their meals.

"Ben."

Ben looked at Saint Patrick, in midbite. "Yeah?"

"Keep your locket close to you."

"Okay, I will. But what about the note?" said Ben, eating a bite of his Irish potatoes.

"Your locket gives you what you want–what you need. Sometimes despite reasonable doubt, it will give you what your heart desires most. That's why the note appeared, and that's why Elizabeth apologized."

"But it was a lie," said Ben. "The note."

"No, it wasn't a lie or an invasion," said Saint Patrick. "Your locket was willing to give you what you needed. Elizabeth only apologized because she chose to. The locket's power did not affect her."

"Saint Patrick's right," said Elizabeth, who overheard the conversation between Ben and Saint Patrick. "I chose to apologize on my own accord; it wasn't the locket's doing."

Meanwhile, in a nearby booth, Hamish was busy scribbling notes on a cloth notepad made of parchment paper. He couldn't help but glance at Ben and his friends every few minutes or two.

"More water?" asked a blonde waitress. She was holding a glass of ice water in one hand and a parchment notepad in the other.

"Huh? Well, yeah," said Hamish, not looking up from scribbling.

She carefully poured ice water into Hamish's empty glass and went on to serving other customers.

A loud blast from a wand immediately cracked the Green Leprechaun's windows. Customers instantly barricaded themselves under freestanding furniture. Ben and his friends quickly hid under the restaurant's bar to seek safety.

"What's happening?" Ben asked Saint Patrick.

"Lyon must've known you'd be here and is now attempting to kill you," Saint Patrick said through the commotion. "We have to leave."

Saint Patrick retreated from under the bar. He tapped the wooden floor with his cane. A mist entered the dusty and chaotic air. Then, as it cleared, Ben heard silence.

"Do you think Lyon will keep attacking the restaurant now that you restored calm here?" Ben asked earnestly.

"I think he will," said Saint Patrick. "So I earnestly suggest we seek safety elsewhere."

"What about all the other customers?" Elizabeth asked. "Will they be all right?"

"I imagine they will," said Saint Patrick. "Lyon was really after Ben."

"But Lyon would have killed every customer here if he'd had the chance, right?"

"Depends," said Saint Patrick.

"Depends on what?"

"Ben, I hate to be the bearer of bad news, but we must go before all chaos breaks loose again; the customers are in continued danger."

"Okay," said Ben. "You're right."

Ben and his friends quickly left the Green Leprechaun in the hope of seeking shelter elsewhere–away from Lyon's awful wrath.

CHAPTER VIII

Mystic, the Green Pixie

IN THE DISTANCE, a tree house quickly came into view; its greenery and sunflowers were slightly visible from a forest clearing. A rope ladder lay just inches from the base of the tree. It was thick and elongated, stretching to the sky. Ben and his friends had never in their life seen so much foliage; it was prosperous and lively.

"Where are we?" Ben asked.

"We are at Mystic's," said Saint Patrick. "She's a friend of mine, and she's a pixie. I thought her house would be a perfect hiding spot for you and your friends, as the naked eye does not so easily see it."

There was a low but distinctive growl. In the bushes, a shadowed figure slowly approached Ben and his friends.

Ben's heart leaped.

Wolf silhouettes were everywhere.

"What do we do?" Ben asked Saint Patrick.

"The locket, Ben. Use your locket."

Then—without delay—a blinding light hit Elizabeth, causing her to scream.

"*Elizabeth!*" Ben yelled.

Ben's adrenaline was pumping. The wolves had injured the one person he could not live without and cared for deeply.

"We need to ward off Lyon's magical wolves," said Saint Patrick at once. "Ben and I will ward off the wolves while you"—Saint Patrick pointed to Jeremy and Christine—"take Elizabeth to a safe spot, near Mystic's tree house."

"No," said Ben. "I want to stay with Elizabeth. I will not leave her injured here—or worse, be killed by Lyon's ravenous wolves."

"Ben, I'm okay. You must do what Saint Patrick is instructing you to do."

"Elizabeth, No! I won't leave you."

"All right, Ben, you may stay with Elizabeth," said Saint Patrick. "I can handle Lyon's wolves on my own."

"Let me help," said Jeremy. He stood stoic and proud.

"You'll be dead before you have a chance. I won't risk your safety," said Saint Patrick.

"I can handle it."

"Jeremy, I said no."

"Honey, please listen to Saint Patrick," said Christine. "He's only trying to keep you safe from harm. You may get hurt trying to battle dangerous wolves."

"You think Ben here won't get hurt, too?" Jeremy asked. "He would, and you know it."

"Yes, I know."

"Then allow me to battle."

"It's very gallant of you to want to take Ben's place in battle, but it's not up to me," said Christine. "It's up to Saint Patrick, and he said no. And you know what? I agree with him."

"You know what, Jeremy?" said Saint Patrick. "I'm only trying to spare your life by not allowing you to battle Lyon's dangerous wolves, but if you want to so badly, be my guest."

"Really?"

"If you want to fight so badly, be my guest. But be forewarned: Lyon's wolves are unpredictable creatures. They'll blindside you when you least expect it."

"Okay." Jeremy was unsure of himself. "You know what? I'm going to opt out of fighting dangerous wolves. They seem so … so dangerous."

"That's what I thought," said Saint Patrick.

Ben managed to avoid the specks of light caused by Lyon's magical wolves, and he gently guided Elizabeth to a nearby log where she could rest her injured ankle. Blow after blow of light entered the dusty air. Ben and Elizabeth, horrified, could see the scene before them.

Jeremy and Christine were barely visible, hidden behind a tall and thick tree just beyond the forest clearing. Wolf shadows continued to move swiftly in the darkness.

Saint Patrick wasted no time. He tapped the grass, and immediately the wolves that were once growling went silent. They lay on the grass, still.

"Let's hurry, before Lyon's wolves are aroused from their dreamlike state."

The wolves lay in a dreamlike state, just as Saint Patrick had mentioned, but Ben was unsure for how long they would stay that way.

"Are you all right?" Ben asked Elizabeth, to keep himself distracted from the arousal of Lyon's wolves.

"I'm fine," she said. "You don't need to worry about me."

"But I do worry about you," said Ben. "I love you. To see you hurt was the worst thing I could have experienced."

"Ben … really … I'm all right. I have a sprained ankle."

"You're a trooper," said Evan. "I know that if I got my ankle sprained, I'd cry like a baby."

"Evan!"

"Ben, what! I'm only stating the obvious."

"Elizabeth does not need your comments right now," said Ben. "Her ankle hurts bad enough as it is. She doesn't need a reminder from you."

"Ben, it's all right," said Elizabeth.

"No, it's not all right," said Ben. "With the added pressure of Lyon's wolves following us at every turn, I don't know how much more I can take."

"Ben, what do you mean?" Evan asked.

"I never signed up to be a 'protector of Ireland,'" said Ben.

"But you chose to be one," said Evan. "If I were in your shoes, I don't–"

"Evan!" said Ben.

"–know what I'd do."

Saint Patrick quickly tapped the grass. Instantly a large basket made from the excess tree limbs from Mystic's tree house appeared. It looked strong enough to carry two people.

"It'll be all right," he said after finishing the woven basket with his magic. "You're not alone with defeating Lyon. I know a heavy burden is on your shoulders now; I'm partly to blame for that, and I am sorry. But listen, Ben; it's an honor to serve as a leaf'd prince. Many princes who have come before you have successfully proven themselves to be legendary. You are just one of a long line of Leaf'd princes."

"Tell me, this, Saint Patrick: did all the leaf'd princes have to deal with evil wizards like Lyon?"

"Well, honestly … no, they didn't. These wizards had similar foes."

"We need to hurry," Saint Patrick added. "Lyon's wolves will wake at any moment."

He gestured for Ben and Elizabeth to get into the premade basket. As soon as they stepped into the basket and Saint Patrick used his magic to hoist them into the air, Ben saw a spectacular view of Ireland's countryside: the lush scenery of the fields, the green foliage of the trees, and the forest-cutters' cottages were in the distance. Further along, people were small dots. A river lay just inches from the forest-cutters' cottages, flowing onward like a ship onto the sea.

Jeremy and Christine were already on Mystic's front porch by the time Ben and Elizabeth reached the top. Ben helped Elizabeth out of the basket, leaning on him for support. Saint Patrick knocked on Mystic's old front door.

Opening it, she glanced around nervously and then quickly gestured for Ben and his friends to come in.

"Sorry about that," she said. "You never can be too careful with an evil wizard on the loose."

"Mystic, that is why we came," said Saint Patrick. "Ben and his friends need a place to hide until further notice. What do you say?"

"Well, I guess that'll be okay," said Mystic, sighing. "I was going to prepare my tree house against the incoming raid of Lyon's attacks on my own, but since you're here, you may help me."

"So how have you been lately?" Saint Patrick asked as he carefully raised a kitchen chair on a dining room table. "I don't see you much anymore due to Lyon's continuous attacks on the village people."

"Well, it is to be expected. Now I don't much go out into the countryside due to risk of being captured by Lyon. I spend my days here by my fireplace, trying to keep warm. It's tough, you know? One day you're fine, going out into the countryside, mingling with the other pixies … the next …"

Mystic trailed off, teary-eyed, trying to regain her composure from remembering such a horrible incident.

"Excuse me, Mystic," said Ben. "Whatever happened to the other pixies? Do you miss them?"

Saint Patrick glanced at Ben crossly. "Mystic does not wish to recall the incident with her brothers and sisters," he said. "Sometimes it is best if one leaves questions unanswered for the time being."

"No, Maewyn, it's quite all right," said Mystic. "I don't mind retelling what happened."

Saint Patrick glanced at Mystic wearily. "Please call me Saint Patrick. Everyone else does. And are you sure?"

"Yes, I'm positive."

Mystic wiped the corner of her eye with a small tissue made of thin wool.

Ben and his friends sat down on several wooden dining room chairs and listened intently.

"Where to begin … hmm … first I should tell you that I was out enjoying the countryside with my brother, Mauve, and my sister, Paltry." She wiped another tear. "We were getting some exotic plants for a sultry soup we were having for our family of pixies who was coming over for our yearly reunion. 'It's so beautiful here,' Paltry said. 'It sure is,' agreed Mauve. Then, as Mauve was picking the last of the exotic lettuce, shadowed figures—maybe wolves— came from out of nowhere and attacked Paltry. She tried to fight back, but it was useless. The shadowed figures instantly killed Paltry. She was no match for them."

"I'm sorry," said Elizabeth. "What about Mauve? Whatever happened to him?"

"He died after defending himself from the shadowed figures," said Mystic. "He, like Paltry, had no chance."

"I'm sorry," said Ben.

"It's okay," said Mystic. "I'm fine. I quickly flew away secretly to avoid harsh attacks. Luckily I was able to get away without any physical damage. Although I do have emotional scars from the incident, that's all I have. I was lucky."

"I'd say you were," said Ben.

"That's not all," said Mystic. "The shadowed figures were not done with me yet. They tried to burn down my tree house. This tree house is my only place of shelter—of comfort. They were unsuccessful, but if they had succeeded, I don't know what I'd do."

She tried to stop herself from crying, but it was not possible. Big, soggy tears fell to the floor.

"Mystic, it's going to be all right," said Saint Patrick. "You know your sister and brother are in a better place, right?"

"Yeah, I know," said Mystic through sniffles. "It's just hard to get through something that difficult, you know?"

"Yes, I know."

***

Mystic could still remember the lush greenery of her flowers, the vibrant colors of the plants native only to Ireland. She remembered how, as a child, her mother would tend to the plants hanging aloft in the kitchen her father had built for his wife years earlier. She could still smell the sweet and distinct aroma of perfume lingering in the dusty and old tree house. Oh, how she missed her mother!

If only she could get a glimpse of her mother once again. She would tell her mother sorry she had argued with her. They had different opinions about how she wanted to live her life; Mystic was a free spirit, always desiring to see different lands and other exotic creatures. Her mother, though, tried to keep her grounded and hidden away to avoid danger.

Mystic understood that there was more to her life than living in her tree house. She wanted to explore the boundaries beyond her tree house. She never realized why her mother had strict ways, but now reflecting, she understood. Mystic's mother's mother had done the same thing to her. She, like Mystic, had desired to see the world beyond the comfortable boundaries of her tree house. And so Mystic's mother vowed she would run away, never looking back. And she did.

***

Ben noticed that Mystic's house was cluttered with an odd assortment of plants; some of them were hanging from the ceiling, and others were in flower pots. He had not noticed them when they first stepped inside. Perhaps it was because he was distracted by Lyon's impeding wolves and Elizabeth's injured ankle that he had completely missed seeing them.

"Nice plants," said Ben, glancing around.

"Thank you," said Mystic. "I had some of my plants imported from foreign countries. I love plants; they're so exotic."

"So do you think Ben and his friends could stay the night?" Saint Patrick asked. "It looks like Lyon's magical wolves are not going anywhere anytime soon, and we need a spot to evade Lyon's wolves," Saint Patrick added, looking out of a small glass window down at Lyon's medicated wolves.

"I don't see why not," said Mystic. She turned to Ben and his friends. "Do you want some herbal tea? It's mint flavored, and I make it myself."

"I don't believe I want any, Mystic, but thanks anyway," said Saint Patrick.

"I don't want any tea," said Elizabeth. "Thank you anyway."

"Me, too," said Evan. "I'm not keen on the taste of tea."

"I'd rather not have any, thanks," said Ben. "But I think Elizabeth should have some to raise her spirits."

"Oh, Ben, I'm all right," she said.

"Elizabeth, it'd be wise of you to have some liquid. You look flushed."

"Ben … I'm okay. There's no need to worry about me; I'm fine."

"But I disagree," said Ben. "You need to regain your strength."

"Ben's right, you know," said Saint Patrick. "Lyon's wolves are fierce creatures. They'll attack anyone if Lyon gives them a command to do so."

"Okay … I guess one cup of tea wouldn't hurt," said Elizabeth.

Mystic stirred the tea in a brass pot hanging aloft on the arm in the fireplace. Mystic poured some of its contents into a chipped teacup and handed it to Elizabeth.

Elizabeth reluctantly drank the tea. "Oh, this is good." she smiled. "Is that mint I taste?"

Mystic nodded. "Yes indeed."

"It's my favorite."

"I'm glad. Do you want another cup?"

"Oh, no thank you."

Scratch. Scratch.

Ben glanced out the kitchen window. Lyon's wolves had regained consciousness and were now clawing at the base of Mystic's tree house.

"What'll we do?" asked Christine, looking out of Mystic's kitchen window and seeing several wolf silhouettes.

"We must stay here until Lyon's wolves have passed," said Saint Patrick. "Nightfall is approaching, and we must sleep here until morning. It's too late now, and we must sleep."

"We must stay here?" said Ben, looking at Elizabeth, concerned for her ankle.

"Yes, we must," said Saint Patrick. "I think that for everyone's safety, we will stay put."

***

Whoosh.

Ben awoke from a deep slumber.

Sitting up, he looked around in the room, which was dimly lit by candles. There seemed to be nothing out of place. Elizabeth had soon fallen asleep next to him on a cloth couch, her injured ankle elevated on a chair. Blankets lay on her. Ben slowly and carefully got up from the sofa where Elizabeth was and crept to the kitchen window. There was nothing he could make out to suggest that Lyon's magical wolves were out in the shadows.

Then he heard it: a whooshing sound—the same one he had heard at the start of nightfall. Something was inside the tree house.

"Ben?"

Ben turned from the window and saw that Elizabeth had awakened. Her voice was soft.

"Yeah?" he said.

"What are you doing?"

"I thought I heard something."

"Saint Patrick seems to think Lyon's magical wolves are still at the base of the tree house, and I do too. Be careful. I don't want you hurt."

"I'll be fine."

"Come back to the couch. The least we can do is to wait it out, just as Saint Patrick mentioned."

"All right."

Ben settled back on the couch with Elizabeth, his thoughts racing about whether Lyon's wolves were indeed inside the tree house. Surely Lyon's wolves could not get inside Mystic's tree house. After all, Saint Patrick had subdued them, and they lay unconscious.

But for how long?

"Ben!"

Evan's voice came in and out as Ben heard it. Then it came into focus.

"Yeah?" he said.

"Lyon's wolves are inside the tree house!"

"What?"

"Lyon's wolves! They're inside the tree house!"

Whoosh.

There were wolf shadows dodging in and out of the dim candlelight. Their eyes shone a deep green.

He knew he would have to fight off the wolf shadows, but his anxiety got the better of him.

"Do something! Anything!" Elizabeth cried as a wolf inched its way toward her.

"Ben!"

Saint Patrick stood in the threshold of the sitting room, glancing at Ben and the wolf silhouettes and then back at Ben, concerned. "Use your locket to subdue the wolves," he said.

Without question, Ben opened the locket around his neck. A sword, encrusted with a burgundy and gold handle and shaped like a three-leaved clover, appeared. With only seconds to react, Ben waved the sword back and forth.

Flashes of green light from the wolves' mouths entered the dusty air, almost hitting Ben in his head, and knocking him nearly unconscious. Ben stood up straight, trying to keep his balance. The blast from Lyon's wolf silhouettes proved to be too much for Ben. Then, taking a deep breath, he swiftly moved the sword in fluid motion.

A burst of green light again shot from the mouths of Lyon's wolves. Loud commotion echoed in the sitting room, which shone a deep glow from candles scattered across the room.

Ben continued to struggle. "Help me, Saint Patrick."

Saint Patrick stepped forward and tapped his cane on the carpet, and a burst of light immediately appeared in brilliant colors of several shades of green. At this, Lyon's wolves winced. Jeremy, despite his earlier warning from Saint Patrick, grabbed pots and pans from Mystic's kitchen countertops and threw one after the other at the wolf silhouettes, but the pots and pans went through the wolf shadows as if they were thick smoke.

Lyon's wolves were relentless, and Jeremy, Saint Patrick, and Ben fought tirelessly to subdue them. The burst of light exploded everywhere in the small, dimly lit sitting room.

"Jeremy …"

Jeremy rushed to his wife, Christine, and saw that she was lying on the carpet, injured from her waist down. Scratches were visible down her legs.

"Don't."

Jeremy moved away from aiding his wife, looking intently at his spouse, tears pouring down his face. "But I want to help you. I need to help you."

"I'm fine," said Christine.

"But you're hurt," said Jeremy. "What must I do to help you?"

"Nothing."

"Nothing?"

"Yes, nothing," said Christine. "It's too late for me. Listen, honey; I'm too old to fight. You'll be fine; I know it."

"Please don't go," said Jeremy. "I need you. I love you."

"I love you, too," said Christine. She gazed into her husband's teary eyes. "You'll be fine; I know you will."

"No … no, I won't," Jeremy insisted. "I can't live without you."

"You can, and you must."

"No. No, I won't let you leave me."

"But … you … must …"

Lyon's wolves were silent. For a second, all Ben and his friends could hear were Jeremy's soft sobs.

Moments passed, and Christine's face became pale. Her body fell limp in Jeremy's arms. Tears flowed down Jeremy's face as he realized that the love of his life, whom he had known ten years, was gone.

"I'm sorry for all of this," said Ben. "If I could help you, I would."

"But you could," Jeremy insisted. "You could help Christine and me."

Ben blinked. "Excuse me, what?"

"You could bring Christine back from the dead."

"What is he talking about?" Elizabeth asked.

"Jeremy, you know that is impossible," said Saint Patrick. "The resurrection spell is tricky and is too advanced for Ben to cast."

"It is?" said Ben.

"Yes, it is." Saint Patrick turned to Jeremy. "I'm sorry," he said. "I know you're disappointed, but Ben's focus is to defeat Lyon."

"I understand," said Jeremy, sighing.

For a second time, Ben heard a low growl; he knew Lyon's wolves were not silent any longer.

Mystic, who had been occupied in the other room, ran into the sitting room; without delay, she put her hands up in the direction of Lyon's wolf silhouettes. Green mist immediately shot from her fingertips, subduing the wolves for only a moment.

Jeremy took Christine's body away, getting out of the way, afraid that the chaotic blasts of light might hit him. Together Ben, Mystic, and Saint Patrick finally had the upper hand, and they used their combined powers to hold back Lyon's wolves. Then they lay panting, out of breath. In a hazy blue mist, they disappeared, leaving a dusty residue behind.

Once calm was restored and it was quiet, Mystic turned to Jeremy and asked, "Are you all right?"

"Yeah," said Jeremy through sobs, "I'm fine."

"Ben?"

Ben looked at Saint Patrick. "Yeah?"

"We must move. I don't know whether Lyon's wolves will attack again or whether Lyon himself will show up and kill you and your friends."

"I don't think it's safe for Elizabeth to travel in the condition she is in," said Ben.

"Oh, she'll be all right," assured Saint Patrick. "I'll protect her with my life; I promise."

Ben was slightly hesitant. "You will?"

"I swear on my life. Now we must go forth and be on the move lest we come across more dangerous hazards caused by Lyon or his wolves."

"All right," said Ben.

Ben and his friends left Mystic and Jeremy and ventured into the unknown, searching for safety in the green foothills of Ireland, with Saint Patrick as their wise guide.

CHAPTER IX

Ben McNealy

Prince William's castle, Medieval Times. 1865.

THE LUSH GREEN of the hills was nothing like any of Ben and his friends had ever seen. A medieval castle with olden stones, etched with history, lay beyond the hillside. As they reached the castle, Ben noticed the more delicate details: images of past leaf'd princes were ever so carefully etched in stone as if carved by an old, steady hand. Some princes were riding on horses; others were shooting bows and arrows.

"Now Ben, you must be in disguise when entering this castle," said Saint Patrick. "I will use my magic to turn you into your father, Prince William."

"Why?" Ben asked.

"Lance, the Rowzand family servant, will explain further," said Saint Patrick. "Oh, I see him now."

A tall, skinny servant with dirty brown hair approached Ben and his friends. "Oh, it's you, Ben. It has been a long time. Too long."

Ben glanced at Saint Patrick and then at Lance. "Excuse me, who are you?"

"Oh, pardon my rudeness. My name is Lance Brogtrott," he said. "I'm your family's servant. I deal with the daily tasks of the castle. By the way, Queen Kathrynne, your grandmother, thinks Prince William is missing. She doesn't trust anyone until her son returns. She refuses to lead the Irish people until her son shows up."

"Lance, I'll offer you a deal: Ben will pretend to be Prince William until further notice, or until Queen Kathrynne has figured out that Ben is his father," said Saint Patrick.

"No, I refuse to be a part of your crazy scheme," said Ben. "I don't feel comfortable with the idea. I don't know Queen Kathrynne all that well. Will she punish me by putting me to death?"

"I don't think Queen Kathrynne will throw you in the castle's dungeon or put you to death," said Saint Patrick. "Yes, she might be angry at first, trying to process everything. It'll take time for her to get used to the idea that her son is gone, but I think she'll be grateful for your presence. She'll love you, just as she loved her son—and still does."

"I appreciate your confidence," said Ben. "But still … deceiving a queen … my grandmother … I can't do it."

I agree with Ben," said Elizabeth. "Deceiving a queen is tricky, and I, for one, think it is a mistake. She's fragile."

"As for me, I think it is a good idea to deceive Queen Kathrynne," said Evan.

"That is a terrible idea," said Elizabeth.

"Not necessarily," said Evan. "Have you ever considered that if Ben decides to be his father, it will help Queen Kathrynne to be a better leader?" He turned to Lance and added, "Didn't you just say that Queen Kathrynne missed her son?"

"Yes, I did," said Lance.

"Then I think it'd be better for all of us if Ben pretends to be his father for the time being," said Evan. "Queen Kathrynne will be overjoyed that her son is back in her life, and she'll be able to lead the Irish people effectively because of it."

Ben heard the argument between Elizabeth and Evan for a few seconds more before Saint Patrick tapped the grass with his cane. Sparks and loud noises entered the sky.

Elizabeth and Evan stopped arguing.

"Ben, please reconsider Saint Patrick's plan," said Lance. "It would mean a lot to Queen Kathrynne to see her son again—even if only for few hours."

"Okay." Ben sighed. "I'll do it—to spare my grandmother's feelings."

"Are you sure?" asked Elizabeth wearily.

"Yes," said Ben.

Okay, great," said Lance.

***

A grand ball was a tradition and exciting night for Three-Leaf'd Tournament participants and their dates. For Ben, it was the first time he had heard of such a thing. All the princes from across the Irish plains were expected to attend, dancing and feasting all evening. Flowing medieval dresses with crystals made every girl envious about the one girl who'd wear such garb and show off her curves. For the guys, their tuxes were equally elaborate with shades of dark green and blue.

Elizabeth saw a dark green satin dress hanging on clothespins near the edge of a large window. Ben and his friends were in a large bedroom in a tall tower. Lance stood near the dress, fluffing it every moment or two with his long, delicate fingers.

"This," he said to Elizabeth, "is what you will wear to the Leaf'd Ball; Queen Kathrynne must announce its inception."

"It's beautiful," said Elizabeth nervously, admiring the elaborate and delicate craftsmanship. "But I can't wear it."

"Oh, nonsense," said Saint Patrick. "Ben's date has to be equally impressive, and this dress qualifies.

"And for you, Ben, a dark green satin suit to match your date's dress." Lance pulled a dirty white sheet off a large stone mannequin.

"Queen Kathrynne will be expecting her son's wife, a peasant," Lance added. "She isn't thrilled her son married a peasant. She may ask you intrusive questions. Don't mind it, though. She means well."

"You ready?" said Saint Patrick to Ben and Elizabeth.

"Yeah, I guess," said Ben.

Elizabeth nodded.

Saint Patrick tapped his cane on the floor. Smoke covered Elizabeth.

When the smoke cleared a little, Elizabeth noticed at once that her clothing had changed; the dark green satin dress that was once on the mannequin, hung loosely on her slim figure.

Ben was astonished. Then it was his turn. With another tap of his cane, Ben's hair was pushed back, slick. A dark green dress suit shone magnificently in the sunlight through the impressive glass windows.

"Now," said Saint Patrick, "will you two follow me, please?"

Saint Patrick led the way to the castle's garden where a cobblestone patio surrounded a brass fountain. Several chairs were arranged around the fountain's perimeter. In the distance, a gazebo stood on a grassy hill, surrounded by lilacs and sunflowers.

"Oh, William, my son, it's you."

A woman in a long, flowing gown walked out onto the patio. She held out her arms, hugging Ben as she approached. Ben felt a bit awkward. Hugging strangers was too much for him. Queen Kathrynne held Ben a few seconds more before turning her attention to Elizabeth.

"And you, my dear, what is your name?"

"This is Bridgette Greenhouse," said Lance before Elizabeth could answer. "She's your son's wife."

"Is she rich?" said Queen Kathrynne at once. "You know I don't allow my son to marry someone who has no money, power, or prestige."

"No, Your Majesty," said Lance. "She hasn't got money, power, or prestige."

"No royal inheritance?"

"No, Your Majesty."

Queen Kathrynne looked over Elizabeth as if deciding whether she was a thief who had stolen her son's heart. "Explain yourself. Why, exactly, did you marry my precious and only son?"

"I think she—"

"Lance, enough!"

Lance parted his lips, almost making them disappear.

Queen Kathrynne's tone made Elizabeth jump. "I don't know," she said. "I love him, I guess."

"You love him, *you guess?* That wasn't confident, my dear," said Queen

Kathrynne, circling Elizabeth, her gaze upon Elizabeth's medieval dress. "Tell me, Bridgette, why have you dressed up? Is it, perhaps, because you want to impress me?"

Elizabeth was speechless.

Ben was too afraid to say anything.

"Uh, no, Your Majesty," said Elizabeth.

"It's for the Leaf'd Ball," said Saint Patrick, who had heard the conversation between Queen Kathrynne, Lance, and Elizabeth and decided to say something before things became too awkward. "Tonight, if you allow it."

"Really? Is that so?" said Queen Kathrynne.

"Yes, Your Majesty," said Saint Patrick.

"And are you sure this is Bridgette, an Irish farm girl who lives just beyond the forest clearing?"

Queen Kathrynne wasn't a fool. She knew everybody's rank and lifestyle— even those of the lowest of peasants. And Bridgette was no exception either.

"Yes, Your Majesty," said Lance.

He continued to trim the bushes from earlier in the day.

"What was it your father did, my dear? Wasn't he a farmer?"

Elizabeth didn't know what to do; she nodded in agreement.

"Lance, won't you escort my son to the castle's courtyard while I chat with my daughter-in-law?" asked Queen Kathrynne.

Lance escorted Ben to the courtyard. Saint Patrick and Evan followed closely behind.

Ben whispered, "What do you think Queen Kathrynne will say to Elizabeth?"

"I wouldn't worry about Elizabeth," said Saint Patrick in Ben's ear, "Queen

Kathrynne is a dignified woman. She doesn't make irrational decisions. Elizabeth will be fine."

"Let's sit." Queen Kathrynne gestured for Elizabeth to sit.

She sat.

"Now," said Queen Kathrynne, taking a seat herself, "why the sudden interest in my son?"

Elizabeth was silent; she didn't know what to say. Then she finally said, "I love your son, Your Majesty."

"You love my son?"

"Yes."

"Yes, well, I'm sure that as a peasant you have learned to adapt over the years," said Queen Kathrynne quickly. "Now a handsome prince has landed in your lap and has asked you to be his bride. And looking at his compassion and wealth, you considered all your options: not marry him and remain a servant, or marry him and become a queen and inherit his money, power, and prestige. Then you decided on a whim to marry him because of his money and entitlement."

"With all due respect, Your Majesty," said Elizabeth, "I did not marry your son for his money or entitlement. I married him for him. I love him. Pardon my saying this, but I think you won't respect any girl who comes from a different background than you. Maybe you're afraid of losing your family's reign. Just know I'm not interested in taking away your family's reign; in fact, I'm doing the contrary. I'm embracing it, taking it in, and enjoying it. You may not like me, and I respect that, but please know I do love your son and I would do anything for him."

Elizabeth's story was convincing—even for her. Bridgette would have been proud, she assumed.

Queen Kathrynne was taken aback by Elizabeth's boldness. "That is far from the truth. I want my son to be happy with a girl who has the same wealthy status as mine."

"Have you ever asked Prince William want he wants in a bride?" said Elizabeth.

"What are you getting at?" Queen Kathrynne asked.

"Maybe if you had asked him–I'm not saying you have or have not–then you probably would have discovered that he wants someone who isn't rich or well off."

"You mean someone like you?"

"Well ... yes."

"I think I know my son well enough to know what he likes in a bride," said Queen Kathrynne, pouring a glass of tea from a large cup and taking a sip.

"With all due respect, Your Majesty, you don't know your son at all," said Elizabeth. "Have you ever really listened to what he wants, instead of assuming you know what's best for him?"

"Why should an Irish farm girl like you, who knows little about how a kingdom should be running, give such advice? I am knowledgeable and have the resources to wage war on other foreign countries," said Queen Kathrynne. "I know many things about being a queen and governing a peaceful society. What are you–a peasant who waits on those who are higher in rank than yourself? You are in no position to give me advice."

As soon as Queen Kathrynne said it, she knew Elizabeth was right. Prince William was giving her hints all his life; he did not care for princesses who showed the slightest interest in him. He wanted someone who didn't care about his royal stature, and Bridgette was it.

"Well, let's check up on your husband."

Queen Kathrynne got up from the chair, and she and Elizabeth walked to a courtyard where Ben, Saint Patrick, Evan, and Lance were.

"I wish to see my son's progress," said Queen Kathrynne. "How's he doing?"

"Prince William's not ready to show his progress at this time," said Saint Patrick.

"Oh, nonsense," said Queen Kathrynne. "I wish to see my son's progress now—something worthwhile like archery or jousting, perhaps?"

Ben turned to Saint Patrick and whispered, "What do I do? I haven't advanced any further than archery. What if Queen Kathrynne wants to see something more than just archery?"

"It'll be all right," Saint Patrick whispered back. "Trust your gut and believe in yourself."

Ben took a deep breath. He raised the bow and arrow, feeling the strong bow in his hands, and with one loud smack, its arrow zoomed past Queen Kathrynne's ear and hit a target.

"I'm impressed, my son," said Queen Kathrynne. "How about jousting? Have you improved since then?"

"Well, yes, I have," Ben lied, to spare Queen Kathrynne's feelings. "Every day."

"Well, let's see it, then," said Queen Kathrynne.

"Prince William has only mastered a few moves," said Saint Patrick.

"Oh, that's good," said Queen Kathrynne. "I want to see my son's progress."

Ben shot a worried glance at Saint Patrick.

"Well, I don't want to spoil the surprise," said Saint Patrick.

"Surprise?" said Queen Kathrynne.

"Yes, surprise," said Saint Patrick. "I want you to be surprised once you see your son compete. Now, it wouldn't be a surprise if you already saw him jousting, would it?"

"No. I guess not." Queen Kathrynne sighed. "I think it only fits that we have a ball to celebrate the Three-Leaf'd Tournament participants, I've decided. We shall invite all the potential hopefuls and their dates."

Queen Kathrynne turned to Lance and said, "Plan a ball."

"But Your Majesty ... I don't know how–"

"Figure it out," said Queen Kathrynne. "And by the way, Lance"–he turned from walking away–"if anything goes wrong, it'll be your head that's going to roll. I'm going to supervise everything, so it'll be like I was planning it."

"Yes, Your Majesty."

Lance left the courtyard.

Queen Kathrynne turned to Ben and said, "Oh, by the way, Princess Lexis Tanglewood wants to dance with you at the ball, and I told her you would."

Ben felt sick. He was being pulled in too many directions. On the one hand, he didn't want to dance with Princess Lexis, whom he had met at the Green Leprechaun just days ago. He was afraid Elizabeth would get the wrong idea about the two of them. He didn't want her to feel anxious. But on the other hand, if he didn't dance with Princess Lexis, she would inevitably draw attention to the fact that he was not Prince William, Ben assumed, and Saint Patrick's plan of deceiving Queen Kathrynne would not work.

So Ben touched his lips together, almost making them disappear, and kept quiet and nodded at Queen Kathrynne's request, even though he hated the idea of dancing with a snobbish princess.

Ben and his friends went inside the back entrance of Prince William's castle to ready themselves for the Leaf'd Ball, which was just hours away.

CHAPTER X

Ben McNealy

"YOU READY?"

Saint Patrick stood at the doorway of Ben's room.

"Just about."

"Well, hurry! Guests are already arriving."

"Ben, are you all right?"

Evan stood at the bathroom threshold with a toothbrush he had brought along in his mouth.

"Yes," he said.

"No, you don't seem fine," said Evan. "I know when something's wrong. Now, what's wrong?"

"Nothing."

"Something's wrong. What is it?"

"I said nothing's wrong."

"Let me get Saint Patrick. He might be better at getting you to say what's on your mind."

Evan set down his toothbrush on the edge of a brass sink; he spat mint-flavored toothpaste into it and crossed the room. He was about to open the door when Ben stopped him.

"Wait! I'll let you know what's wrong."

"Okay." Evan sat down on a nearby cloth chair. "All right, tell me."

"I'm afraid Elizabeth will be jealous of Princess Lexis hanging all over me while we're dancing."

"That's it?" said Evan. "That's not so bad."

"Well, it is for me," said Ben.

"It'll be fine," assured Evan.

"You ready now?" said Saint Patrick through the door. "Important guests are waiting."

Ben opened the door. "Yes, now I am."

The hallway was small and decorated with ornate details of Irish heroes etched in stone. Leprechauns and other creatures littered the castle's entrance. Ben found it hard to get past a cluster of leprechauns who all seemed to be excited about the ball because, Ben assumed, they had never been to one.

Ben managed to squeeze through the cluster of Leprechauns to a long and ornate door. They were all talking at once; however, he could make out what they were saying.

"… Yeah, I never expected the prince would be back so soon."

"I agree," said one leprechaun, who was pushed against the door by another leprechaun, both of them trying to go through the long, ornate door.

"One rumor I heard was that Prince William abandoned his post in favor of peasant life. He married that peasant girl … what was her name? Bridgette Greenhouse? Yes, I believe that was her name."

"As far as I'm concerned, Prince William deserves to be a peasant," said a stout leprechaun with large nostrils. "No sane prince would abandon all he knows for a poor, old peasant."

"That's not true."

For a moment, the leprechauns stood silent. Then one brave leprechaun stepped among the crowd of the other leprechauns and asked, "Who are you to question the prince's decisions? We're just pondering the reasons Prince William left his post as prince of Ireland."

The stout leprechaun with the large nostrils stepped in front of the leprechaun who had spoken and looked intently into Ben's face. He asked, "Isn't *he* Prince William?"

There was more jibber jabber among the leprechauns until one leprechaun from the back of the crowd said, "Yes, I believe that is him."

The crowd of leprechauns stepped away from the door to let Ben to the door.

He quietly turned the knob of the door and stepped through, closing the door behind him.

"Why are there leprechauns guarding that door?" asked Ben, pointing.

"They are trying to escape Lyon's wrath, as we are trying to do," said Saint Patrick. "Queen Kathrynne insists that every leprechaun and creature stay here for the Leaf'd Ball."

"Are they guests?" Ben asked.

"Yes," said Saint Patrick.

"When does the ball start?"

"In an hour or so."

"Okay."

"Ah, here we go."

Ben heard faint violin music playing in the background of the large room. Then it got louder, and louder still. Then creatures appeared with violins and long bows moving slowly like graceful swans on a lake. Treats shaped like various Irish symbols, such as three-leaved clovers, gold, and top hats, were at the edge of the table; green colored punch was set at the side of the buffet table, with parchment paper cups surrounding it.

"Ah, there you are, my son," said a voice.

Ben looked in the direction of the voice and saw Queen Kathrynne coming over to him.

"Glad you are home, my son."

"Me, too."

"Oh, here comes Princess Lexis."

"Why is she here early?" Ben asked.

"She came to perfect the waltz with you," said Queen Kathrynne. "All the princes dance with their potential queens."

"But I'm not marrying Princess Lexis," Ben insisted. "I don't love her."

"Well, not yet, anyway," said Queen Kathrynne. "Give her a chance. Who knows? You might fall in love."

"But I don't love her."

"Where's Bridgette?" Saint Patrick asked Queen Kathrynne.

"I honestly don't know," she said. "She was supposed to be here."

Saint Patrick disappeared down the hall, in search of Elizabeth. He finally found her sitting on a chair in the parlor, dabbing her eyes with a large cloth. He stepped inside the room.

"What's the matter?" he asked.

"Nothing."

"Oh, come on, tell me. You wouldn't be here if nothing were wrong."

"All right. It's Queen Kathrynne. I overheard her talking with Princess Lexis. She promised Princess Lexis Ben would marry her by the end of the night."

"You shouldn't worry, my dear," said Saint Patrick. "Ben loves you. I can sense it by the way he looks at you."

"I know he does," said Elizabeth. "But it does make me think Princess Lexis might influence him; and let me tell you, a man can't resist a beautiful and rich princess."

"Maybe another man would be influenced–one who hasn't had any moral standards and one who only cares about rich princesses," said Saint Patrick. "Tell me, is Ben a man who would lust after rich princesses?"

"No."

"Then why are you worried?"

"I don't know."

"You shouldn't be."

"All right."

"Now let's go forth to the ballroom," said Saint Patrick. "Ben is waiting for you."

Elizabeth and Saint Patrick entered the castle's ballroom. Saint Patrick went straight to the buffet table to get some snacks and punch.

In the background, Elizabeth could hear faint violin music. Ben was off to the side, watching various princes mingle with their dates. Elizabeth was about to walk over to Ben, but Princess Lexis whisked him away to the dance floor.

"Dance with me," she insisted. She put her arms around Ben's neck, but Ben immediately peeled them off.

"Please, I don't want any trouble from you," he said. "My wife's here, and if she gets the wrong impression, she—"

"She won't," said Princess Lexis quickly. "I promise."

"You sure?"

"Yes, I'm sure."

"So did our previous date alter your perception of me and our future marriage, perhaps?"

Ben didn't expect the question. "Huh? Excuse me?"

"So did our previous date alter your perception of me?" Princess Lexis repeated.

"Uh, no. It didn't. It was okay."

Ben saw Elizabeth's angry expression. She was crossing her arms, pouting, not even looking at him.

"Could we skip our dance?" Ben asked, glancing in the direction of Elizabeth.

"Why? Aren't you enjoying my company?" said Princess Lexis, biting her bottom lip flirtatiously.

"Yeah, I am, but—"

"Please stay." Princess Lexis placed her cheek on Ben's shoulder, and he could smell the intense aroma of sweet perfume.

"I can't. I must talk to my wife. Excuse me."

Ben quickly pulled away from Princess Lexis's loose grip on him and walked over to the wall near the buffet table, where Elizabeth was standing.

"Are you all right?" he said.

"Oh, I'm all right."

Before Ben could respond, Princess Lexis grabbed him close and said, "Please continue to dance with me. I'm lonely without you there."

Princess Lexis then whirled Ben across the dance floor. Elizabeth watched at a distance, sulking. She couldn't bear seeing the love of her life being whisked away by a princess who barely knew him or knew his identity. She finally stormed off to the courtyard balcony, where she sat down on the edge of a fountain.

"Elizabeth, you okay?"

Elizabeth turned, startled, and saw that Evan was there.

"Yeah, I am. You can go now. I'm fine."

"No, you're not fine. You're crying."

Elizabeth immediately wiped a tear from her face with the back of her hand. "I'm not crying."

"Yes, you certainly are," said Evan. "Is there something you want to talk about? Ben, perhaps?"

"Evan, I said I'm fine!"

"Okay."

There was silence between Elizabeth and Evan until Elizabeth said through tears, "Ben's dancing with a princess, and I think he's enjoying her company a little too much."

"Oh, I'm sorry," said Evan.

"Well, I can't blame him," said Elizabeth. "Queen Kathrynne wants Ben to dance with her. Although if she knew that Ben wasn't Prince William, she wouldn't have suggested Ben dance with her."

"Elizabeth, you know Ben loves you," said Evan. "He wouldn't suddenly fall out of love with you, right?"

"Yeah, I suppose you're right," said Elizabeth.

She stepped into the ballroom from the courtyard.

She overheard Princess Lexis talking with Ben. She immediately had a lousy remembrance of the earlier encounter he had with Princess Lexis; she hated it. She knew Ben loved her, but seeing Ben with Princess Lexis again hurt her deeply.

She watched, crossing her arms; she tried not to look, to see if that would somehow mask her pain.

"Do you think we can have another date since our last one was disastrous?" she asked Ben.

Princess Lexis could sense that Ben was confused–that she needed to remind him of the events that occurred on their date.

"You remember we were at the Green Leprechaun enjoying ourselves when a floozy of a Princess named Princess Taylor came in. She spotted you among the leprechauns, and she began flirting with you. A fight broke out with our wands, with light shooting everywhere, and you left, embarrassed. 'Course, I couldn't blame you. I'm sorry for my rude behavior at the Green Leprechaun. Would you like to go on another date with me?"

Ben didn't know what to say. He didn't want to hurt Princess Lexis's feelings, but he didn't want to go on a date with Princess Lexis either.

"Sure," he said, to spare Princess Lexis's feelings.

Princess Lexis smiled. "Great. I'm looking forward to it."

Meanwhile, Princess Taylor entered the ballroom. She was looking for Prince William so she could apologize to him. She felt awful about the incident that had occurred at the Green Leprechaun, and she was hoping she could start anew with Prince William. Scanning the ballroom filled with creatures, she spotted Ben, dressed as Prince William in disguise, and walked over to him. She tapped Ben on his shoulder.

"Hi," she said. "May we talk for a second?"

Princess Lexis immediately whirled Ben around to get a frontal view of Princess Taylor.

"No," she said, "he's busy at the moment."

Princess Taylor scoffed. She knew Princess Lexis was only trying to make her jealous. And so she decided that she would compete for Prince William's affection by grabbing the first prince she saw and dancing with him. The only thing she failed to realize about her plan was that Prince William wasn't Prince William; he was Ben, and Ben loved Elizabeth.

"Dance with me," she said, grabbing a Scottish prince who was eating at the buffet table. He was very lean for his age and was wearing a plaid kilt.

"But I don't want to dance. I don't know how to waltz."

Princess Taylor wasn't paying attention to what the Scottish prince was saying. Instead her focus was on Ben and Princess Lexis. She whirled the Scottish prince around the ballroom floor, almost making him dizzy.

Ben, meanwhile, wasn't focused on Princess Lexis at all. His focus was on Elizabeth and how she must have felt. Would Elizabeth forgive him for dancing with Princess Lexis–a princess whom he barely knew?

"I can't dance with you. My wife is over there."

Ben withdrew from Princess Lexis's grip and walked over to Elizabeth in the corner of the ballroom.

"May we talk?"

"Sure."

As Ben turned to escort Elizabeth to the ballroom's balcony, Princess Lexis followed them. She, in turn, gave Ben a passionate kiss.

As they walked back into the ballroom, Princess Lexis was out of sight.

"I can't believe you let that awful and deceitful princess kiss you," said Elizabeth. "After all we've been through … the dates, the late nights staying up …"

"First of all, it was a surprise kiss; I wasn't expecting it. And second, are you going to let a princess like that get to you?" said Ben.

"Well …" Elizabeth began, but she was cut off by Ben.

"Elizabeth, I love you, and I always will," he said. "What do I have to do to show you I love you? There is no other person in my life. Do I have to shout on a mountaintop, tell random strangers … what?"

"You don't have to prove anything," said Elizabeth. "I know you love me."

"Then what's the matter?"

"I don't know." Elizabeth sighed. "But kiss her anyway."

"What?"

"I want you to kiss Princess Lexis," said Elizabeth.

"No! Why?" Ben asked.

"I saw how you were with her; you love her," said Elizabeth. "I know you do."

"No! I won't. I love you; I don't love her." Ben leaned forward and kissed Elizabeth on her lips.

Ben's lips were warm and familiar to Elizabeth. She longed for a kiss that was warm and comforting. It had been too long since she and Ben had kissed unexpectedly.

She smiled. "Wow. Okay," was all she could muster.

Evan stepped out on the balcony where Ben and Elizabeth had been kissing moments ago.

When he found his voice after a small bit of shock, he said, "Are you coming back into the ballroom?"

"Yeah, I am," said Elizabeth.

Elizabeth walked into the ballroom, where much loud merriment was taking place and music was playing.

Evan grabbed Ben's arm. "You came a bit late, my friend."

"What do you mean, Evan?" Ben whispered, not wanting to make his voice audible to Elizabeth, who was out of earshot of them.

"I saw you with a princess, and that got Elizabeth upset. She was crying, you know."

"I know."

"Did you guys make up?"

"Yeah, what did you think?" Ben was becoming aggravated.

"So do you love this princess?" said Evan.

"No, Evan, I don't!"

"Why did you kiss her, then?"

"She kissed me. It was unexpected. I told Elizabeth that, and she believed me."

"She did?"

"Yes, she did," said Ben. "What's with the probing questions all of a sudden?"

"I care about Elizabeth—and you too."

"Okay ..."

Evan followed Ben to the ballroom, feeling a rush of disappointment. He still had doubts about Elizabeth and Ben's relationship, but he reluctantly accepted Ben's explanation of the princess's kiss. After all, they were best friends.

At Evan's departure from the castle's balcony, Elizabeth felt a pulsating pain. Looking down, she realized that Saint Patrick's spell had begun to wear off, and her ankle, which once had appeared to be fine, now had a bruise.

"Ben, Saint Patrick's magic—it's starting to wear off."

At Elizabeth's words, green mist surrounded her like fog.

Ben was stunned. He knew Saint Patrick's plan of deceiving Queen Kathrynne was too good to last.

Ben knew he had no choice. He had to warn Saint Patrick before things got more out of hand. He ran over to the buffet table where Saint Patrick was and tapped him on the shoulder.

"It's Elizabeth, she's—"

"Ben …" Saint Patrick glanced, his mouth agape at the sight before him. In the threshold of the castle's balcony, Elizabeth stood by herself, trying to cover her throbbing ankle with her long green dress.

"What is she doing here in the castle, and who is she?"

Saint Patrick recognized the voice at once. It was Princess Lexis, who at that moment had passed the castle's balcony threshold, her mouth agape.

Elizabeth had no idea what to do. She stood there, unable to fathom all that was going on.

"I think it is time for me to explain our plan to Queen Kathrynne," whispered Saint Patrick, who had passed Ben on his way to the ballroom door, out in the hall.

On Saint Patrick's way, he spotted Queen Kathrynne. She glanced at Ben, seeing green mist rising from his conscience and his surroundings. Her mouth fell open.

"Who is he, and what is he doing here in the castle?" Queen Kathrynne asked.

Saint Patrick's voice became uncomfortably dry. Then he found his voice. "This is Ben, your grandson."

"My what?"

"Your grandson," Saint Patrick repeated. "He was only pretending to be your son to save you from grieving. We didn't mean to cause any harm, if that's what we've done."

"And what about the girl in the dark green dress? Was she an imposter too?" said Queen Kathrynne, sounding offended.

"Oh, no, she wasn't an imposter," said Saint Patrick. "And neither was Ben. She's Ben's girlfriend."

"And why is my grandson here, and not my son?" said Queen Kathrynne. "Did something happen to him?"

No one spoke. Ben glanced at Saint Patrick for guidance.

"He's dead," said Saint Patrick boldly.

Queen Kathrynne's mouth was ajar. She gazed beyond Ben and Saint Patrick's shoulders to her husband, King Diamond, who had just come over to break the news to his wife.

"You knew?"

"Yes, of course, I knew," said King Diamond. "I didn't want to worry you. The kingdom is already falling to pieces, and I didn't want to add one more thing to your worry list."

"And I'm sure you knew about our plan to deceive your wife, huh?" said Saint Patrick.

"Yes, I did."

"How?" said Saint Patrick.

"I was in the shade of a tall tree; I heard everything."

"And you just let it happen?" Ben asked.

"Yes, I did," said King Diamond. "Like you, I thought it was a good idea at the time. She loved our son, as did I. I didn't want her to grieve—at least for a while."

"Then you must know that the wizard Lyon killed Prince William and his wife," said Saint Patrick.

"I knew he died, yes," said King Diamond.

"I'm sorry it happened," said Saint Patrick.

"Thanks. I appreciate it."

Queen Kathrynne had conflicting emotions; she was sad about her son's unexpected death, and then she was angry at Lyon's cruel act. She screamed, finally sobbing. She kneeled, wailing now. Everyone, including the leprechauns, stopped their merrymaking and enjoying themselves to gaze at Queen Kathrynne, their mouths agape. She had her head buried in her hands, wailing louder than ever before. King Diamond started to rub his wife's back to comfort her, but she put her hand up to stop him.

"Stop," she said.

She didn't want her husband's comfort now. She wanted to cry.

Ben felt a bit awkward, as he had never seen a queen of such high authority be in a vulnerable state of mind. He could not blame Queen Kathrynne for her heartbreak. She loved him dearly, and not having him with her now made everything worse.

"Your Majesty, everything's going to be all right," said Lance, who had come over to console her.

"No, no it's not," she sobbed. "No one can bring back my son."

Then, pulling herself together, Queen Kathrynne declared, "Find Lyon, the wizard, and kill him for the crimes he committed against my son and my kingdom."

"I'm sorry, Your Majesty," said Lance, "but that is nearly impossible."

"And why is that so difficult?" said Queen Kathrynne, her voice hoarse.

"Because Lyon is no ordinary wizard," said Saint Patrick. "He's cunning and smart and will blindside you if you're not carefully looking out for him."

"Then we must be diligent in looking for Lyon," said Queen Kathrynne.

"You're right, Your Majesty, which is why your grandson, Ben, must compete in the Three-Leaf'd Tournament," said Saint Patrick. "This is the only way to defeat Lyon. I'm sure Prince William would've wanted this."

"I'm sure he did," said Queen Kathrynne. "But I'm not comfortable with my grandson competing in such an unsafe tournament. He may get hurt, and I don't want another tragedy to mourn over."

"I see why you're concerned, Your Majesty," said Saint Patrick, "but I must assure you that Ben must compete in the tournament. And by my training, he will be able to defeat Lyon and win the Three-Leaf'd Tournament confidently."

Queen Kathrynne seemed unconvinced. "You sure?"

"Yes, I'm positive."

"Isn't Ben too young to compete in the Three-Leaf'd Tournament, though?"

"No. Your Majesty, I'm sure you're aware of the rules of the tournament, then?" said Saint Patrick.

"Yes, I'm quite aware of the rules," said Queen Kathrynne.

"Then you must be aware that any participant that is unable to fulfill the duties because of injury or death is replaced with a blood relative, such as an uncle or a prince's son, right?"

"Yes."

"And don't you worry, Your Majesty," said Lance. "A trainer who knows the tournament and the layout of the arena must be the one who trains many participants for the difficult feats ahead, and Saint Patrick surpasses the qualifications of a trainer in my book; I trust him with my whole heart."

"I don't know whether I can enter such a tournament and defeat Lyon," said Ben.

"Oh, Ben, don't worry," said Saint Patrick. "With my aid, you'll be fine; with my aid, you'll sure to win."

"I still have doubts about Saint Patrick's training skills, but I must trust you," Queen Kathrynne disclosed, turning her attention from her husband to Saint Patrick.

"Thank you, Your Majesty," said Saint Patrick. "I won't let you down. Ben will be ready for the Three-Leaf'd Tournament when the time comes; I promise."

Queen Kathrynne nodded her approval. "I will be checking your progress with Ben."

"Sure. No problem."

Elizabeth felt her ankle growing worse by the minute. Tears began to fall from her eyes. "Ow, it hurts ... so badly."

"Saint Patrick, I'm still concerned about Elizabeth's ankle," said Ben, who watched Elizabeth wince from the pain.

Taking an oblong bottle from his pocket and a cloth from his other pocket, Saint Patrick said to Elizabeth, "Find somewhere to sit. I'm going to bandage your ankle."

"I don't know," said Elizabeth warily. "Will it sting?"

"A little, but the swelling will go down, and it won't hurt as much," said Saint Patrick.

Still wary, and hurting from her ankle, Elizabeth reluctantly found a seat in an armchair. The armchair was inches from a footstool, which Saint Patrick scooted near Elizabeth's feet.

"Try to relax," said Saint Patrick.

"What's in the bottle?" Elizabeth asked, looking at the bottle and Saint Patrick suspiciously.

"Healing properties," said Saint Patrick. "Don't worry. You'll feel better soon."

Saint Patrick gently poured a clear liquid on the cloth; he then dabbed the substance on her ankle. He cut a thin string off his garment and tied it securely upon her ankle and around the cloth so it would stay in place.

Immediately Elizabeth felt the intense pain subside. "Thank you," she said with a sigh of relief.

"No problem," said Saint Patrick. "Make sure to leave the cloth on overnight. The liquid, as I have said, has healing properties that will help your ankle."

Elizabeth felt a sense of calm. She took deep breaths, letting the liquid seep into her swollen ankle.

"We might have to stay the night," said Saint Patrick, looking at Ben and his companions. "Lyon is unpredictable, and with Elizabeth's ankle recovering, there is no use in moving. When the morning dawns and Elizabeth's ankle has healed, we can move on."

"I agree," said Ben, who sat by Elizabeth in the nearest armchair.

"There is a bedroom down a hallway, there," said Queen Kathrynne, who had stepped in a few minutes prior and overheard Ben and his friends' conversation. "It is spacious and will fit all of you comfortably."

"Great," said Saint Patrick. "Shall we go?"

"We shall," said Ben.

Ben carefully guided Elizabeth down the hallway to where the bedroom was located, with his friends and Queen Kathrynne following closely behind.

CHAPTER XI

Ben McNealy

"THE MOST IMPORTANT thing is to be diligent and cautious about whom you're jousting."

Saint Patrick's voice faded in and out like static on a radio. Ben put his mind back on what Saint Patrick was telling him.

"Jousting can be tricky, but with the right mindset and drive, any prince may win a sparring match," said Saint Patrick. He demonstrated by using his sword, waving it quickly in a fluid motion. "Lance, will you come here please?"

Lance had been listening quite intently about what he was telling Ben, all the while trimming the hedges with a large bolt cutter. (He had to cut the hedges because Queen Kathrynne had asked it be done, and the gardener was on vacation for a week in a nearby town.)

"Yes?" he said.

"Will you spar with me?"

"I don't have any sparring experience," Lance admitted.

"It doesn't matter," said Saint Patrick. "I just want to show Ben techniques of sparring, and the best way to do it is to show him."

"All right. It's worth a shot."

Ben watched in earnest as Saint Patrick and Lance moved in all directions. He could hear the clanking of metal as they went along.

Finally Lance lay on his back, his eyes on Saint Patrick. His arms were at his sides, and he was out of breath. His sparring stick lay inches from his face. Straining, Lance tried his best to reach for his sparring stick, but almost immediately Saint Patrick seized it, grabbing it in midair with a snap of his fingers.

"Thank you, Lance. Your jousting skills amaze me."

"Thank you," said Lance.

"You're welcome."

Saint Patrick turned to Ben and said, "Now I want you to spar with Lance."

"Why do I have to spar? Isn't it only on horses?" Ben asked.

"Yes, indeed, sparring on horses is very popular among the Irish people," said Saint Patrick. "There's a chance that Lyon might spar on foot, and I want you prepared for anything he throws at you."

"Okay." Ben sighed. "I'll give it a try."

Ben grabbed a sparring stick lying on the ground beside him, and feeling a bit uneasy, he waved it around a bit. Taking a deep breath, he aligned his sparring stick with Lance's, and before he knew it, there was a sound of clanking metal.

After a few minutes, Ben started to lose his breath. Lance's tricky skirmishing continued to tire him.

After some time, Lance pinned Ben to the ground, with just his sparring stick in his sweaty face.

"I'm done," said Ben breathlessly.

"You can continue. You're doing fine."

"No. I'm not. Jousting is difficult."

"Ben, you can do this," said Saint Patrick. "Every great prince who has been in your shoes has failed at jousting at first."

"Did you know that every sport I've tried, I've failed at?" said Ben.

"Ben ..."

"Try it again, but this time try to keep your negative thoughts out of your mind, and instead focus on succeeding," said Saint Patrick.

Brushing himself off, Ben gripped his sparring stick and continued to joust with Lance, despite his continued uncertainty of himself.

After some time, and with trial and error, with one last ounce of strength, Ben managed to knock Lance to the ground.

Lance lay breathless, arms and legs sprawled on the ground. "Nice job," he said. As soon as he got up from the field, he brushed himself off. Lance had cuts and bruises from jousting and appeared to be out of breath.

"Thank you for your heroic efforts," said Saint Patrick, and he bowed humbly to show his gratitude.

"You're welcome," said Lance. "If you need me further, I'll just be trimming these bushes."

Lance walked feebly over to the bushes, grabbed a small bolt cutter, and began to trim the thick growth.

"Shall we continue your training?"

"Okay."

As Saint Patrick continued to explain what the Three-Leaf'd Tournament would consist of, Ben could not help but be amazed at Lance for his willingness to participate in such a dangerous feat as jousting. He was willing to sacrifice his time and suffer a couple of scratches and bruises just for him.

"Archery, as you know, is a favorite among the Irish people," said Saint Patrick, "and is a favorite of the Three-Leaf'd Tournament. I want to see how far you've come thus far."

A small bow appeared in Saint Patrick's hands, and he handed it to Ben.

Upon seeing Ben's confused expression, Saint Patrick decided once again to demonstrate how to shoot a bow and arrow. He took the bow from Ben, carefully stretched the string back, and released it. It flew at lightning speed, hitting a target a few yards away.

"Now you try." Saint Patrick carefully handed the bow back to Ben.

Ben, filled with some anxiety, released the fragile string. It flew a few feet away, barely missing the target. He released another one, this time more relaxed. The arrow flew at the target and hit it square in the middle.

Saint Patrick smiled. "Very good. Now for your next feat."

Ben watched Saint Patrick earnestly as he walked, cane in hand to guide his stride, over to a corral of majestic horses near the edge of the garden.

It was Queen Kathrynne's corral of horses, and she loved and cared for them dearly. She didn't allow her servants to take care of them—as she was scared they may not care for them as she would have, Ben assumed.

Saint Patrick took one of the horses from the corral and guided it gently to where Ben was standing. "In the tournament, you will be expected to joust on horseback," he said.

"But I don't know how to joust on a horse," said Ben.

"No problem," said Saint Patrick. "That is why I'm here to teach you, is it not?"

Saint Patrick mounted the horse. He put his cane into a small satin bag attached to the horse's saddle; the cane instantly collapsed as it touched the lining of the bag. Saint Patrick rubbed his palms together. A jousting lance appeared.

"Watch me," Saint Patrick instructed. "Jousting on a horse is a very different skill to master than jousting on foot."

Ben watched.

Saint Patrick once again recruited Lance's aid, and once the two of them were across from each other, a half mile apart. He called to Lance, "You ready?"

Lance nodded. "I am."

Saint Patrick made the first move. He pressed his heels into the horse's sides, and it grunted, neighed, and trotted at a quick pace. As soon as he got within earshot of Lance, he poked him in the ribs. When this happened, it made Lance lose his balance, and he landed on the soft grass, beside his horse.

Several attempts later, Lance was getting the best of Saint Patrick, finally knocking him to the ground.

"Oh, I'm so sorry, Maewyn," said Lance, who attempted to lend a hand to him.

"I'm okay, really," said Saint Patrick, getting up with his cane, which appeared to assist him. "But please do try to remember to call me Saint Patrick. The people of Ireland prefer to call me that, and I do too."

"Sorry again," said Lance.

"Don't apologize. I'm fine."

"You ready to give jousting on a horse a try?" Saint Patrick asked, his gaze fixed on Ben. "Again, you will be expected to joust on a horse in the Three-Leaf'd Tournament."

"It looks harder than jousting on foot," said Ben, looking warily at the horse.

"Oh, I'm not going to lie to you; it's harder than you think. But you'll be fine."

He gestured for Ben to get on.

Ben mounted the horse; anxiety filled his conscience, but he brushed it away quickly.

After several attempts at jousting, Ben was able to knock Lance off his horse.

"Very good, Ben," said Saint Patrick. "Your father would be proud of you. You know your father had a natural talent for jousting. He always had his opponent to the ground.

"Now, let's continue your training, shall we?" Saint Patrick added. "Now, I'm sure you heard of mystical dragons throughout the misty ages of history?"

Ben slowly nodded. "Yes," he said.

"Well, there are two types of Irish dragons: one on land and one in water," said Saint Patrick. "I'm sure you're most familiar with land dragons." Ben didn't speak, so Saint Patrick went on. "And of course, land dragons have four legs and have long, delicate iridescent wings, and they are most familiar to those who remember them.

"In Celtic lore, Irish dragons are gatekeepers to other worlds and guardians to the secrets and treasures of the cosmos. They are represented side by side with the Celtic gods.

"As creatures that protect the earth and all creation, they are considered to be the most dominant of all the Celtic symbols," said Saint Patrick. "It is important for you, as the leaf'd prince to know and study Celtic dragon lore, as some higher authorities see it as a symbol of power and wisdom."

"Will I have to study Celtic dragon lore?" Ben asked.

"Yes, eventually you will have to study Celtic dragon lore," said Saint Patrick, "however, not for the Three-Leaf'd Tournament. I'm just preparing you for what comes after the Three-Leaf'd Tournament, as I confidently know you will win and become a leaf'd prince for the Irish community. Ben, the rulership of the leaf'd prince is seen as a great and wonderful responsibility, and I want you to treat it as such."

"I will."

"Shall we continue?"

Ben didn't know what his training would consist of next. He dismissed many new questions that had just entered his head and instead focused on Saint Patrick.

With a tap of Saint Patrick's bejeweled cane, an Irish land dragon appeared before them. It was the biggest creature Ben had ever seen. Its skin was green-tinted; it had long, spiked scales along its back. Smoke filled the fresh, brisk air. Stricken with fear, Ben backed away; his breath was short and shallow.

"Do not be afraid," said Saint Patrick. "This is just a simulation of what you might be encountering in the Three-Leaf'd Tournament."

"Is it dangerous?" Ben asked warily.

"Oh, the simulation? Oh, heavens no! An Irish dragon is a symbol of power and wisdom. The Leaf'd Council, who judge the participants in the tournament, want to see whether you can outwit one or kill one."

"I don't think I can outwit a massive dragon," Ben disclosed. "Just look at it. It's huge!"

"You'll be all right," said Saint Patrick. "Just believe in yourself."

Taking a deep breath, Ben opened his locket. A burgundy and gold-encrusted sword appeared. Ben remembered it was the same one he had used to fight off Lyon's wolves. He shook the sword back and forth, as if that would distract the creature. He could feel his legs buckle as the dragon's tail smacked the ground. He lay on the grass, somewhat disoriented. Looking up, he saw the dim outline of a dragon's green eyes. In the center of its pupil, a black dot was staring back at him; it was as if he saw an endless void of space, soulless.

Ben waved the sword in the dragon's face again. A roar echoed in his eardrums. He stepped back, stumbling upon a root and falling upon the grass.

"What do I do?" Ben yelled, turning to look at Saint Patrick, who was nearby. "I can't do this!"

"You *can* do this," Saint Patrick encouraged. "Every prince has used some form of a magical object in some shape or form. Use your locket."

Without question, Ben opened the locket again. A long braided rope appeared in his free hand. Attached to its end was a glistening medal hook–a grappling hook! Ben looked around but saw nothing. How was he supposed to distract a massive dragon?

In the distance, Ben saw a dim outline of an oak tree standing alone. Using all the strength he had, he threw the grappling hook toward the tree. It wrapped itself around its limbs.

Ben pulled the rope back and let it go. Immediately he was thrust upward, in a straight line, toward the tree. When his foot hit one of the tree branches, Ben breathed a sigh of relief. He had made it–but only just.

Ben coughed. He looked up and saw the massive creature that had hurled him to the ground. Was it going to kill him right here?

Ben looked at the belt loops of his pants. In one of them was a sword, much like a knight's halter. He slid it out carefully, thrust it toward one of the dragon's eyes, and pierced it, and before he knew what he had done, the creature yelped in pain. It pulled back from the tree, unable to spot Ben's presence in its blurry vision.

Ben opened his locket again.

A gust of wind entered the quiet atmosphere. Ben watched, mesmerized, as the dragon's blurred image slowly moved toward him and the locket, like a magnet, finally closed itself, leaving just a burnt ash smell and red sparks behind.

"Well, Ben, congratulations," said Saint Patrick. "You did great. Averting Irish dragons is only half the battle. The other half is successfully navigating through an unfamiliar maze with all sorts of dangerous obstacles."

Ben was worried.

"Oh, no matter, Ben," Saint Patrick added with a smile. "If you can distract a massive Irish dragon, you can certainly navigate through an unfamiliar maze. No problem."

Saint Patrick tapped his cane on the grass. A 3-D map was barely visible in front of Ben's sight. It quickly became visible as Ben's eyes adjusted to its accurate placement of locations of Ireland.

"This map's important," said Saint Patrick. "It's only visible in the dark. It has a depiction of a maze, which you will be expected to navigate through in the tournament."

Ben felt flushed. He hadn't expected to navigate through a significant and unfamiliar maze.

"Every great prince," continued Saint Patrick, hardly noticing Ben's uncomfortable conscience, "has made it successfully through a maze of his own, barely unharmed. Your task is to get through a maze, find a tower, climb it quickly, and rescue a maiden in distress (chosen by the Leaf'd Council), and bring her safely back to the maze's entrance in the allotted time you'll be given."

"I'm not a fast runner," Ben disclosed. "How can I rescue a maiden in distress when I can barely climb?"

"Don't worry. Plotting a course through a maze is not about speed; it's about smarts. I'm confident you'll get through it quite easily."

Saint Patrick's words made Ben feel at ease. He gazed past Saint Patrick to a tall flower, its petals drooping, near the edge of the castle's patio.

"Whose flower is that?" he asked, pointing.

"Queen Kathrynne's," said Saint Patrick. "She treasures it, the flower. It was her son's—your father's. He gave it to her."

"Oh."

"How's the training going?"

Ben jumped.

Saint Patrick jumped too, because the voice touched Ben's shoulder.

Ben and Saint Patrick turned and saw that Queen Kathrynne was standing there.

"Fine," said Saint Patrick.

"Does Ben know who he is facing in the tournament yet?" Queen Kathrynne asked.

"Well, I haven't told him that yet, but I will."

"You'd better tell him; the sooner, the better."

"You know I will tell him, Your Majesty," said Saint Patrick.

"What about the rest of his training?" Queen Kathrynne asked. "Is he improving?"

"Everything's going as planned, Your Majesty," said Saint Patrick. "Don't worry."

"What about jousting? Has Ben mastered it yet?"

"He's close."

"And the jousting on a horse? Is he getting close to mastering it?"

"Yes, I think he's improving."

"All right," said Queen Kathrynne. "Make sure my grandson doesn't dawdle, as the tournament is less than a month away. I don't want my kingdom and its subjects to be the laughingstock of the Three-Leaf'd Tournament if he's ill-prepared to participate."

"I'll make sure Ben's prepared; don't you worry, Your Majesty," said Saint Patrick.

"Okay."

"Don't worry about our grandson. He's in good hands," said King Diamond, who was behind his wife, hearing the exchange between Saint Patrick and her. They disappeared in the confines of the castle, leaving Ben and his friends by themselves.

***

"How did your training go?" Elizabeth asked, taking a sip of her lemonade in a large tin cup, hours after Ben's training session with Saint Patrick.

He and Elizabeth were seated at a round brass table in his grandmother's garden patio.

"Fine," said Ben. "Saint Patrick thinks I'm improving."

"Oh good." Elizabeth took another sip of her lemonade.

"What did you do—?"

Ben didn't get to finish his thought. Instead he stared at Elizabeth, whose mouth fell open.

Elizabeth continued to look at Ben's neck closely and realized that he wasn't wearing his locket. Elizabeth remembered it was Saint Patrick who had told him to keep it safe and out of the hands of foes who'd use it for their evil purposes.

"Ben—your locket. It's missing!" Elizabeth gasped.

"What? How?" said Ben. His stomach lurched. What would Saint Patrick think, say?

Saint Patrick entered the patio. "Queen Kathrynne wishes for you and your friends to join her for dinner," he said, gazing at Ben.

"Saint Patrick ... Ben's locket—" Elizabeth gasped.

Saint Patrick noticed the reason Elizabeth had gasped. Ben's neck was bare.

"What happened here? Why doesn't Ben have his locket? You know it is important that Ben has his locket. Why, then, is it missing?" Saint Patrick gazed at Ben and his friends, expecting either of them to answer him.

No one answered. None of them thought they could. They seemed disappointed in themselves. According to Saint Patrick, they had a great responsibility to keep Ben's locket safe, and they had failed.

"What's wrong? Why is everyone silent?"

Ben turned and saw that Evan stood at the garden archway, holding a brass pot filled with large, draping flowers.

"Why are you holding that pot?" Ben asked, trying to distract himself from the apparent silence.

"I was helping Queen Kathrynne," said Evan. "Lance was tired of gardening, so I thought I'd help."

"Ben's locket is missing," said Saint Patrick. He glared at Evan, making him uncomfortable. "Do you know what happened to Ben's locket?"

Everyone looked earnestly at Evan. Evan felt the pit of his stomach gurgle. "I-I don't know," he stammered.

"You don't know?" said Saint Patrick.

"Yes," said Evan.

"Well, I think you know where Ben's locket is," said Saint Patrick. "You see, Evan, Lance told me that you were the last one to see Ben's locket."

"I never saw the locket."

"Evan, I know you saw it–or at the very least you know who took it."

Evan gazed at Ben, and then at Elizabeth, and he continued to stay silent.

"I think he knows something," Elizabeth finally said.

"Evan, please tell us," said Ben.

Evan didn't know what to do or say. His eyes wandered and met Saint Patrick's brown ones that glared at him disapprovingly.

Evan blurted, "Hamish Greentines! I think Hamish Greentines stole Ben's locket!"

"Well, I'm not surprised," said Saint Patrick. "Hamish has always had a knack for stealing items that aren't his. At least that's what I've been told."

"Do you think we can get Ben's locket back?" Elizabeth asked.

"Yes, it's certainly possible," said Saint Patrick. "But first we must travel to Hamish's. I imagine he has every item he has stolen stowed away there in his house. If Ben's locket is there, I believe we'll find it.

"The thing you must know about leprechauns like Hamish is that they never apologize for their mistakes. They're greedy–always snagging the latest precious and valuable thing. So, keeping this in mind, we must be diligent and mindful of what he might do."

"Do you think Hamish will hurt us?" said Ben.

"He might. That's why it's crucial that we get your locket back. Without it, I'm afraid you won't be able to compete in the tournament and defeat Lyon."

And so Ben and his friends set out in the early dawn of the morning to retrieve Ben's locket from Hamish Greentines, the leprechaun.

CHAPTER XII

Hamish Greentines

THICK GREENERY AND moss hung over a long, winding dirt path as Ben and his friends walked along. A short distance away, they heard birds chirping and frogs croaking.

Hamish Greentines lived in a tree stump. Once a lively and prosperous tree, hunters had knocked down Hamish's tree home, leaving a stump, which Hamish now occupied. The blow to his tree home devastated Hamish and his family. But over time, he adjusted to his newfound home and made it his own.

Hamish loved his grandfather, Earnest Greentines. He remembered from an early age that Earnest had built the tree home with just his bare hands. Then he remembered that Earnest had gotten sick, and the other leprechauns in his family had no clue what his sickness was. He remembered that his mother, Evie, had cried upon Earnest's unexpected death.

Just about dark, Hamish, who was about twelve, saw his mother gazing through a large round window at the sunset, just beyond the mossy trees and foothills. He saw that she had tears in her eyes.

Soon after that, Evie moved on from her father's death and told Hamish— then thirteen—to steal for their family to survive.

And so that is what he did. And that is what he was known to do.

Saint Patrick tapped on the green moss with the tip of his cane, near the path. It slowly fell, piece by piece. Through an opening where the moss once was, Ben and his friends saw what seemed to be a small but sturdy stump.

"This," said Saint Patrick, "is Hamish's home."

Further along, Saint Patrick led Ben and his friends to the village square. Here Ben and his friends saw many creatures holding large parchment bags filled with what looked like produce and knit clothing. In the middle of the village square, a large fountain stood by many carts. Some Irish peasant children were sitting on the fountain's edge, throwing tarnished gold coins into its clear water, while others were chasing chickens throughout the square.

Irish women in large straw hats hurried along the path, eyeing carts as they went. Some stopped to browse, while others bought produce and knit hats and bags. Saint Patrick led Ben and his friends through the chaos of the square to Hert McGawn's produce cart.

"Is this tomato good?" asked an Irish woman. She eyed the tomato and then looked at Hert suspiciously.

"Depends what you call 'good,'" said Hert.

"Is this tomato good for pasta?"

"I'm sure it is."

"What about this zucchini?"

"Yes, that one is good, too."

>139

"And what about these peppers?"

By this time, Hert McGawn was red-faced. He looked into the woman's brown eyes and asked as politely as he could, "Ma'am, are you going to buy any product or haggle me all day?"

"Well, yes, I am," said the woman. "But first I want to know if all your food is on sale."

Hert sighed. "Yes, it is on sale."

"Okay. How much?"

"Eight gold coins."

Ben watched as the woman searched through the contents of her parchment bag, taking out a few coins.

"Is this enough?" she asked Hert.

Hert took out a small magnifying glass from his pocket and examined the coins that the woman placed on the edge of his cart. "Ma'am, what type of coins are these?"

"Silver ones."

"I don't accept silver coins."

"Oh."

"Do you have gold ones? I accept those."

The woman searched her parchment bag, finally finding several gold coins at the bottom. "Here you go. Is this enough?"

"Yes, I believe it is," said Hert. "Thank you."

After taking a handful of tomatoes, zucchini, and green and yellow peppers and placing them into her parchment bag, she soon was out of sight, disappearing through a crowd of shoppers mingling with each other along the path.

"Hi."

Hert jumped and saw Saint Patrick and Ben and his friends a few feet away from his cart.

"What do you want?" Hert asked grumpily. "Can't you see I'm busy?"

"I know you are busy," said Saint Patrick, "but I was wondering if Hamish had already gone by your cart."

Hert glared at Saint Patrick suspiciously. "Why?"

"Well, I know he irritates you, taking gold coins from your cart," said Saint Patrick. "I also know you have a keen eye for gold. Do you happen to have seen a gold locket lying about in the village square?"

"Ugh, no, I haven't," said Hert.

"Hert, I think Hamish might've stolen a gold locket," said Saint Patrick.

"And why is it my problem?"

"You see Hamish almost every day. I thought you would have some insight on when he shows up."

"Do I look like a fortune-teller to you?" Hert didn't even look up. He continued to count gold coins in his wicker basket.

"Uh, no, you don't," said Ben awkwardly.

"How am I supposed to know when Hamish shows up at my cart?" said Hert. "He shows up at odd times during the day, sometimes when creatures are busy browsing. Sometimes he doesn't show up at all."

"But you can't deny Hamish was here today and took some of your coins," said Saint Patrick.

"Yes, I can't deny that. Hamish was here."

Ben wanted to ask Hert why the Irish woman had given him silver coins when there was a sign that said "Gold Coins Only" on the edge of Hert's produce cart, but he thought it was rude. He was still curious about it, so he asked Saint Patrick instead.

"Hert, despite his old age, has identified with old people, the wiser group. This Irish woman comes by his cart every day to buy the same vegetables." He turned to Ben and whispered, "Plus, this Irish woman's his mother. She has dementia. Poor thing. He treats her with the utmost kindness and respect because he feels like he owes her that."

Ben felt empathy toward the old Irish woman and to Hert. To go through the same routine would drive Ben mad, but he had a large amount of respect for Hert's gentle nature.

"Do you mind if we stay here until Hamish shows up again?" Saint Patrick asked Hert.

"I don't care."

"Okay. Thanks."

In the confines of the crowd, Saint Patrick and Ben and his friends watched Hert's cart. Several creatures came and went, browsing and buying. Then, just as Ben and his friends seemed to lose all hope, a small white-faced leprechaun with curly brown hair and big brown eyes emerged out of the crowd a few feet from Hert's produce cart. When Hert turned his attention away to count several coins an old Irish man had left him, Hamish snatched several gold coins near the edge of the cart. When Hert turned around again, he saw Hamish smiling gleefully, as if he had stolen the last cookie from a cookie jar.

"What did you do?" Hert asked sharply.

"I didn't do anything," said Hamish innocently.

"I know you have stolen some of my coins," Hert insisted. "I know you did."

"I didn't."

"I know you did."

"Hamish."

Hamish turned, realizing who had spoken, and froze. Saint Patrick fixed his eyes on Hamish. Ben and his friends joined Saint Patrick near Hert's produce cart moments later.

"Hamish, I know you stole Ben's gold locket," said Saint Patrick.

"I don't know what you're talking about," said Hamish.

"I know you know what I'm talking about," said Saint Patrick calmly. "A locket of great significance doesn't just disappear, does it?"

"I'm sure you just misplaced it," said Hamish.

"Misplaced it?" Saint Patrick's face was beet red. "Misplaced it? I think not! Hand me Ben's locket!"

"I don't have it."

Hamish snatched a few more gold coins off the edge of Hert's produce cart and disappeared.

"What do we do now?" Ben asked wearily.

"We entice Hamish to come back and steal more coins," said Saint Patrick.

"I don't want Hamish back here," said Hert, glaring at Saint Patrick with the utmost disgust.

Hert feared that Hamish would continue his raid of thievery attempts. Taxes in the kingdom had slowly but surely gone up in the past year, and because of the high demand for produce within the country, Hert had to cut back on the food.

King Diamond and Queen Kathrynne had promised Hert that taxes would not hurt his business, but their promise merely served as padding for more complaints. His produce had soon rotted in the summer heat, and the customers did not like their food rotten and stinky. Without realizing it, Hamish had set in motion a domino effect of misfortunes on Hert and his produce cart business.

"He won't steal any more of your gold coins; I promise," said Saint Patrick.

"I don't believe you," said Hert.

"Oh, don't worry," said Saint Patrick. "Everything will be just fine."

After digging in this pocket, Saint Patrick placed some of his gold coins on the edge of Hert's produce cart. They shone with a golden appearance, reflecting in the sun's light.

Hert saw that Hamish had returned to his cart, enticed by Saint Patrick's fake gold coins.

"Hold on," he whispered to Ben and his friends.

Saint Patrick touched the edge of Hert's produce cart with just his fingertips. Green smoke instantly surrounded Saint Patrick and Ben and his friends. For a moment they couldn't see anything except green smoke.

When it cleared, they saw what seemed to be at first glance a stump Saint Patrick had shown them hours before going to the village square.

With a pop, Saint Patrick and Ben and his friends landed with a thud on the grass beside the tree stump.

"Wait here," Saint Patrick demanded.

He tapped his cane on the grass. Ben and his friends saw the stump expand into a small log cabin.

Saint Patrick tapped his cane on the grass again. With a click, the front door of Hamish's stump home unlocked.

It was a small place except for a stone fireplace. Hamish hardly noticed Saint Patrick and Ben and his friends. He had his back turned to them, stirring a pot of herb tea in a large brass pot hanging aloft on the arm in the fireplace.

"Hamish."

Stunned, Hamish turned and saw Saint Patrick glaring at him. "What are you doing here?"

"I'm here for Ben's gold locket," said Saint Patrick. "Is it here?" He looked around the room and saw that dust covered chairs, tabletops, and bookcases. "I see you haven't touched anything in weeks. Have you got it hidden somewhere?"

"I don't know what you're talking about," said Hamish. "I never took Ben's locket."

"Of course you did," Saint Patrick insisted. "You can't resist gold. Leprechauns can't help themselves. They steal gold if it's in their sight. Now don't lie to me. Where is Ben's locket?"

"I don't know."

"I know you took Ben's locket. If you tell me now, I'll forget you ever took it."

"I told you," said Hamish, "I don't know where the locket is."

"Saint Patrick, let's go," said Ben, turning his back toward the front door. "Hamish doesn't know where my locket is."

"Ben, he does know where it is," said Saint Patrick. "He's just not telling me."

Hamish went over to the fireplace and very carefully poured Irish tea into a chipped teacup he got from the hearth. Hamish nonchalantly took a seat in an armchair by the fireplace and sipped his Irish tea.

Saint Patrick tapped the floor with his cane. Seconds later, Ben heard the crash of coins and glass breaking. In an instant, Hamish tipped his Irish tea on himself, cursed himself, and then turned his head and gazed in horror at his precious coin collection, which was now covered in glass shards near the back of his kitchen.

"Why did you do that?" Hamish asked tearfully, looking at Saint Patrick.

"I did that to teach you a lesson," said Saint Patrick. "Have you learned your lesson about taking people's things?"

"I didn't take Ben's locket, all right!" Hamish yelled.

"Then who did?" Saint Patrick asked.

"I don't know," said Hamish.

A spurt of hot tea boiled over the brass pot in the fireplace, gushing onto the floor. Hamish felt his feet growing numb. A hot stream of Irish tea swept over the floor like a sea over sand. He could feel his insides burning; he could feel the numbness of his feet growing more intense.

Then Hamish heard the screeching of bats. Above his head, he saw black shadows among the dimly lit room. Sitting among the ceiling beams were many bats. There was a rustle of bat wings, and Hamish screeched.

"Please don't let these bats get me!" Hamish begged.

"Sure. I won't let these bats get you," said Saint Patrick.

"You won't?"

"Yes, I won't. On one condition, though."

"What?" asked Hamish, on edge.

"Hand over Ben's locket, and I'll forget you ever took it."

"I don't have it, I said."

"Suit yourself," said Saint Patrick. He tapped his cane on the floor again.

Hamish could feel his eyes slowly shutting. He tried to open them, but it was impossible. The force of Saint Patrick's spell prevented Hamish from opening his eyes.

"I can't see a thing!" cried Hamish.

This must have amused the bats or at least aroused them from their sleep. In the dimly lit room, Ben and his friends heard the swooshing of bat wings. Before Hamish knew what was going on, swarms of bat-like creatures paraded on his head like torpedoes on enemies of war. He stepped back, still blinded by the heaviness of his eyelids, tripping over himself, finally stumbling to the floor.

"Please help me," he begged.

Hamish sat crouched down on the floor, still remembering the bat-like creatures flying in the darkness in his childhood room.

Bats terrified Hamish. He could still envision the eerie shadows of bats looking at him from the corner of his room, where they hung from a beam, sensing his presence. They haunted him then, and they still haunt him now.

Hamish shuddered.

"Are you ready to give up and tell me where Ben's locket is, or not?" said Saint Patrick. "Just know that if you don't tell me, more chaos will surely happen to you."

Drenched in hot tea, blistered, and terrified of bats, Hamish said, "All right. I'll tell you where Ben's locket is. It's in the kitchen, in one of the drawers. Excuse me."

After carefully crossing the room, Hamish opened the drawer, cautiously took out a golden locket on a golden beaded chain, and handed it to Saint Patrick. "Here you go," he said.

"Thank you," said Saint Patrick. "And in turn I'll restore calm and order to your house."

"You're welcome," mumbled Hamish, "and thank you for restoring calm and order to my house."

Saint Patrick nodded but did not elaborate. Instead he tapped his cane on the floor one final time. Instantly calm and order were restored: the hot tea evaporated, there was a sound of tea filling the brass pot, and the sound of coins filling a corner cabinet filled the dusty air.

With a tap of his cane, Saint Patrick and Ben and his friends were magically on the path, near the village square. Creatures were going about their own business, barely even noticing they were there.

Then Ben heard it: a low but distinctive growl.

The creatures in the village square hardly noticed the growling at all, but then a small girl screamed. It was so loud that Ben almost lost his hearing. Looking among the crowd of creatures, Ben saw that the little girl who screamed appeared to be kneeling on the edge of the fountain now, near a woman Ben guessed was her mother. She was holding the little girl, comforting her as best she could. Tears were flowing from her eyes, and her nose was red and puffy, but Ben was not sure. The distance gave him little to no clarity. In the silence, Ben had an eerie feeling that something was there: something invisible—something dangerous. Shadowed figures quickly moved through the crowd of creatures, hardly touching them. They appeared to be searching for something.

They dodged in and out of the crowd, going through them as if they were smoke. Ben tried to piece together where he had seen the unknown beings, but he couldn't remember. It was all a surreal blur to him.

Then, as the cloaked figures got closer to the fountain, Ben was able to faintly make out the creatures' reflection in the fountain's pool of water. Ben assumed that these creatures were standing upright, but on closer inspection he saw they were on all fours. Overall, they looked like dogs—poorly clothed dogs, Ben assumed.

But why would dogs be wearing cloaks, anyway? he thought.

A flash of green light exploded. Ben gazed in shock at the scene before him: Amid the chaos and destruction of the village square, Lyon's wolves' eyes glowed madly. They appeared to be ghosts, not solid at all.

Dark clouds filled the once bright atmosphere. Ben felt the hair on the back of his neck stand up. The sudden coldness in the atmosphere here was too much for Ben to take.

Lyon's wolves swiftly moved about in the dim light. The fountain that was once solid as a rock had split in two from Lyon's wolves' dark magical energy. The girl and the woman, afraid that the fountain's heavy stone would impact them, ran. Ben felt his blood pumping inside him. He was starting to run toward the falling fountain. He didn't know why, but he knew he needed to stop the falling stone debris. Behind him he heard Elizabeth's faint scream in the distance.

"Ben! No! Don't do it!"

Ben ducked as stone and dust fell in heaps around him. All that was left of the fountain was chipped stone pieces and powder.

There was a rush of wind. Ben saw Lyon's magical wolves surrounding him and his friends. He fumbled with his locket for a few seconds before finally opening it.

"Nothing's happening," said Ben, looking over his shoulder at Saint Patrick for guidance.

"Be patient. The locket's magic will work."

"How?"

"Just be patient."

Sure enough, a thick white feather wand appeared in Ben's dominant hand–his right hand.

Lyon's wolves slowly moved toward Ben; he turned in the other direction to run, but Saint Patrick grabbed Ben's arm and said, "You can't just abandon the fight with Lyon's evil magical wolves. You must be persistent and devoted to winning the fight."

"I don't know if I can," said Ben quickly.

"But you must," said Saint Patrick. "Your father would have wanted you to finish what you started for him and defeat Lyon's wolves."

"I don't know if I can," said Ben.

"You can," said Saint Patrick. "I believe in you. Elizabeth believes in you. Everyone here believes in you. Trust yourself, and let the locket's magic aid you."

There was no time for any further protest from Ben, because several of Lyon's wolves howled and a burst of light entered the air, almost blinding Saint Patrick and Ben and his friends.

They immediately stepped back, covering their ears from the shrill noise. Ben, despite the ear-splitting pain of the sound, stepped forward and flicked the feather wand. A spark of yellow light shot from the wand's end, instantly silencing Lyon's wolves. The light continued, and Ben saw that the fountain, once in shambles and unrecognizable, was immediately put together into a glistening stone fountain.

"Let's go," said Saint Patrick, "before the feather wand's magic wears off and Lyon's wolves are after us again."

"You mean they could be after us again?" said Ben, who was running past Evan, not looking back over his shoulder.

"Yes, that could be a possibility," said Saint Patrick. "That is why we must keep moving."

There was a low but distinctive growl.

Looking over his shoulder, Ben saw that Lyon's wolves had become unfrozen and were following him and his friends. Still running, Ben flicked his wrist. A yellow burst of light went over his shoulder, hitting the wolves. Ben heard a yelp.

There was a second growl. A third.

Elizabeth screamed. A blast of light from Lyon's wolves flew past her ear.

Evan ran ahead of Ben and Elizabeth, afraid that Lyon's magical wolves would injure him.

Ben flicked the feather wand again, and then a third time.

The blast of light hit Lyon's wolves.

Crack.

A tree limb fell in front of him. On it was one of Lyon's magical wolves. Its eyes gazed into Ben's terrified brown ones.

With a flick of his wrist, Ben managed to injure the wolf. It lay motionless beside the tree limb. Ben could hear the wolf's heavy breathing.

"Ben! Look out!"

More wolves approached the tree limb. Ben turned, and with quick thinking, he flicked the feather wand. Several bursts of light hit the wolves directly; they yelped in pain.

Seconds later, it seemed the wand's spell had merely served as a temporary distraction. Lyon's wolves were stronger than ever before. They howled, splitting Ben and his friends' eardrums.

Finally, after what seemed like hours, Saint Patrick and Ben and his friends escaped Lyon's wolves. They were on a hill just beyond the village square.

"Do you think they'll follow us?" Ben asked.

"They might," said Saint Patrick. He smiled. "You were brave to fight against Lyon's wolves. I'm proud of you. Your father would be proud of you, too."

"Thank you," said Ben.

"I suggest we make camp here," said Saint Patrick. "Lyon's ex-girlfriend, Suzette, lives just beyond this hill." He pointed to a small cluster of maple trees just below the hill. "She might know Lyon's weakness, so it would be easier to defeat him."

"Lyon had a girlfriend?" said Ben.

"Yes, he did," said Saint Patrick. "There is a rumor that he and his ex had a child, but that is merely speculation."

"And who was that child?" Ben asked.

"I don't know," said Saint Patrick. "No one knows except Suzette herself."

Saint Patrick then tapped the grass. A campsite appeared with folding chairs, a picnic table, and two huge tents. On the picnic table was a spread of grilled meats and side items such as potato salad and coleslaw.

Ben was hoping Lyon's wolves would not find them. He wondered if Elizabeth and Evan were thinking the same thing.

CHAPTER XIII

Suzette Polish

A CABIN LAY just beyond the grassy hill. In the background, Ben saw a windmill. Attached to it was a bucket, scooping up water. The land beyond the cabin was vast, stretching for miles. Greenery covered the area surrounding the cabin and beyond; many vegetables of colorful varieties surrounded its exterior.

Coming closer, Ben, and his friends saw a small woman kneeling; she was placing dirt into a circular flower bed.

"Ah, who are you?" She turned, startled. She held a large hand shovel high as a weapon.

"Suzette, I'm sorry we startled you, but we need to talk to you about Lyon," said Saint Patrick.

"No, I don't think that'll be all right," said Suzette. "I swore that I wouldn't talk about him. That part of my life is over, and I prefer it to stay in the past."

"Suzette, this is very important. We need to know Lyon's weakness," said Saint Patrick.

"Lyon doesn't have a weakness." Suzette glanced at Ben and his friends suspiciously. "Why do you want to know whether Lyon has a weakness?"

"To defeat him," said Ben.

"Oh." Suzette sighed. "I can't help y'all. I'm sorry."

Suzette knelt and continued tending her plants.

"If you know something–anything at all–about Lyon's weaknesses, please tell us," said Ben. "You know, the sole responsibility to defeat Lyon rests upon my shoulders. I'm scared to death. I never knew how scared I'd feel about defeating such an evil wizard. I get it. You're scared too."

"I'm not scared," said Suzette at once.

"Really?" said Saint Patrick. "I'm scared."

"I refuse to talk about Lyon, so don't ask me again."

Suzette could sense the desperation in Ben's eyes; she decided she would talk. "Okay. I'll talk about Lyon," she said. "If it helps you in defeating him, I'll be happy to help. It'll be painful for me to relive those memories, but I'll try to keep it together."

"Won't you come inside?" Suzette added. She gestured toward her house.

Saint Patrick and Ben and his friends entered the small cottage. A wicker couch lay near the front door, with an identical wicker chair at each side of the sofa.

Elizabeth sat on one of the wicker chairs, while her companions sat on the couch and the other wicker chair.

"What do you want to know?" Suzette asked, taking a seat on a third wicker chair opposite Ben and his friends.

"I want to know the reason you fell in love with an evil wizard," said Elizabeth.

"Lyon was not always an evil wizard," said Suzette. "He was kind. He fashioned flowers of rich detail and gave them to me as gifts. Then, afterward, things started to go downhill."

"What kind of things?" said Ben.

"On the night we went to a carnival, things changed. It completely altered my perspective about who Lyon was as a wizard.

"Lyon had become spiteful and hateful when Dawnsy, a girl, asked for directions to the Ferris wheel. I showed Dawnsy where it was located, and Lyon, despite himself, flicked his wand. A red, fiery spark entered the cloudy air, and the poor girl was dead. I told Lyon I had had enough of his evil, spiteful ways."

"I know you want to put that awful incident behind you, but would you consider seeing him again?" said Saint Patrick.

"No, I won't. Not after what I've experienced; I don't want to be stressed. I'm peaceful now, with myself," said Suzette.

"The reason I ask is that you may prevent more deaths," said Saint Patrick.

"How can I do that?" said Suzette.

"You could tell him you still love him and you want him back," said Saint Patrick. "Of course, you won't mean it, but Lyon won't realize that."

Suzette looked warily at Saint Patrick. "I don't know."

"You said yourself that he loved you once, did you not?" Ben asked.

"Well, yes, I did," said Suzette, "but that was before I knew his true evil nature."

"So will you do it?" said Ben, on edge. He wanted the demise of Lyon as much as anyone in Ireland. All of this had become too real to him when Elizabeth was injured by Lyon's wolves.

"No. I won't," said Suzette.

"No? Why not?" Elizabeth asked.

"It's too dangerous," said Suzette.

"Don't you want to stop Lyon from hurting any more creatures?" said Saint Patrick.

Suzette had a sick feeling in the pit of her stomach. She knew Saint Patrick was right. There was no guarantee she'd be safe from the hateful wrath Lyon had planned for the Irish people.

"You know," said Suzette after an awkward silence, "my husband, Tucker, hated Lyon with a passion."

"He did?" said Ben.

"Yes," said Suzette. "He'd gaze out of the windows day and night, looking for any magical hint that Lyon was nearby."

"How did he feel about you dating Lyon?" Elizabeth asked.

"I never told him."

"Why not?" said Ben, his curiously aroused.

"I didn't want our marriage strained. I loved Lyon so much, and if I had told him, he'd probably have gone crazy."

"You talk about your husband as if he's gone. How did he die?" said Ben.

Suzette sniffled. "He died from cancer."

"Oh, sorry," said Ben.

"May I ask what kind?" said Elizabeth.

"Throat cancer."

"Oh, dear."

"It's quite all right." Suzette sighed. She didn't want to talk, as it was growing more painful, but she felt she had to; the impending silence here was driving her crazy. "I expect you heard I was pregnant, right?"

Ben shook his head. "No."

"Did you tell him—Lyon?" said Elizabeth.

"No, I didn't, and I don't plan to."

***

Suzette remembered how scared she had been at the prospect of Lyon as a father. She had pictured his face, angry and confused. Once he was over the shock of her pregnancy, he'd want to immediately try to manipulate the child into doing dark magic and sorcery. To prevent this, she knew she had to go away.

At the break of dawn, Suzette walked to the nearest village. There she asked a man passing in a covered carriage for a ride. He happily obliged.

"So what's your name?" the man asked. He had a thick Irish accent, and it got on Suzette's nerves, but she took it in stride.

"Suzette."

"Where're you going, Suzette?"

"Don't you think that's personal?"

"Oh, I'm sorry. Trying to make casual conversation, that's all."

For the rest of the carriage ride, Suzette was silent. In the silence, she could hear the roughness of the trail road as they journeyed on. Looking out the covered window, she saw the vast countryside with its rolling green hills and small forest-cutter cottages. Finally, after some time, the man stopped the carriage at an Irish country inn, Lottie's, a few miles past the village square.

"Is this where you wanted to go?" the man asked.

"This'll be fine," said Suzette. She got out of the carriage.

"Ma'am."

She turned to face the man.

"I know this isn't my business or anything, but is the father of your baby meeting you?"

"No. My husband's busy. I'm fine."

"Well, let me at least pay for your stay. It's the least I could do, having taken you thus far."

The man climbed out of the carriage. He took out a few gold coins and handed them to Suzette.

"You don't need to pay for my inn stay," she said.

The man smiled warmly. "Well, yes, of course, I do."

She turned to thank the man for his generosity, but he was gone. The only thing left was an imprint of carriage tracks on the damp grass.

***

Despite her unwillingness to do so, Suzette had reluctantly agreed to see Lyon—on the condition that Saint Patrick would wield his magic to protect her from harm.

"Yes, of course, I will," he said.

"Thank you," said Suzette.

"You're welcome." He turned his attention to Ben. "Lyon will most likely show up at the Three-Leaf'd Tournament. There might also be the possibility Lyon might send a decoy in his place to harm you. If I were you, I'd be on my toes."

"Okay," said Ben. "Will you be on the lookout too?"

"Oh, yes, I will; don't you worry."

"All right," said Ben.

"Now, Ben, you didn't think I'd leave you with Lyon on the loose, did you?" said Saint Patrick.

"Well, no, I didn't," said Ben.

"Exactly," said Saint Patrick.

After an awkward moment of silence, everyone agreed that Lyon needed to be defeated and killed, and soon, with the aid of Ben's locket.

CHAPTER XIV

Suzette Polish

SUZETTE STRAINED IN her chair. The stiffness had become too uncomfortable for her as she drew a deep breath. "I think I know some of Lyon's weaknesses," she said. "Well, one weakness, anyway."

Ben leaned forward. "Really?"

"Yes," she said. "Lyon may be still in love with me."

"Why do you think that?" Elizabeth asked.

"When Lyon killed Dawnsy, and when I ended our relationship, I could sense his disappointment," said Suzette. "In his view, as I presumed later, he wanted a relationship with me so badly that he'd do anything to have it—even kill."

Ben felt uneasy. He didn't think an evil wizard like Lyon could love another without something in return. Evil wizards, as far as Ben knew, were selfish magical beings, always thinking of what they could get from another, without merit or explanation of their actions.

"Are you sure Lyon loved you?"

Ben's question shocked Suzette, and she herself leaned forward, looking at him with such intensity that he was sure she'd kill him with her stare.

"Yes, he did," she said.

"And you think you'll persuade him not to hurt other Irish people?" Ben asked disbelievingly.

"Yes, I'll try."

Evan, who had been listening to the conversation between Suzette and Ben eagerly for a few moments, finally spoke.

"Sometimes evil wizards don't have weaknesses," he said. "They are strong and will-minded and will not give up a fight without a long, drawn-out battle."

"Well, in this case, Lyon has a weakness," said Saint Patrick. "He still loves Suzette and wants her approval."

"Do you think Lyon will continue to attack me even if I win the tournament?" Ben asked.

"I'm afraid he will," said Saint Patrick. "That is why I'm preparing you for the after-effects of the Three-Leaf'd Tournament. That way you will be better equipped for whatever hazardous spells he will shoot at you."

Ben looked warily at Saint Patrick. The pressure of defeating such an evil wizard was wearing Ben thin; Saint Patrick smiled warmly, slightly calming Ben's fragile nerves.

Saint Patrick took out an old gold pocket watch from inside his cloak pocket and glanced at its face. "Blimey, is that the time? We'd better go, lest danger follows us."

CHAPTER XV

Ben McNealy

A WHOOSH FILLED Ben's ears, and he fell back on the soft grass. In the distance, a hazy image of a stone castle lay just beyond Ben's view.

"Ah, you're all right." Queen Kathrynne leaned forward, stretching out her arms. "Thought you'd never get here."

"Did something happen?" Saint Patrick asked wearily.

"Yes," said Queen Kathrynne. "The castle's gardens got mangled."

Queen Kathrynne led Ben and his friends to the garden's patio, where there was a vast array of plants scattered about. Ben felt a sick feeling in the pit of his stomach. The once lively and prosperous garden had been turned into a desolate wasteland.

"I'm sorry," Ben finally said.

"Well, what can you do when all of your beautiful flowers have been crushed?" said Queen Kathrynne, sighing.

She picked up a fan from a wicker table weathered with age and fanned herself. It was delicate in its design. A rose was carefully stitched on the front of it, and at the bottom were initials: K. D. and Q. K. Queen Kathrynne remembered that her husband had given the fan to her for their twentieth wedding anniversary.

The fan was rare, but Queen Kathrynne was unsure where her husband had gotten it. All she knew about it were the tidbits her husband had told her. She pictured a man in the foothills of Ireland fashioning it with delicate tools. She assumed he was a crafter working for extra money. The fan was special to her, and she treasured it ever since.

"Lyon tried to burn down the castle's exterior while you were gone," said Queen Kathrynne quickly. "But it was protected by Rowzand family magic. I suggest you flee from here; it is not safe."

"I agree," said Saint Patrick.

"But where would we go?" Ben asked with a sigh.

"You leave that up to me," said Saint Patrick. "You and your friends will be much safer once we all flee from this place."

"I agree with my wife and with Saint Patrick," said a voice behind Ben and his friends.

Ben looked beyond Queen Kathrynne's shoulders and saw a man dressed in regal robes that were red, gold, and green. He had a golden crown with emerald stones on his head. In his left hand, a glistening golden staff shone with such brilliance and color that Ben was sure it was rare. He looked every bit a king.

"Lance will accompany you on your journey to find a safer location," he said.

Lance stopped trimming the garden's bushes and glanced at King Diamond. "What?"

"That's right."

"With all due respect, Your Majesty, I refuse to go on a dangerous journey."

"Lance, you will go with Ben and his friends, and that's my final word."

Lance glanced wearily at Queen Kathrynne, but she nodded her head to show her approval of her husband's order.

"Well ... if you think it's best."

"I know it is best," said Queen Kathrynne.

"I will have to pack a suitcase," said Lance. "I don't know how long I will be with Ben and his friends."

"Oh, you'll be with Ben and his friends for as long as Saint Patrick says," said Queen Kathrynne. "I made prior arrangements with Saint Patrick, and he has agreed to report to either my husband or to me if you decide to bail on Ben and his friends."

"Why are you doing this to me?" Lance asked tearfully.

"For your protection, and for the safety and prosperity of the kingdom, you will go with Ben and his friends," said Queen Kathrynne. "I don't want you to die from a careless act of violence. You are my best servant and friend. If I lost you, it'd be just devastating."

"Really?" said Lance.

"Yes," said Queen Kathrynne.

"Well, since there is a long journey ahead of us, we need some food, don't we?" said Lance, and he retreated to the kitchen, bidding farewell to Queen Kathrynne and King Diamond. Ben and his friends instantly smelled the sweet aroma of baked goods lingering in the air: muffins, cupcakes, and small apple pies. Within moments, Lance returned with a full plate of baked goods wrapped in thick parchment paper.

"Here you go," said King Diamond, and with a snap of his fingers, a couple of cloth suitcases appeared.

"Thanks, Your Majesties," said Lance, and he bowed humbly.

"Shall we go?" said Saint Patrick, and he beckoned toward the door.

Ben and his friends were about to leave when there was a knock at the patio door leading out to Kathrynne's garden. Then Ben and his friends heard the voice of a female servant.

"Won't you come in? Queen Kathrynne and King Diamond will be with you in a moment."

"Excuse me." Queen Kathrynne stepped into the study leading to the patio door. There she found a tall but skinny man sitting on the wicker couch. He was wearing a colorful garment: red, purple, indigo, yellow, green, and blue. In one hand, he held a rolled piece of parchment; the other hand held a golden pocket watch. He wanted to be anywhere other than his present location at the castle, Queen Kathrynne guessed.

"Oh, Mr. Brytant," said Queen Kathrynne. "What brings you here?"

He put his pocket watch back inside his pocket and turned his attention to Queen Kathrynne.

"I'm here to see Ben."

"Why?"

"To talk about the Three-Leaf'd Tournament. To give him written rules and regulations."

"Very well, Mr. Brytant; you may see him," said Queen Kathrynne.

Ben and his friends entered the study where Mr. Brytant and Queen Kathrynne were located.

"Who's this?" asked Ben.

"This is Mr. Brytant," said Queen Kathrynne. "He came to give you a piece of parchment that has the rules and regulations inscribed upon it. He will be one of the judges who will judge you based on your efforts in the tournament."

"Okay." Ben wasn't sure he liked Mr. Brytant too much.

Mr. Brytant looked Ben over as if he was trying to memorize his appearance. "You look like your father," he said. "Very scruffy looking, hair matted and pinned down … not like a prince at all, but the features are there." He seemed to be muttering to himself, probably thinking of more insulting things to say to Ben, when he said at once, "Here you go."

Ben grabbed the parchment from Mr. Brytant. It was thick in texture, and when Ben unrolled the paper, it spilled onto the polished dingy floor.

Ben handed the parchment to Saint Patrick.

"Did Ben start his training?" said Mr. Brytant.

"Yes," said Saint Patrick.

"Did you tell him about the Irish dragons?"

"Yes."

"Have you told him that Irish dragons are symbols of loyalty and courage?"

"Yes, I did."

"Great." Mr. Brytant seemed greatly pleased. "The first task on this list is Celtic dragons. Please be sure Ben is prepared to face one."

Saint Patrick nodded.

Mr. Brytant turned to leave but turned back around almost at once and said, "And before I forget–more tasks will appear as Ben completes them. This map shows only one task at a time. That way no one is tempted to skip a task."

"Are you assuming Ben will skip a task?" said Queen Kathrynne, who had been silent before this time but was now glaring into Mr. Brytant's accusing eyes. "Because I find that highly offensive. No one in my family has ever been accused of such a monstrosity."

"No, I'm not accusing Ben of such a thing, Your Majesty," said Mr. Brytant. "But I, as leader of the Leaf'd Council, have to take everything into account."

Mr. Brytant turned toward the castle's entryway, walked out of the study, and disappeared.

CHAPTER XVI

Karoline Brickswough

"**Y**OU FINISHED?"

Karoline glanced at the old man, who appeared scruffy and dirty from his job as stone smoother. He was covered in cement and dried glue.

He smiled. "Yes."

Karoline took his plate.

The old man then took a few handfuls of coins from his large jacket pocket and placed them on a round table. He mouthed, "Thank you," to Karoline, who momentarily looked up from wiping a table and smiled. He left the Green Leprechaun and trudged into the rain lackadaisically.

Meanwhile, Saint Patrick, Lance, and Ben and his friends entered the Green Leprechaun. They were dripping wet from the rain. A tarp lay inches above the restaurant's windows because glass that was once there had been blown out by a strong force of some kind.

Karoline, busy picking up used plates and utensils, had hardly noticed at first the new arrivals to her father's restaurant. Had she seen them at first glance, she would have been grateful to see them, Ben assumed.

With a wave of Saint Patrick's hand, the tarp that once covered the Green Leprechaun's windows was replaced with thick glass. He pressed his palms together. A parchment cloth became visible. He wiped his face and his hands with the fabric, dampening it. Within seconds, it was dry again, as if it had not been wet at all. Saint Patrick pressed his palms together once more, and the cloth vanished.

Karoline didn't notice Saint Patrick's magic. She kept her attention on her chores.

Saint Patrick cleared his throat.

Karoline looked up from wiping a table. "Oh, it's you, Saint Patrick. What are you doing here? My father thought you'd show up."

"He did, did he?"

"Yes. My father overheard a customer saying there was a boy you'd be training for the Three-Leaf'd Tournament." She continued to wipe the table, and then she glanced at Saint Patrick. "Prince William's boy. So is this him?"

"Yes. It is. Well, Ben, his friends, Lance, and I would like to hide in the Green Leprechaun's cellar to seek refuge from an evil wizard named Lyon. Have you heard of him?"

Karoline stepped back, aghast. "Yes," she said.

"Then you must know he is a very dangerous wizard?"

"Yes, sir."

"What are you talking about?" A small man with a long beard appeared from the restaurant's back room. In his pocket, a dirty rag was barely visible. Ben saw that the man's face was flushed from sweat, his trousers tainted from dirt and grime.

"Daddy, our visitors want to use our cellar," said Karoline.

"That's fine," said Raymond, his voice low and tired.

"You are not worried about Lyon?"

"Of course I am." Raymond placed his rough hand on his daughter's shoulder. "But we must keep our guests safe. It is our utmost priority."

"Let me just finish wiping the tables from the day of customers," said Karoline, "and I'll meet you guys in the cellar."

"There's no time for that, my dear," said Raymond at once. "Your safety is all I'm concerned about. Those tables can wait."

"But I don't want our customers to come in the morning and have dirty tables," said Karoline.

"Those tables can wait," repeated Raymond. "Now come and hold the door to the cellar; it's too heavy."

Karoline dropped the rag she was using to wipe the round tables, and without any further objection, she followed her father to the back room, where the cellar was located. She knew her father well. He would surely give her a nasty look if she did not follow through with his request, and she did not want to see it. She had endured too many dirty looks already as a young child. Saint Patrick, Lance, Ben, Elizabeth, and Evan followed suit.

Raymond rummaged through the contents of his pocket and pulled out a brass skeleton key shaped like a leprechaun. He placed it into the lock and turned it. Karoline pulled on the knob of the door, opening it and holding it in place with her body.

"Hurry," she said. "I don't think I can hold the door any longer."

Everyone stepped through the door; Ben heard it slam shut as soon as Karoline moved away.

The cellar was damp and dimly lit with lanterns as Ben and his friends stepped down steep steps. They were all about to step down the last step when they heard a terrifying scream.

"*Help me, Ben!*"

Ben turned instinctively. There among the shadows of the lanterns, on the steps, stood a cloaked figure. Its face was hard to see because its hood was too big, but Ben recognized the voice.

"Shut up, girl!" it spat. "One more cry for help and I'll kill you right here!"

A gleaming knife shone through the dim light of the cellar, its blade touching Elizabeth's perspiring neck.

"Please don't hurt her," Ben said. "I love her."

"Figure," said Saint Patrick, "let Elizabeth go."

The figure pulled back its large hood to reveal a small leprechaun, its face glistening like stars in pitch blackness, in the dim light.

Hamish glared at Saint Patrick and said, "I have a job to do, and I won't leave here until it's done."

"And what job is that?" asked Saint Patrick.

"I can't reveal that," said Hamish. With a wave of his cloaked hand, Hamish and Elizabeth disappeared in a cloud of hazy green mist.

"We have to get Elizabeth back!" said Ben, his gaze not leaving the spot where Hamish and Elizabeth had disappeared. "I love her, and I can't lose her!"

"I will rescue her," said Saint Patrick.

"I will go with you," said Ben.

"You will not," said Saint Patrick.

"Why?"

"I refuse to see you get hurt," said Saint Patrick. "With Lyon out in the open, you're more vulnerable than ever. I refuse to see you hurt–or worse, killed. I refuse to let that happen."

"But Elizabeth needs me," Ben insisted. "If what you say is true–that I'm such a hero for the Irish people–why not let me save them … save Elizabeth from an evil wizard?"

"Because it's more complicated than just a few waves of a wand," said Saint Patrick. "Lyon has gotten craftier and slyer over the years; he has killed many magnificent and respected creatures–some of whom cannot be replaced. I want you to be ready to face Lyon with enough confidence and knowledge of what he will throw at you that you'll win, and the Three-Leaf'd Tournament will accomplish that feat."

"Please let me go with you to rescue Elizabeth," said Ben, this time on his knees on the step. "So that I know for sure she's safe from any harm."

"You know, Saint Patrick, Ben will not let this go until you allow him to go," said Evan. "Take it from me; I should know."

Saint Patrick wavered in his options. He sighed. He knew Evan was right. Ben would indeed not heed the suggestion of just him rescuing Elizabeth; the idea was beyond comprehension. Ultimately deciding Ben should go with him, he said, "Yes, you may go."

Saint Patrick, Lance, Karoline, Raymond, Ben, and Evan ventured into the night, each hoping that the group would find Hamish and Elizabeth.

***

High on a grassy hill, surrounded by the Irish community, a castle stood magnificently at the edge of the mountain. Its stones had been weathered with age. Hamish took Elizabeth, his small arms holding her tight like a rag doll, near Lyon's feet on a weathered stone path.

Lyon grinned, and Elizabeth saw his crooked teeth. She desperately wanted to flee, but the tightness of the small but strong leprechaun was preventing her from escaping. Besides, she could not think of running now—not when a cliff was underneath the castle's grassy hill.

"Put her here," Lyon commanded, pointing to the path beside him. "I want a good look at her."

Hamish did as he was told.

Elizabeth flinched. "What are you going to do to me?" She felt her throat close; she could scarcely breathe.

"Oh, nothing now," said Lyon calmly. "I will have to wait until your friends rescue their precious one."

Elizabeth saw in the distance a few small dots venturing up the grassy hill. She felt an overwhelming sense of excitement and yet of fear. Her friends had come to rescue her, but she was uncertain how their rescue attempt would pan out.

"Let her go!"

Ben stood high on the hill's tip; his arms were stretched out in desperation and longing.

No. I won't." Lyon turned to Hamish. "Kill Elizabeth. Throw her off the cliff if you have to."

Hamish grabbed Elizabeth; she fought with every ounce she had in her but to no avail. He had her pinned to his chest, his arms wrapped around her waist. With a hard push, Elizabeth was probed to the edge of the cliff.

She could hear her heart pulsing in her eardrums. "Please don't kill me …

please …" she sobbed. Looking down, she saw the razor-sharp edges of the cliff and the rocky bottom. She felt her heart pulsing in her throat.

Was she going to die?

"Hamish—release Elizabeth at once," said Saint Patrick. His voice was firm and unapologetic, almost like that of a parent scolding a child.

"I can't," said Hamish, "I must do what I am told."

"Oh, let me do it."

Lyon held his lit wand, motionless, at Hamish's loosened grip. Elizabeth was lifted out of Hamish's grasp and moved toward Lyon. With a flick of his wrist, Elizabeth was hung in midair off the cliff, with nothing but wand sparks holding her up.

"Please help me!" she screamed.

Hamish watched, transfixed.

Ben lurched forward, his adrenaline pumping. As soon as he went a few steps farther, Saint Patrick pushed him gently back with his hand.

"Don't do it," he said. "Lyon might blindside you."

"What am I supposed to do—let Lyon kill Elizabeth?" said Ben.

"I know it's hard, but trust me; everything will be all right."

"I just can't let Elizabeth die at the hands of an evil wizard like Lyon."

Ben instinctively opened his locket. A thin white feather wand appeared. Despite Saint Patrick's warning, Ben flicked the wand. Red and green sparks shot from the end of it, barely missing Lyon's head. Ben was about to flick the wand a second time when a voice rang out.

"Drop your wand."

Ben stood frozen, his wand still in midair.

"Drop your wand, I said," Lyon said again, his voice just as bloodcurdling as his wolves' howls. "Do it *now!*"

"No."

Ben flicked his wand. A bright light shot from it; Elizabeth was pulled toward Ben and his wand like a magnet. Despite this, Lyon turned and flicked his wand, and the strong currents of the two wands collided with each other: Elizabeth was instantly pulled back and forth by an invisible current of wand sparks.

"Let Elizabeth go!" said Ben desperately.

"No," said Lyon.

"You must … please …"

"No. I won't."

The wand sparks continued for a few seconds more until it broke violently; red and yellow flashes dissolved into nothingness, and Lyon's wand sparks became weaker. Ben flicked his wand again, and its current pulled Elizabeth safely into his presence.

Lyon watched at a safe distance, his expression turning stale. He lifted his wand in the direction of Ben and flicked it.

Elizabeth screamed; a red spark jolted past her eardrums, almost making her deaf.

Ben, desperate for guidance, gazed at Saint Patrick, who lifted his jeweled cane and tapped the damp grass. A blow of wand sparks hit Lyon so hard it nearly knocked him unconscious.

"We have to go," Saint Patrick urged.

And so Ben and his friends ran.

A dark and grim atmosphere greeted Ben and his friends as they rushed along in Lyon's tower. Ben could feel the rush of wind on his back and neck. He scarcely looked behind him, while running, and just beyond the dim light provided by lanterns mounted on the cobblestone walls was a dim wand's light. Lyon had managed to rouse himself from Saint Patrick's injury to him and was after them.

Light engulfed the whole tower, and Ben could barely see in front of him.

"I can't see. What do I do?" said Ben, his voice in a sudden panic.

"Keep going," said Patrick. "It'll be fine as long as we keep going."

Lyon's wand sparks became spurts of light, cascading upon Ben and his friends like a comet rushing across the sky. He turned and saw Lyon racing down the tunnel, his wand aloft, pointing at him, its tip glowing. He tried to fight back with his wand, but its sparks were too far away.

He could feel his heart race as they ventured further and further still into a dim tunnel. Some time passed, and the sound of Lyon's wand sparks seemed to have faded.

Had Lyon gone? There was no way of knowing whether this was true. All Ben could sense was that Lyon's tunnel was growing eerier by the minute.

An entryway appeared. In the tunnel, Ben could barely see a faint light. He felt a sense of warmth within his conscience. Ben and his friends made it to the end of the tunnel—or so he thought.

"Hurry, Ben! We can't afford to tarry," said Saint Patrick, rushing his friends along.

Whoosh.

Ben tapped the feather wand on the edge of the tunnel's entryway. A wrought-iron door materialized.

A scream from the other side of the wrought-iron door pierced Ben's eardrums.

It was familiar—a voice Ben knew.

"Evan!"

"Ben, please help me! I can't get through!"

"What do I do now?" said Ben. He desperately tried to tap the feather wand on the edge of the entryway frame again, but nothing happened.

"There's nothing you can do for Evan at this present time," said Saint Patrick. "The only thing you can do now is move on and hope for the best."

"You're not going to do anything?" said Ben.

"I can't do anything," said Saint Patrick. "My magic repels iron. All it will do is bounce off its surface. So does yours. If you keep trying to use the feather wand, nothing will happen. You'll only grow more frustrated."

"And what about Evan?"

"He'll be all right."

"No, no he won't," said Ben, in a tirade. "Lyon will get him and certainly kill him if I'm not there to save him."

"We'll save him," said Saint Patrick. "But not now. My most important goal now is to keep you and the rest of your companions safe from harm. I can't do that effectively if you're this upset."

Ben looked at Saint Patrick wearily.

"Promise me you'll calm down and forget about Evan for the time being."

"I can't. I just can't."

"You must."

Ben burst into tears. "I can't forget. How can I? Evan's my best friend. How can I abandon him?"

"Ben, look at me."

Ben obeyed.

"Evan will be fine," said Saint Patrick. "We'll get him as quickly as we can. Do you doubt me?"

"Uh … no."

"I sense hesitation in your voice. Remember I helped you this far, didn't I?

And when things went awry, I helped you with my knowledge and expertise, did I not?"

"Yes, you did."

"Now we must get out of here lest we get captured by Lyon."

"Ben, help me … please …" Evan's voice was slowly slipping away.

"Do not fight me."

Ben could hear Evan's struggle with Lyon. He fought intensely to escape, but it was useless. Lyon grabbed Evan, leading him out of sight.

"I promise you, Ben. We'll find and rescue Evan."

Saint Patrick's voice was calm and relaxed.

Ben was still unsure about Saint Patrick's repeated promise to find and rescue Evan, but he felt as though he had no other choice.

"Okay," he said softly. "I believe you."

"Oh, good," said Saint Patrick. "Let's go."

Saint Patrick led the way out on Lyon's cobblestone pathway, with Ben and his friends close by near the edge of the hill cliff, disappearing into the night.

CHAPTER XVII

Saint Patrick

BORN IN ROMAN Britain at Banna Berniae, a location few people are familiar with, Saint Patrick lived quietly. But it wasn't always this way.

At sixteen, he was captured from Wales by Irish raiders who made him their slave, taking him to Ireland. He was a slave for six years before he escaped, returning to the safe confidence of his family.

He entered the church, and many years after that, he returned to Ireland. After much deliberation and soul-searching, in his latter years of his life, he became an ordained bishop. Saint Patrick's real name was Maewyn Succat, but the Irish people referred to call him Saint Patrick.

Little is known about places where he had worked. Even so, in the seventh century, he had come to be revered as a patron of Ireland. Details of his life were written in hagiographies from the seventh century. Most of his writings are now widely accepted without too much criticism.

He ministered in what is known as modern-day Ireland. His life cannot be fixed with certainty, but his ministry was active during the latter part of the fifth century. March seventeenth is the date of Saint Patrick's death, and it is remembered as a holy day—a non-liturgical or liturgical holiday—as well as the celebration of all things Irish: the wearing of the green, the symbol of the three-leaved clover, and feasting and drinking.

Saint Patrick's father, Calpornius, was a deacon; his grandfather, Potitus, was a priest. In captivity as a slave, Saint Patrick was a herdsman.

After six years, Saint Patrick heard a voice telling him he'd soon return home, for his ship was ready.

He fled his master and traveled two hundred miles and found a ship. Many years after that, having had many adventures, he returned to his family, now in his early twenties. After remembering a vision he had after returning home, Saint Patrick recalled seeing a man named Victoricus who had handed one of his letters to him. It appealed to him, saying that the Irish people needed a voice and that he was that voice.

Saint Patrick did not accept gifts or money from wealthy women for his services of baptism or ordaining priests even though he was a bishop and could have done so if he had chosen to. His mission was to baptize people and ordain priests to help lead the new Christian communities.

He converted wealthy women, some of whom became nuns in the process. He dealt with sons of kings, converting them to Christianity too.

Saint Patrick used the three-leaved clover as a tangible way for the people of Ireland to understand the Trinity: Father, Son, and Holy Spirit. Thus, the three-leaved clover is used as a symbol of Saint Patrick's Day.

Much of what is understood about Saint Patrick banishing snakes from Ireland is a myth. No serpent has successfully migrated to a new environment, and the only reptile in Ireland is the viviparous, or common, lizard. No snakes have been found in Ireland, so the theory of Saint Patrick banishing them from Ireland is merely speculation.

The three-leaved clover has been sacred since pre-Christian days. Owing to its green color and size, many viewed it as a symbol of rebirth and eternal life.

Some Irish legends say that during his journey back to Ireland from his family home at Birdoswald, Saint Patrick carried with him an ash stick or staff. He'd thrust it into the ground, trying to send a message to the people that the stick itself had taken root by the time he was ready to journey forth from that place; it was called Aspatria (also known as Ash of Saint Patrick).

A twelfth-century work, Acallam na Senórach, tells of Saint Patrick meeting two ancient warriors, Caílte mac Rónáin and Oisín, during his many travels. The two travelers were once members of Fionn mac Cumhaill's warrior band the Fianna, and they somehow survived to Saint Patrick's time. In the work, Saint Patrick sought out to convert the warriors to Christianity, while they defended their pagan past.

Moreover, Saint Patrick set out to find a druid named Cleary, who was a teacher of all things Irish, from its knowledge to Irish prophecies. He wished to pay a visit to him to see if he knew whether Lyon had been thorough in his quest of ridding the Irish people of all they held dear—their families, animals, and farms—or just bluffing.

Cleary was the only druid in Ireland who was willing to give some confidence to Saint Patrick so he could travel forth from that place to find

Prince William's son, Ben McNealy, because he felt he was the only one who could rid Lyon of his evil plans and kill him.

Cleary lived in a separate part of the forest, where he studied Irish lore to be well versed in Irish literature. His collection consisted of books that told of the pasts of magical beings, including when they were born, who their parents were, who their ancestors were, and what their lives were like. It included the wizard Lyon's past.

***

A small cottage came into Saint Patrick's view. He knocked on an old and scratched door, and after a few moments, a little druid answered. He was wearing a long purple robe that hid his feet, and on the bridge of his nose were wire spectacles.

"Oh, Saint Patrick, how are you? It's been a while. What are you doing here?"

"Well, to be honest, I want some guidance," said Saint Patrick.

Cleary closed the door behind Saint Patrick to keep the warm air from escaping his cottage. "What's this about?"

"Well, it's about Prince William's son, Ben," said Saint Patrick.

"Hmm. Interesting. Does this have to do with the current wrath of Lyon's wolves?"

"Yes. How did you know?"

"Well, a druid knows a thing or two about creatures' habits—and that includes Lyon's magical evil wolves," said Cleary. "I've been following their movements for the past couple of days, and I must say it isn't looking good. Ever since Prince William's son was born, chaos has broken loose. Lyon will not stop until Ben is dead and out of the way."

"That's the reason I'm here," said Saint Patrick. "I'm afraid I'm making a mistake in recruiting Ben to defeat such a dangerous wizard on his own."

"But he won't be on his own," said Cleary. "He'll have you. With your experience and expertise in training him, he'll be fine. Besides, he's got his father's magic in his father's locket, should he accept the task of defeating Lyon."

"I don't know."

"Do you remember the time you baptized people and ordained priests to lead the new Christian communities?"

Saint Patrick nodded. "I remember."

"And do you think those wealthy women in our small Irish community would have become nuns if you had not influenced and inspired them?"

"Probably not. It's my calling, though."

"True, it is. It was indeed your influence and intelligence that brought those wandering souls to the Creator," said Cleary, "and those people are better off now that you aided them. The same goes for Ben. He'll thank you in the long run, but for the time being, he'll not fully understand the significance of what you're doing for him."

"So you think I'm doing the right thing in recruiting Ben to defeat such an evil wizard?" Saint Patrick asked, still unsure of himself.

"Yes, frankly, I do," said Cleary.

"Well, thanks for your vote of confidence."

"Anytime."

And with his newfound confidence intact, Saint Patrick traveled forth secure in the knowledge that Ben would make the wise decision to train with him to rid the Irish communities of Lyon.

CHAPTER XVIII

Raymond Briskswough

THE GREEN LEPRECHAUN was left in shambles. Among the dust and debris were traces of magical wolf substance in the dense air. Ben surveyed the scene before him: nothing seemed to be untouched; there were shards of glass everywhere. The place he once knew was now a war zone.

Raymond ran up to the debris, and among it he saw pieces of the Green Leprechaun's furniture scattered across the dead grass. The restaurant Raymond once knew–the place he grew up with, which his parents had given to him to keep running–had been taken from him. He turned to Karoline, who sobbed.

"What are we going to do?" she asked her father, still sobbing.

"I don't know, honey," said Raymond, Karoline's father. "I honestly don't know."

Elizabeth asked, "Well, do you have any relatives who might want to take you in?"

"No, we don't," said Raymond. "Unfortunately all of our relatives died from the wrath of Lyon."

"Oh, I'm sorry," said Elizabeth.

"We fled Lyon years ago," Raymond continued, apparently unaware no one was listening to him, but he seemed to take it in his stride. "We didn't know how long Lyon would send his wrath upon our poor Irish communities.

"It finally died down, so we decided to come back to the Irish isles, but as soon as we heard rumors of Lyon continuing his wrath upon the Irish communities, I didn't know what to do. Rumors surfaced that the reason Lyon had continued his wrath was that a boy was born to Prince William. Lyon hated the boy because he was rumored to want to 'finish him off.'"

"I sympathize with you, Raymond, Karoline," said Saint Patrick. "Yes, it is true that there was a boy born to stop Lyon from destroying any more lives. He's right here—Ben McNealy, formally known as Prince Benjamin Rowzand."

Ben thought it was weird to be called "Prince," but he took it as a compliment.

"I think we should all go to my cabin—just until the chaos with Lyon has subsided and there is a free moment to escape," said Saint Patrick. He turned to Raymond and Karoline. "You may stay at my cabin for as long as you need to."

"I don't know. I don't want to impose," said Raymond.

"Oh, it's no trouble. You won't be imposing."

"Well, if you insist."

"I do insist."

Ben would be in the safety of Saint Patrick's cabin as he prepared for the

Three-Leaf'd Tournament in two days, and so Ben and his friends journeyed forth, without haste, into the forest just beyond the Green Leprechaun.

***

Saint Patrick's cabin was made of trees that surrounded the cottage itself and the wood. He took pride in his cabin, as it was the only home he felt that had any normalcy in his life. He was always on the run, baptizing and ministering to those who needed it. And now his cabin felt warm and safe from the elements.

Saint Patrick and Ben and his friends finally came to a clearing. It was barely visible, but as soon as they came closer, it was clearer. A log cabin stood by itself, its small windows providing little light. Next to the cabin lay a lush green landscape.

"This is my home," said Saint Patrick. "I live here when I'm not helping the queen, baptizing, or ministering to the people."

"You baptize? And minister?" said Ben.

"You sound surprised," said Saint Patrick. "Didn't you take history in school?"

"Well, yeah, but–"

"He didn't pay attention to history in school," said Elizabeth.

"That's too bad," said Saint Patrick. "As I said at an earlier time in your training, you'll have to study Irish lore to be a better leaf'd prince."

"I can handle it."

"I know you can. Oh, it's not important now," said Saint Patrick. "The point is you'll be a better leaf'd prince in due time."

"You think so?"

"Yes, I do," Saint Patrick replied. "Your father would be proud of all you have accomplished thus far—and I am too. Well, let's go in, lest we want Lyon's wolves to find us." He took a skeleton key out from his cloak pocket, placed it carefully into a keyhole, and turned it. Immediately Ben and his friends were greeted with the warm, fiery glow of a fireplace and the smell of herbal tea. As soon as they stepped further into the room, Ben noticed that the furniture was carefully placed throughout the room; in the middle was a dingy, stained couch. The place, as far as Ben was concerned, seemed lived in.

Saint Patrick placed his cloak on a coat rack by the cabin's front door and turned his attention to Ben and his friends.

"Tea?"

"No, thank you," said Elizabeth.

"No, thank you; I'm fine," said Ben.

"Let me know if you change your mind. My tea is made of the purest herbs. The Irish love my tea."

"Okay. Thank you."

"Sure."

Saint Patrick went over to the fireplace; hanging above it was a large wooden spoon. With it he stirred the tea slowly, allowing the aroma to seep into the dusty air. He took a seat in a green-stained armchair and sipped his stirred concoction. Ben smelled the aroma, allowing it to seep into his nostrils. It smelled of mint and berries.

"Oh, before I forget: the sleeping arrangements," said Saint Patrick. He placed a chipped teacup he was drinking from on a small table by the fireplace, grabbed a cane lying by itself near the armchair, and stood up. "There are two bedrooms down the hallway there." He pointed to a long, narrow hallway near the back of the cabin.

Meanwhile, Raymond and Karoline took it upon themselves to tour Saint Patrick's cabin.

"Very nice china," said Raymond, glancing at an antique-looking plate with a yellow sunflower printed upon its surface.

"Thank you," said Saint Patrick. "It was my grandmother's. She passed it down to her daughter, now down to me. I have a set, which I plan to use for dinner tonight."

Karoline made her way to one of the bedrooms, and upon entry she realized it was small with only one window. She was not used to this. Raymond spoiled her with a spacious bedroom and bathroom, and this one seemed cramped and unwelcoming.

As Raymond went by her bedroom, Karoline called out, "This bedroom is too small. May we go somewhere else?"

Raymond stepped into the room. "Please make the best of what we were given," he said. "Saint Patrick has graciously offered for us to stay with him in his cabin. He didn't have to offer it, but he did. It is dangerous outside this cabin. You realize that, don't you?"

"Yes, I know, but I'm used to–"

"I know you're used to spacious rooms, but we don't have that here," said Raymond. "Please, and I ask that you make the best of what we were given."

"I'll try."

"Thank you."

"Sure."

"Oh, you're back here. I was looking for you two." Saint Patrick stood in the hallway, holding his cane, to keep himself upright. "Dinner's almost ready. I think you're going to like it."

"What is it?" Karoline asked warily.

"Don't worry about it. It's Irish food; you'll love it."

***

Hours later, the smell of Irish food tickled Karoline's nose. As she stepped into the main living space, a large wooden table came into her view. From the fireplace, a dull glow illuminated the room. On top of the table, a large tablecloth hung loosely from the edge. Coming closer, she noticed that Ben, his friends, Saint Patrick, and her father had already taken their allotted places at the table.

Raymond glanced at his daughter lovingly. "How was your nap?"

"Good."

"You were out the moment I left the room."

"Yeah, I know. I guess the added stress of an evil wizard on the loose has gotten to me."

"That's fine."

There was a spread of the most heavenly smelling food imaginable. Irish soda bread, glazed corn beef, Irish lamb stew, and Irish shepherd's pie were spread across the table. On the edge of it, delicate china and silverware were in front of each person, each bearing a subtle sunflower pattern Saint Patrick had mentioned before.

Saint Patrick, afraid that Hamish would find them, snapped his fingers. Immediately Ben heard the shutters close, darkening the room. Even if Hamish attempted to invade the cabin, he would not be able to succeed.

"We need to keep you safe," Saint Patrick said, turning his attention to Ben. "If Hamish is anywhere close to this cabin, he's bound to show up here. And with Lyon's influence, there's no telling what he may do." With a wave of his hand, candles immediately lit themselves, providing some light to the room.

"Well, this food is delicious," said Raymond, smacking his lips.

Saint Patrick smiled. "Thank you. That means a lot to me."

"Well, I have an announcement," said Raymond.

The room fell silent. All the occupants were looking at each other. Finally, in midbite, Karoline asked, "What is it, Father?"

"I've decided to sell the Green Leprechaun."

"But why?" Karoline asked, shocked that her father had come to such a decision.

"With what's going on, and with such a dangerous wizard on the loose, I don't want to risk the lives of our customers and employees. It's not fair to them, to you, or to me."

"But the restaurant was given to you by Grandpa. He expects you to keep it running."

"That's just it, Karoline. I can't keep it going."

"But you must."

"No, I can't."

"But you must," repeated Karoline, her voice shaking.

"Now Karoline, you knew this day was coming."

"No."

"Karoline …"

"Well, you could keep it going."

"Karoline, the answer is no."

"But we can rebuild it," insisted Karoline, "the Green Leprechaun. Once the chaos has subsided, and Lyon is defeated, it'll be fine."

"Karoline, no. It's true we could rebuild it, but I don't want the financial burden resting upon my shoulders. I'm too old, and it's emotionally draining. It's too painful to think of all the memories," said Raymond.

Karoline opened her mouth to argue once more, but Raymond said, "I've made my decision. I will not rebuild the Green Leprechaun, and you should respect my decision."

Karoline sighed. She knew not to argue further with her father. After all, he was a stubborn but fair man. If the Green Leprechaun could be rebuilt, she knew he would do it quickly.

"This dinner is fantastic," said Lance, taking another helping of Irish lamb stew.

"You're very welcome. It was my mother's recipe," said Saint Patrick.

"Do you think I'm ready to compete in the Three-Leaf'd Tournament? I don't feel like I am," said Ben, once silence had come and gone.

"Every great prince who has ever entered a tournament of this great magnitude has faced his doubt, Ben," said Saint Patrick. "Don't ever doubt yourself; you'll be fine."

***

A draft filled Saint Patrick's cabin as evening settled in.

"This'll be your room," said Saint Patrick.

Ben pushed an oak door open just a crack. Two twin beds were at each side of the room, with a comforter softer than silk draped over each bed frame.

"Here."

A burgundy sheet appeared in Saint Patrick's palm. He handed it to Elizabeth. Clothespins appeared in his palm; he gave them to Elizabeth.

"What do you want me to do with this?" she asked.

"I got you this sheet for privacy," said Saint Patrick.

"Thank you," said Elizabeth.

"You're welcome," said Saint Patrick.

A wire appeared inches above Elizabeth's bed. She draped the sheet over it and placed the adjacent pins on the sheet securely, creating a barrier between the two twin beds for privacy.

"Here, take this."

"What is it?"

"It's a scarlet night robe," said Saint Patrick.

"I don't want it," said Elizabeth at once.

"Take it, please."

Elizabeth took the scarlet night robe without question.

In silence, Saint Patrick left the room.

"Elizabeth?"

"Yeah? Ben, is that you?"

"Yeah."

"Hold on."

"All right."

Elizabeth pulled the scarlet night robe over her head, pulled back the sheet, and turned her attention to Ben. "Yes?"

"I'm going after Evan, to rescue him," he said.

"But Saint Patrick specifically told you not to worry about him; he said he'd rescue him. Don't you remember?"

"Yes, he did, I remember, but I don't want Evan to get hurt or—even worse—die at the hand of a menacing wizard."

"I don't want it, either," said Elizabeth.

"Then come with me," Ben insisted.

"Go with you?"

"Yes."

"I can't."

"Why not?"

"Saint Patrick said it was too dangerous," said Elizabeth. "And besides, you need Saint Patrick's guidance in case something goes wrong. And besides that, he promised to take us to rescue Evan when he feels it's safe enough."

"Well, I can't wait that long. Evan might be dead by the time we try to save him."

"I feel partly responsible that Evan is even missing," Ben added. "If I had done something more, maybe–"

"Nothing you've done would've stopped Hamish from taking Evan; you know that," said Elizabeth.

Ben sighed. "I guess you're right." He turned to Lance, who at that moment entered the room. "What about you? Are you going to help me?"

"No. I can't. I can't risk my loyalty to Queen Kathrynne and King Diamond. It is too dangerous. The queen and king would not be happy with me if I chose to help you."

At dawn, when everyone was asleep, tucked in their beds, Ben set out on his own, braving Lyon's magical wolves to save his best friend, Evan, whom he cared for and loved. And as he journeyed through the forest, the brisk air at his back, he wished Elizabeth was with him to help him along.

CHAPTER XIX

Elizabeth Motts

"SAINT PATRICK!"

Elizabeth's voice lingered down the hallway toward Saint Patrick's bedroom. She walked blindly toward Saint Patrick's bedroom with the dull light provided by the wall lanterns as her guide.

"Saint Patrick! Hurry, please!" she yelled as she banged the door.

Saint Patrick quickly opened his bedroom door. "What is it?"

"Ben is missing!"

"He's what?"

"Missing. Ben said he wanted to save Evan. I tried to stop him, but he didn't listen."

"When did he leave? Last night sometime?"

"Possibly."

"Then we must act quickly," said Saint Patrick. "By now he could be deep in the forest, near Lyon's castle."

Elizabeth and Saint Patrick walked through the forest without delay. Karoline and Raymond were left behind, waiting for Saint Patrick and Elizabeth's safe return.

The night air was crisp, making Elizabeth pull her burgundy hood up on her head, drawing its strings to make it stay in place.

"Do you think Ben will be all right?" Elizabeth asked Saint Patrick as they traveled farther into the forest.

"I wouldn't worry about Ben. He can be stubborn at times, but I think he'll be all right, given he doesn't run into Lyon's wolves."

"Do you think he *will* run into Lyon's wolves?" Elizabeth asked.

"He might," said Saint Patrick. "That is why it is vital that we find him before Lyon does. I still cannot believe Ben disobeyed me after I specifically told him not to look for Evan."

"He cares about Evan," said Elizabeth, "and so do I."

"I know you two do. But it is dangerous out here; Lyon is dangerous."

"I know."

"You know, when I met the two of you, I knew at once Ben was stubborn, just like his father," said Saint Patrick. "When I met you, I could sense your gentle spirit, which is like that of his mother, Bridgette."

"Really?"

"Yes."

"Thank you."

"You're welcome."

***

Ben felt a slight chill as he stepped upon Lyon's drawbridge, heading toward his castle.

Elizabeth and Saint Patrick were close by in the shadows, watching intently while camouflaged by the darkness.

In the night, shadows were moving swiftly.

By this time, Ben had made it to the front door of Lyon's castle. Lightly turning the knob, he stepped inside. Elizabeth and Saint Patrick closely followed; both were silent to avoid getting caught.

The halls of the castle were uncomfortable and damp. Ben felt his neck stiffen. As he turned a corner and moved toward a door to another room, a figure heretofore unknown to Ben grabbed him; he fought back, kicking and screaming at the top of his lungs, but whoever had him would not loosen his or her grip. He felt his whole body go limp.

Hazy, but still conscious, Ben looked at the figure once more before passing out.

***

"Do you remember this place, Ben?"

The voice came in and out as if it were static on a radio playing inside his mind. He opened his eyes and saw a familiar sight before him. He was on the cliff rooftop of Lyon's castle. Overlooking the tower room he was in, he could barely see the cliff's edge. He remembered saving Elizabeth's life from Lyon hours before that, right here on this very cliff. Now he was here at this cliff again, and this time he wasn't saving Elizabeth. He was a prisoner of an evil wizard.

"Why did you bring me here?" Ben asked, his voice hoarse.

Ben was flung, limp, toward one of the walls of the tower. He was too weak to move–even to escape.

"Who are you, and what do you want from me?" Ben added.

"Who am I? *Who am I?*" asked the figure.

"Yes."

The figure slowly uncovered its hood. In the gloom, Ben saw a man's silhouette.

"L-Lyon?"

"The one and only."

Ben finally found his voice. "Why did you kidnap me?"

"I had to. You were snooping upon my property. I don't take kindly to those who snoop."

"I didn't mean–" Ben began.

"Don't worry about it," said Lyon. "I have already forgotten about it. But here's my proposition for you: I will release you from this wall, and you'll be free to go, if you drop out of the Three-Leaf'd Tournament."

"No, I won't. Too many people depend on me," said Ben. "Saint Patrick–"

"Do you think that crazy old man knows how to train princes properly?" said Lyon. "No! He's just wasting your time. Why else would he not allow you to save your only true best friend?"

"How did you know that?"

"A wizard is all-powerful and knows everything that concerns princes," said Lyon. "Besides, would a best friend get himself kidnapped by an evil wizard? I think not!"

"Evan didn't get kidnapped! Hamish took him! Where is he?"

"I don't know where he is."

"Liar! You know where he is! You're just holding out on me."

Ben regretted his words almost at once. Lyon snapped his fingers. A sharp pain instantly shot through Ben's stomach, and he was lifted by a jet of red sparks. He winced because the pain was too great to bear.

"Ben! No!"

Elizabeth stood inches away from Ben, her eyes filled with tears. Saint Patrick stood beside Elizabeth, his jeweled cane holding him up. From the look upon Ben's face, Elizabeth was confident he was ready to attack Lyon with every ounce of his strength.

Just then Lyon turned from the wall to Saint Patrick. Ben slid down the wall; he was slightly disoriented from Lyon's rough treatment.

Elizabeth watched in horror as Lyon pushed at the air in front of Saint Patrick. He was thrown to a brick wall on the other side of the tower room, across from Ben. His feet and hands were glued to the wall as if he were a fly on sticky paper.

"Let me go, Lyon!"

"I can't do that, Saint Patrick."

Saint Patrick felt his own body grow numb.

"Lyon, I promise you Ben will withdraw from the Three-Leaf'd Tournament if you release him from this wall," said Elizabeth.

"How can you make such a promise, girl?" said Lyon, gazing at Elizabeth with squinted eyes.

"He will; I promise."

Ben could not believe what Elizabeth was saying. "Elizabeth … no! What are you doing?"

"Saving your life."

"I don't believe you," said Lyon. "Ben will never give up his position in the Three-Leaf'd Tournament."

"What if I told you Ben would give up his position if he didn't have me to worry about?" said Elizabeth.

Lyon looked at Elizabeth with such intensity that it made her sweat. "What are you getting at, girl?"

"I'll break up with him."

"Elizabeth … No! You can't do this!"

Elizabeth ignored Ben's plea. Instead she turned her attention to Lyon, who smirked.

"You're serious, aren't you?"

"Yes."

"Elizabeth … you can't do this! He's tricking you!"

Lyon quickly took out his wand, and with one casual flick, a cloth bandana appeared around Ben's mouth, silencing him.

Lyon pondered Elizabeth's suggestion. "You mean to tell me that if you break up with Ben here, he'll be vulnerable and too distracted from winning the Three-Leaf'd tournament?"

"Yes, he will. And you won't kill him, right?"

"I can't promise anything," said Lyon, "but yes, I won't kill Ben."

Elizabeth uttered the words "We're done" before she knew they were out of her mouth. She stood there, frozen, her eyes locked on Ben's terrified ones.

Just then, there was a crack. Everyone looked around to see what had made the noise.

Then they saw it.

Saint Patrick had managed to break free from the wall; his oak wand was inches from Lyon's now frightened face. "If you harm Ben and his friends, you will regret it," he said.

There was an exchange of wand sparks, crackling and hissing as they bounced off the walls of the tower room. The noise proved deafening to everyone's ears. The quarrel between Lyon and Saint Patrick went on for a few seconds more, the crackling of wand sparks growing louder.

With a pop, Lyon flew back on the stone floor. Sparks flew above his head and hit the wall behind him. Stunned, he gazed at Saint Patrick with fear and trepidation.

"Now I want you to get Evan, bring him to us, and leave this place, never to return," he said. "If I hear that you've not done this, I will report to Queen Kathrynne and King Diamond about your refusal to leave. You're lucky I have a good heart toward my foes. You have caused so much damage here in Ireland, and it's high time for the people to grieve their loved ones and thank their Creator for those who were spared from your heartless acts."

"I won't leave Ireland until I have what I desire: the title of leaf'd prince," said Lyon, his voice cracking. "I will be the leaf'd prince. I will destroy all who get in my way, and that includes Ben McNealy."

"That's what I thought you'd say," said Saint Patrick, expecting nothing less from Lyon. "Ben will destroy you, and he will be a hero."

"Not on my watch, he won't."

Just then, Lyon disappeared, leaving only a trace of smoke, ashes, and soot behind.

"Why did you have compassion on Lyon?" Elizabeth asked. "You know he was going to attempt to kill Ben and everyone here."

"Sometimes you have to have compassion for those who refuse to have it themselves," said Saint Patrick. "I knew he was still going to murder those who were brave enough to face him, but I must show compassion to foes and friends alike. Let's get out of here."

Elizabeth untied the bandana around Ben's mouth, and Saint Patrick used his magic to release Ben from the wall. When he did, Ben asked, "What about Evan?"

"We'll get him later. It's too dangerous to get him now."

"Will Evan die at the hands of Lyon?"

"I don't know," Saint Patrick said honestly. "I don't know."

CHAPTER XX

Ben McNealy

Tournament day I

SUNLIGHT BEAMED UPON the autumn leaves of the trees surrounding Saint Patrick's cabin. In the distance, people were buying goods for their homes from carts at the town's square. One woman snapped at a merchant for providing few pears to sell, because she had known him to have more pears than she was used to.

"Sorry, ma'am; I don't have many pears," he said. "Here's what I have."

She glared at the display of pears and turned up her nose in disgust. "Why fewer pears today? You know I love my pear cider every morning, Pete."

"I know you do, but this is all I have." Whilst the exchange of the woman and the merchant was going on, peasant children were by the fountain, splashing in its cold, refreshing waters. Occasionally they splashed each other, often carelessly splattering some of the water over the sides of the basin, upon the cobblestone path. Dogs were frantically barking and licking up the excess water near the fountain's perimeter.

Among the chaos of the town's square, Ben, Saint Patrick, and his friends found themselves in a dirty place. Farther along, Ben and his friends saw a row of yellow-tinted tents scattered across a grassy field. When they approached the area, Lance, the Rowzand family servant, greeted them with a warm and sincere smile.

"Hi, glad you're all here," he said. "Ben's friends, will you follow me? There is an invisible barrier here." He took them to a green part of the field where people were already getting comfortable on padded bleachers. They had face makeup on symbolizing different participants' colors. Ben stood back, watching the chaos, anxious.

Lance returned and told Ben and Saint Patrick to follow him.

A stained yellowish tent came into their view as they approached a green part of the arena.

"This is the participants' tent," said Lance, peeling back its flap.

"What's that smell?" he asked.

"Oh, that is just a few participants showering for today's games. After a while, you'll get used to the smell."

Ben was unsure he'd ever get used to the smell, but it was something he'd have to get used to, he guessed.

"And this is where you'll be staying," said Lance, taking out a clipboard made of thick parchment and an ink pen and marking carefully.

"Staying?" *Really? Here?*

A cot stood in the corner of the tent; sweat stains showed on its edges.

"Who else had this cot?" Ben asked, pointing.

"Oh, older participants. I tried to get most of the stains out of the cot, but it was not easy," said Lance.

"Lance, this is unacceptable. Ben can't stay in this tent," said Saint Patrick.

"Unfortunately, it is not up to me who gets nice cots."

"Then who decides?"

"Brytant, leader of the Leaf'd Council," said Lance. "Don't tell anyone I told you. It's against the tournament's rules."

"Will do," said Saint Patrick. He turned to Ben and added, "I'm going to talk to Mr. Brytant myself and see if I can get this cot mess straightened out; don't you worry."

Saint Patrick moved through the crowd, finally finding a small man holding a long piece of parchment. He was talking to a participant. His face, from what Saint Patrick gathered, appeared firm and unwelcoming to passersby.

"Excuse me, Mr. Brytant? May I have a word with you?"

Mr. Brytant, at first glance, had hardly noticed Saint Patrick's presence. After a moment, he glanced at Saint Patrick and said, "Sure. What's this about?"

"Mr. Brytant, I want to commend you for doing such a wonderful job getting together this tournament."

"Thank you," said Mr. Brytant. "I have a feeling that you haven't come over to congratulate me, have you?"

"Well, no, not exactly," said Saint Patrick. "It's about Ben."

Mr. Brytant's eyebrows were raised. "What about him? He hasn't decided to drop out of the tournament, has he?"

"No."

"Good."

"It's about the cot you gave to participants of the tournament. Specifically Ben's. It's disgusting."

"Well, I have no control over who gets what," said Mr. Brytant, sounding stern. "What I can do is forward your complaint to the Three-Leaf'd Tournament Honorary Board, and they can decide whether Ben gets a new cot. I'm sorry I'm not much help. Besides, I'm sure Ben can stay in his family's castle. It's more comfortable there, I'm sure."

"But isn't Ben supposed to stay with the other participants for most of the day until each task is completed for that day?" asked Saint Patrick, a little wary of Mr. Brytant's sudden dismissal of him.

"Yes, that would be ideal," said Mr. Brytant. "However, I can't make Ben stay in the participants' tent if he doesn't want to. Maybe you can convince him to stay in the tent. Now excuse me–lots to do."

Mr. Brytant left Saint Patrick, traveling through a crowd of anxious participants talking among themselves outside the participants' tent.

***

Ben was waiting at the base of the participants' tent when Saint Patrick approached.

"Well, Mr. Brytant says there's nothing he could do," he said. "However, I don't buy it. My advice to you is to stick it out until this is done. I'll see what I can do for future tasks."

"And are you sure I'll have to stay in this tent?" Ben asked anxiously.

"My hands are tied, for now."

"Saint Patrick?"

He turned to face the entrance of the tent, seeing Lance at the base of it. "Yes?"

"You will need to go to the audience area, just beyond the tents. The tournament is about to begin."

"All right."

"Saint Patrick?"

"Yes?"

"I'm scared."

"You'll be fine. Just remember what I taught you. And above all else, have confidence in yourself."

Ben saw Saint Patrick's silhouette fade as the sun's light hit the tent, creating shadows inside. He took a deep breath.

As he drew in one last deep breath, he heard his name over a loud megaphone.

"Ben McNealy, please come to the tournament's main arena. We're ready for you now."

A feeling of adrenaline filled his lungs as he pulled back the tent's flap. The arena that he thought was sparse was now thriving with creatures. Potential participants were waiting anxiously across the spacious grassy field. Lance stood in the center. In one hand he held a long piece of parchment; in his other hand was the brass megaphone he had used to call Ben.

"Ben, here, would you please?"

Lance pointed to the spot next to him; Ben took his allotted place.

"You're first to compete, Ben," continued Lance.

Taking out a small box from his pocket, Lance placed it carefully on the grass in front of Ben.

"This will be your first task, Ben," said Lance. "A dragon. I hope you are familiar with them. I assume Saint Patrick has informed you about them, yes?"

Ben nodded.

"Good."

With a wave of his hand, the box magically disappeared before Ben's eyes. In its place was a massive dragon. Ben saw that the creature before him had sharp scales–sharper than any in existence. The reddish tint and sharp snout made his eyes widen in shock.

The dragon lurched forward, eyeing Ben hungrily.

"Is that my dragon?" Ben blurted.

"Why, yes it is," said Lance. "But be forewarned: this one's an ill-tempered creature, so I'd be careful if I were you."

"Who gave me this dragon?" said Ben at once.

"Ben, I can't say. It's against the rules."

Its nostrils emitted smoke that surrounded the entire arena. Ben's eyes burned, and the feeling of helplessness filled his consciousness. As the smoke began to clear, he was able to make out the scene before him: he was flying high above the arena, his arms and legs sprawled out on its back, his hands gripping tightly on its neck.

Ben's stomach was in knots.

The tiny creatures below him were small to his naked eye. The dragon swayed its weight. Holding on for dear life, Ben could see the vegetation and the tiny houses just beyond the arena.

The dragon dived.

The invisible bleachers unexpectedly cracked, buckling the crowd. Through the fragments of broken shards of wood, Elizabeth could make out Ben's hazy expression: that of fear. She feared for his life; she feared a world without him. Thinking of that was unimaginable to her—at least for the moment.

"Ben, watch out!" Elizabeth called as a pole supporting the area's exterior entrance came into his vision.

Elizabeth's warning proved too late for Ben. He and the dragon hit the pole, nearly knocking both unconscious. He landed on the grass beside the pole. Dizzy and disoriented, he struggled to get up. When he finally did, he saw that the dragon was circling high above him, almost as if it were a buzzard waiting to eat a dead carcass.

Ben suddenly remembered that his first task of the Three-Leaf'd Tournament was to kill or injure a dragon. He decided to damage it.

But how?

Then he recalled how Saint Patrick had told him to have confidence in himself—that nothing and no one could stand in his way to victory.

Acting without haste, he opened his locket; a sword of brilliant colors—red, green, and gold—materialized in his palm. Ben waved the sword, and it got the attention of the dragon. A blast of fire and smoke from its nostrils filled the dark and gloomy sky. Creatures watched in both awe and terror as the dragon dived near Ben, ready to kill him.

Just as it was going to strike, something unexpected happened. The sword, which was glowing magnificently in the darkened sky, acted as if it were an invisible barrier to protect Ben from the creature's fiery blows.

The protection didn't last long. Its fiery essence proved too strong for the sword's magical abilities.

Ben landed on the flat earth. He felt his insides hurt. He tasted blood. All Ben could think about was Elizabeth—oh, sweet Elizabeth—how it was she who (not by her own will, he assumed) had broken up with him. Given a choice, he knew she wouldn't have broken up with him at all. She would've stayed because she loved him so dearly.

Before he had time to react or block the dragon, it took hold of him and the sword, carrying them to the other side of the grassy field. Ben felt his body go limp.

***

"Ben ... do something! Anything!" Elizabeth cried out.

Her cry was useless, as Ben was too far away; besides, if he had heard it, it would have proven ineffective, as Ben's strength could not hold its weight; he was limp from exhaustion.

"Ben can't do anything now," said Saint Patrick, looking at him carefully with a long, thin pair of binoculars.

"Is there anything you can do?" said Elizabeth.

"No, unfortunately I'm not allowed. It's against the tournaments' rules."

"How's Ben going to survive this?"

"Elizabeth, he will."

"How do you know?"

"I just know," said Saint Patrick. "He's got his father's will to keep fighting."

***

Ben felt a sudden smack. The dragon hit the side of the arena's wall. Seeing a tree just a few feet from him, Ben inched himself quickly over to it. He climbed it, hoping it would delay the dragon. It did not. Moments later, it found where Ben was, and using its long, spiked neck, it hit the bark. The tree shook with so much fury that Ben was sure he would fall out of the tree's branches.

Instinctively, Ben unfastened his locket's hinges; a small dagger appeared.

With his last ounce of strength, and on impulse, Ben jammed the sharp end of the blade into the creature's eye. It roared in pain. He must've undermined his strength and realized that the dragon, now injured, was still screaming in pain. He watched the poor creature fall to the grass, buckling.

***

Saint Patrick got up from his seat and watched intently. Lance went out on the field.

"Ben, you won the first task in the Three-Leaf'd Tournament; congratulations," said Lance, kicking the unconscious creature.

Lance turned to the audience in the bleachers and the stunned judges—one of whom was the leader of the Leaf'd Council, Mr. Henry Brytant—and raised Ben's hand. Cheers from the crowd and judges erupted throughout the whole arena.

***

"Do you think I'll be penalized for not facing and killing the dragon?" Ben asked Saint Patrick hours after the first task.

"What are you talking about?" said Saint Patrick. "You did better than I could have done."

"I didn't kill the dragon. I injured it. It could hurt someone else."

"Ben … no. Don't ever doubt yourself. The rules of the Three-Leaf'd Tournament clearly state that one must kill or injure a dragon. They don't say to kill it only."

"I know," said Ben. "I just feel like a fraud."

"You shouldn't feel like that," said Saint Patrick. "You don't need to stress over the details of the tournament. Just the fact that you got past the first task is a huge accomplishment. Most princes are too scared to finish the task of the dragon because it's too dangerous for them. You won. You should be proud of yourself. As for Lance, he thinks you received the corresponding points for your amazing victory over the dragon's demise."

"You think?"

"Yes, I do," said Saint Patrick matter-of-factly.

"Honestly, I couldn't do what you did," said Elizabeth. "I'm proud of you."

"Thank you," said Ben. "Elizabeth?"

"Yeah?"

"You didn't mean to break up with me, did you? Because if you did, I–"

"Don't worry. I am still your girlfriend. I only broke up with you to divert Lyon from hurting you. I love you with all my heart."

"Thank you. I love you too."

"I'm proud of you too."

For a second, no one knew who had spoken. Then everyone turned and saw Queen Kathrynne and King Diamond.

"Honestly, I thought it was a mistake for you to complete. I see now I was wrong," said Queen Kathrynne.

"I agree with my wife," said King Diamond. "You, indeed, were amazing. Your mother and father would be proud of you."

"I didn't know how extensive and dangerous the Three-Leaf'd Tournament was for its participants," said Karoline, walking beside them. "I must say I'm surprised–and a little scared, too–for you, Ben. If given a choice, I wouldn't have competed."

"Ben didn't have a choice. He must compete for the revenge of his parents but also for the safety of Ireland and its citizens," said Saint Patrick.

"Well, it would be a lot of pressure on me if I were competing. I don't think I could've handled it," said Karoline.

"Karoline," said Raymond sternly. "Ben feels the added pressure on him to compete. Don't make it even worse for him than it is."

"Okay, Father." Karoline turned to Ben. "I'm sorry."

"It's all right. I forgive you. Saint Patrick?"

"Yes, Ben?"

"May we please save Evan now?" said Ben. He was anxious and desperately yearned to see his best friend safe and free from harm.

"Only when you've completed the tournament will we rescue Evan," said Saint Patrick. "As I've told you, Lyon is unpredictable and unsteady. I desire you to be prepared for whatever Lyon throws at you, and by completing the tournament, you'll be prepared." Saint Patrick could sense Ben's anxiousness, so he added, "We'll rescue Evan; I promise you."

"Thank you," said Ben.

"Sure," said Saint Patrick.

Ben found it difficult to center his mind on the next task of the tournament because of Evan. Would he die at the hands of the wizard Lyon? All he knew was that Evan was taken by Hamish and could be Lyon's prisoner. Still, as the cold eastern wind blew, he and his companions traveled back from the tournament's arena to Saint Patrick's house.

CHAPTER XXI

Evan Dennrick

Ireland, Lyon's castle, secluded from the Irish community

A DUSTY AND gloomy cell came into Evan's vision. He had been drowsy for most of the night. He thought Lyon had given him a sedative, because the last thing he remembered was Lyon's face slowly going out of focus.

Now looking about, Evan saw through the bars of his dungeon a shadowed figure approaching his cell. It was cloaked and hooded.

"Evan, why the tears? You should be happy you are away from your friends," said the figure.

"I'm not happy. You're a monster," said Evan. "Why was I taken, anyway?"

"Well, you said yourself that you were sick of Ben and Elizabeth's constant cooing over each other. You were taken because of that—to save you from your insanity."

"I never said any of that," said Evan.

"Well, you were thinking it, weren't you?"

"No, I wasn't."

"Oh, don't be coy with me," said the figure. "Any fool with half a brain could have seen it quite clearly: you were—and still are, I assume—in love with Elizabeth."

"I'm not in love with her. Stop saying that."

"You sure? Because I sense you still are," said the figure.

"I'm happy for Ben and Elizabeth," said Evan. "They deserve happiness."

"And you don't?"

"Yes, me too."

The figure pulled back its hood to reveal a man—a wizard. He was wearing a long, tall pointed hat, and in his palm he held a wizard's wand that was glowing with thousands of green sparkles. He looked familiar to Evan, but unfamiliar too.

Evan asked, "Who are you?"

The man said, "The wizard Lyon."

"I want to go home."

"I'm afraid I can't grant your request, Evan," said Lyon.

"Why not?" said Evan, still somewhat groggy from the sedative.

"Because I have big plans. Plans that involve you, Ben, and Elizabeth."

"Please take me home," Evan begged. "I don't want to be here."

"I know you don't want to be here. But in life, you must do things you do not wish to do. And right now, you need to be here with me for your sanity."

"Just know my friends will be diligently searching for me," said Evan.

"If they were diligently searching for you, don't you think they'd have found you by now?" said Lyon.

"You're wrong. My friends are searching for me."

"Now what about your parents?"

"What about them? Did you do anything to them?"

"No, I didn't do anything to them, so calm down," said Lyon. "Won't they be worried too?"

"Why did you bring up my parents?"

"Oh, just casual conversation to keep your mind at ease," said Lyon.

"I barely knew my parents."

"What about your mom?"

"What about her?" Evan snapped.

"Are you close to her?" said Lyon.

"What are you getting at?" Evan asked suspiciously.

"You'll see," said Lyon with a wink. "I don't give away my secrets just yet."

Evan felt awkward, but he thought he had to say something. "Well, no, I'm not," he said. "She didn't even tell me what happened to my father. I don't know whether he's alive or dead."

"What if I told you I was your father?"

Evan gasped. "What? You're my–"

"Father," finished Lyon.

Evan's emotions were running on high. He was confused yet somewhat relieved.

"You're serious, aren't you?" Evan added.

"Of course. Your mother's maiden name was Suzette Katherine Polish, wasn't it?" said Lyon.

"Yes," said Evan slowly.

"Well, when your mother became pregnant, she tried to hide her pregnancy because she knew what I was capable of. However, she couldn't. I knew.

"Your mother thought I was a bad influence on you. She said I couldn't handle the pressure of a newborn. The sad truth was that she honestly couldn't handle you."

"Don't. My mother must have been able to handle my care, right?" said Evan.

Lyon's cheeks turned red. "No. She couldn't. That's the reason she filed for adoption. Evan, you were indeed adopted by the Dennrick family. I heard the husband and wife were excited for a child of their own.

"Suzette said I hurt you as a newborn, but I never hurt you; you must know that. Your mother used you. She manipulated you into believing she was the good person in your life and I was the bad one. I was only protecting you from the ones who got in the way."

"Suzette is a good mom," said Evan.

"To you she was. On the surface she was. But to me …"

"Don't say that. My mother knew my likes and dislikes. And you didn't."

"I do know your likes and dislikes," said Lyon, slightly offended.

"How?"

"I stayed hidden, camouflaged by night. I studied you … at every birthday party, every holiday pageant … everything."

Evan began to cry. The feeling of abandonment was too real for him.

"No, you didn't. You're lying. An evil wizard isn't capable of loving anyone. You'd rather murder everyone–including your son–than offer to be a loving dad to me," he said.

"That's not true. I tried to be a good father, but your mother … she couldn't let me," said Lyon. "She was the one who pushed me out of your life–not me."

"You're lying … again."

"No, I'm not."

"Okay … then what's my favorite color?"

"Is this necessary?"

"Yes, it is. What's my favorite color?"

"I don't know."

"Red. Next, what is my favorite sports team?"

"Evan, this is getting ridiculous," said Lyon, his gaze boring into Evan's brown eyes. "I'm your father, all right? Heck, you may not like it, but deal with the cards you've been dealt. Do you want a date with Elizabeth or not?"

"Uh …"

"Evan, do you or do you not want a date with Elizabeth Motts?"

"Y-yes."

"Then I can help you. If you desperately want a date with Elizabeth, I can make it happen. All I need from you is a small favor in return."

"And that would be …?" said Evan, his heart pounding, for he did not know Lyon's intentions.

"I will make you a deal: I will release you from your cell and allow you to leave my castle if you enter the Three-Leaf'd Tournament and kill Ben," said Lyon.

"I don't know if I can. Ben is my best friend, and I can't betray him."

"You're going to have to if you want a date with Elizabeth. That is my deal. If you do as I say, she'll be more apt to pay more attention to you; she might even coo over you," Lyon said, trying to swindle Evan further with his lies and deception.

"I still don't know if I can do it," said Evan. "It's too risky."

"Dating is indeed risky," said Lyon. "Take it from me. If you want all of

Elizabeth's attention, you must take my advice. I'll ask you again: do you want a date with Elizabeth or not?"

"Yes."

"Then you must do as I say. Enter the Three-Leaf'd Tournament and kill Ben."

Evan was filled with conflicting emotions. True, he desired one date with Elizabeth, but was it worth killing Ben—his best friend whom he had known for years?

Maybe there is a way to get all of us what we want, Evan thought. "Okay, I'll do it; I'll enter the Three-Leaf'd Tournament and kill Ben," he said.

"Excellent," said Lyon. He smiled.

"What will you have me do?" Evan asked nervously.

"Don't worry about that, Evan," said Lyon. "In time you'll understand my scheme in its full entirety; in time you'll thank me for what I've done for you."

CHAPTER XXII

Evan Dennrick

T HE SMELL OF Irish food filled Saint Patrick's cabin as Ben and his friends sat and waited.

"That food smells heavenly," Elizabeth said into the silence.

"Yes, it sure does," Ben finally said.

Karoline and Raymond sat catty-corner of each other in high back cloth armchairs. Karoline had her legs crossed and played with a loose string off the cloth armchair. Raymond was half asleep, using a knitted blanket made of colored wool to cover his legs and torso.

A stone fireplace, located in the center, easily warmed the room. Now and then it popped, making Raymond groan in his slumber.

"Dinner's almost ready," called Saint Patrick from the kitchen.

"Okay," said Ben.

"I don't know how we're going to rescue Evan," Ben added. "Lyon will have the upper hand. I'm afraid we'll be too late and Evan will be dead once we do finally rescue him."

"Don't worry about it," said Elizabeth. "All will work out. And besides, you were fantastic in dispatching the dragon. You'll be able to beat Lyon; I'm sure of it. We'll rescue Evan soon, too."

"You think?"

"Yes."

"I don't know."

"Don't doubt yourself."

"It's hard, you know? I don't think I can be heroic in defeating an evil wizard. Remember: I was at the mercy of Lyon. I was scared. I didn't know whether I'd live or die."

"Ben, you also know I was at the mercy of Lyon," said Elizabeth.

"Yes, I do remember," said Ben. "How can I forget? You know I didn't know what I was doing in saving you."

"Dinner's ready; come all," said Saint Patrick.

"All right," said Ben.

"You trusted your intuition and used your locket's magic to rescue me, and I'll be forever grateful for it," said Elizabeth, as she, Ben, Karoline, and Raymond entered Saint Patrick's dining room.

"I agree. You did great. I'm impressed," said Karoline, who had overheard the conversation between Ben and Elizabeth.

"If anyone deserves to be the leaf'd prince, it is you," said Raymond. "Your gallant act of dispatching the dragon is something I've never seen."

"Raymond's right. I'm proud of you, Ben," said Saint Patrick.

"I don't think I'm ready for the responsibility of the leaf'd prince," said

Ben. "If my sole duty as leaf'd prince is to protect the citizens from foes, and the foes get the better of me, what do I do then?"

"Ben, every great leader has to deal with difficult foes. It is how one deals with them that matters most. You will do awesome as the leaf'd prince; you'll see," said Saint Patrick.

"I think you're ready to take on the duties of the leaf'd prince," said Raymond, "If you saved Elizabeth from falling into an abyss, you are certainly ready to take on that responsibility. I know because I was there and saw it unfold before my eyes."

There was a spread of the most succulent food Ben and his friends had ever imagined possible. Ben had sworn it was the exact food he had seen and tasted before his heroic rescue attempt at saving Evan, but he wasn't sure. All the same, there was Irish soda bread, glazed corned beef, Irish lamb stew, and Irish shepherd's pie, all sitting in large kettles and pots, their steam rising to the ceiling.

"I'm cold. I'm going to get my cardigan," said Elizabeth.

She left the room, heading down the narrow hallway to the bedroom she, Ben, and Lance occupied. She stepped into the room, and lying upon the bed was her cardigan. She attempted to grab it, but as she did so, an eerie feeling fell upon her body. Her hair on her arms stood up, almost as if she were a cat puffing out its fur.

"Don't move!"

The voice was familiar and eerie.

"What do you want?" Elizabeth asked, her voice trembling.

"You know what I want. I want Ben to drop out of the Three-Leaf'd Tournament," said the voice. "I don't like to be hoodwinked, and you, Elizabeth, hoodwinked me into believing you broke up with Ben when in actuality you didn't!"

She felt her throat contract. "I did."

"No, my dear, you didn't. I know the truth. You lied to me. And for that you must be punished."

Elizabeth ran toward the bedroom door, but she misguided her steps; she tripped on the bedpost, landing on the carpet.

In a dark green satin cloak and hood, it seemed all too frightening to Elizabeth.

"You will break up with Ben tonight. Understand?"

Elizabeth didn't know what to do other than nod. Her leg was numb. She tried to get up or to move, but the pain from the fall was too great.

"Then what happens if I don't comply with your request of breaking up with Ben?" Elizabeth asked. "What then?"

The unknown figure waved its cloaked hand, and the bedroom door slammed shut. "You and everyone here will die at the hands of your senseless decision to refuse to aid me."

Elizabeth screamed.

"Don't you scream! Be silent!"

But Elizabeth wasn't listening to the figure at all. Instead, her voice became louder.

The figure knelt and placed its hand over Elizabeth's mouth. "Don't you scream! I'm warning you, girl. Don't you dare! If you do, I'll indeed kill everyone here, including you!"

Elizabeth fell limp, unable to move or even scarcely breathe. She stared blankly at the figure as if deciding what to do next, and as soon as the figure pulled its dull, lifeless hand away from Elizabeth's mouth, Elizabeth bit it.

Instantly it reared back in pain. Moments later, Elizabeth tried to open the door of the bedroom, but it was impossible.

"I'll make you a deal, Elizabeth," said the figure, now pulling back its hood to reveal a shadowed man's silhouette, "If you break up with Ben and go out on a date with Evan, I'll forget murdering Ben altogether."

"No. I won't. Ben is the love of my life, and Evan is my best friend. I can't betray either of them. I love them too much to do that to either of them."

"Now Elizabeth," said the man, his voice now more casual than threatening, "have you ever considered the possibility that Evan may think of you as more than just a friend—that he may want more than a casual friendship?"

"Well … no. He never told me. Besides, I'm in love with Ben, and Ben loves me."

"Don't you think Evan deserves a chance to be with you?"

"But I'm with Ben now."

"But you considered breaking up with him once, did you not?"

"No. You're tricking me. I never considered any of it!"

The man stepped into the dull light of the room, and Elizabeth could instantly see the man's familiar face.

"Lyon! What are you—?" she asked.

"Do we have a deal? You go on a date with Evan in exchange for Ben's life?"

"And you won't hurt Ben?"

"You have my word," said Lyon. "I won't hurt Ben as long as you comply with my request of dating Evan."

"Deal."

CHAPTER XXIII

Evan Dennrick

Tournament day II

A
T DAWN, TRAVELERS moved forth toward a tournament arena. Trees of several varieties had overgrown the path and its wildflowers. If someone did not know his or her way, he or she would easily get lost. Such was not the case for these travelers–a boy named Evan, an evil wizard named Lyon, and a tricky leprechaun named Hamish.

"Why do I have to be tied up again?" asked Hamish, who was stumbling over rough ground upon the path.

"You almost let Evan go free, did you not?" snapped Lyon. "I cannot let that happen. You were supposed to watch him; instead you tricked me, and because of that, and as punishment, you have to be tied up by ropes."

"I didn't mean to; I–" began Hamish.

"Let me out of this cage."

The voice was that of Evan. He looked as if he were homeless: in tattered clothes, hair not brushed. His breath was rotten, as if he had not brushed his teeth since he was kidnapped, which had now been a few weeks.

"I can't do that, Evan," said Lyon, his voice calm. "If I let you out of this cage, you might escape again, and thanks to Hamish, you would've been long gone. Believe me, Evan, you'll be out of this cage soon enough."

"Jousting on a horse and on foot is the next task for participants. Make your way to the arena, princes," Lance announced across the arena.

There, in a green part of the field, Evan saw a blurry image of many princes moving about. Several of them had jousting poles, and from what Evan gathered, these princes were practicing on themselves, as if they were all opponents.

"This," said Lyon, "is very important. You will watch from the sidelines, lest I need you."

"What if I don't want to help you? What'll happen to me?" asked Evan.

"You don't want to know what I'd do to you. Just do as I say and watch from the sidelines, and when I need you, I'll let you know."

"I don't want to be your mule. I want to go home," said Evan boldly.

"You can't go home–yet. You want to date Elizabeth, do you not?" said Lyon.

"Yes," said Evan.

"Then let me take care of it."

CHAPTER XXIV

Ben McNealy

THE YELLOWISH TENT appeared tattered and stained as the noon's sun reflected its thin veil. Ben lay on an old and stained mattress, listening to the other princes' conversations.

"I can't believe how I'm doing. I thought I'd be bad, but surprisingly I'm doing quite well. I killed many dragons and impressed many villagers. I think my father will be proud," said a prince in scarlet robes.

"It beats how I'm doing in the tournament. I couldn't even get past my dragon. The judges only passed me because one knew my father and he asked for a favor," said another prince, in royal blue.

"And why is he here? He isn't a prince. Is he?" The scarlet robe flapped around the first prince's ankles as he slowly moved around Ben while observing him.

"King Diamond seems to think he is a prince," said the prince in royal blue before Ben had time to answer. "It seems he's qualified to compete with us."

"He is, eh?" retorted the prince in the scarlet robes.

"Yes," said the prince in royal blue. He turned to Ben. "Please tell me your name."

"My name?"

"Yes, your name. What is it?"

"Ben."

"Benjamin, eh?"

"No."

The prince in royal blue was taken back. "No?"

"Yes. It's just 'Ben.'"

"Well, I'm going to call you 'Sir Benjamin.' Ben seems so … plain. So, Sir Benjamin, what region of Ireland are you from again?"

"Region?"

"I don't think he's paying attention to you, Jason," said the prince.

"Get out of here!"

Saint Patrick pulled back the thin veil of the tent to reveal two terrified princes. They scurried off, afraid that they would bear the brunt of Saint Patrick's magic.

"You okay?" he asked, coming inside the tent, letting the flap fall closed.

"Yeah."

"I'm sorry about the other princes. They're just jealous of you. Their fathers are nothing to pick a bone to, either," said Saint Patrick. "I helped them with converting their lost souls to Christianity. That's beside the point, though. It's all about you. How are you feeling?"

"What do you think?"

"That nervous, eh? Well, you're going to be all right."

"Trust is not what I want to hear about now," said Ben. He did not want to be told what to do now. He wanted the next task to be done and over with as quickly as possible.

"That's okay. I understand your anxiety."

"You have no idea how I'm feeling."

"You're right. I don't. But I do know you'll be great; I have total confidence in you."

"Thanks," said Ben quietly. "I appreciate it."

Ben heard the voice of Lance outside the tent. "Ben, it's time for you to joust on horseback."

Saint Patrick left the tent knowing Ben would do well.

Ben felt a wave of anxiety fall upon him. He pulled back the thin veil of the tent, and just beyond a grassy field, he saw a corral of majestic, tame horses.

"Here is your horse," said Lance, guiding a gentle white creature toward him.

It neighed, bucked its head, and rubbed its head on Ben's forehead.

"Oh, it likes you," added Lance. He smiled. "Jousting on horseback is about to begin."

Once he got on his horse, Ben was led by Lance to the center of the arena.

"You will joust an opponent on your horse first," said Lance, who took his allotted place in the center of the arena. "The one who takes down his opponent first with his jousting lance wins and thereby moves on to the next task."

A couple of princes nearby snickered.

"That kind of behavior is not tolerated here, understand?" Lance added, giving the princes a piercing look.

"Yeah, I guess," muttered a prince under his breath.

"'You guess'?" said Lance.

"Yeah."

Lance gave another piercing glance. "Yes?"

"Yes."

Then Ben heard it–a rustling sound through the unkempt, tangled bushes. It was from a horse's hoof. Everyone fell silent. Their eyes, including Ben's, craned toward the unknown stranger.

A horse and its rider made its way to the center of the arena, where they were stopped by Ben, stoic and captivating.

The horse had glistening metal upon its bridle and along its flanks. At the end of it, three green ribbons were dangling, each tied so carefully to its harness.

The crowd seemed to be in a trance. The unknown rider had an unusual power of command. He raised his arm, and the crowd cheered excitedly. Then he took it down again, and the crowd quickly fell silent, as if there were evil magic over them.

"Let the jousting begin."

Lance's voice faded as Ben and his opponent moved a short distance away from each other. Ben heard the faint sounds of hoofbeats coming closer– getting louder–as they approached. He could feel the breath of the rider as it inched ever so close to him. Then, in one swift movement, Ben felt a clank as metal hit his side.

"It'll be all right!" yelled Saint Patrick from the bleachers. "Shake it off! Use your jousting lance!"

A stout referee who appeared dirty looked at Saint Patrick and said, "Enough! You're distracting to the tournament participants."

Disoriented and stumbling, and having scratches on his forehead, Ben got back on his horse. He pressed his heels upon the horse's sides with the little strength he had left; it lurched forward, trotting at a good pace. He raised his jousting lance; as he lowered it, he heard the scrape of metal ringing in his eardrums.

Then Ben's horse suddenly hunched back on its hind legs as if spooked. His arm lurched back in response, away from the unknown knight's aim. The knight's jousting lance hit his lance again, knocking him off his horse.

He could taste dirt and grass.

Ben stumbled to his feet. He got on his horse again, still bruised from his fall. There in the distance, he saw the knight laughing, mocking him.

He could sense a long jousting lance barely touching the side of his face. He turned to face the knight, who was now inches from him.

"Are you going to stab me, Ben?"

Ben could hardly comprehend what the knight had just asked him or even understand in its entirely how the knight knew him, because the sharp end of a jousting lance pressed into his side. He buckled to the ground, too much in pain and too stunned to move.

"I will kill you, Ben. It is my right and sole duty to do so," said the knight.

Before the knight's jousting lance hit the grass, Ben's adrenaline kicked in. He swiftly rolled out of the way, missing the jousting lance altogether.

Then something happened. Ben's sword encrusted with gold and red rubies (the same one he had used to fight Lyon's wolves and subdue a dragon) appeared and glowed magnificently, as if it wanted to fight back.

A jet of gold light quickly entered the air.

Great pain entered the knight's body. He was thrust off his horse. As the gold light faded a little, Ben could vaguely make out the knight's strained expression. As it fully cleared, Ben's jaw dropped.

The knight's helmet and silver garments that had once been there disappeared, leaving in its place a tall teenage boy, aged sixteen or so, bewildered.

"Evan, is that you?"

The crowd fell silent.

Elizabeth gasped.

Karoline and Raymond shook their heads.

Saint Patrick was horror-stricken.

"Yeah, it's me. Hi, Ben."

"What are you doing here?"

"I'm competing," said Evan, his voice shaking.

"I can see that," said Ben. "But who put you up to this?"

"No one." Evan did not wish to tell Ben the truth now. It would crush him.

"Evan, please tell me. I deserve to know. Who is it?"

"I said no one."

"Lyon. Lyon put you up to this, didn't he?" said Ben. "He must've. Why else would you have the nerve to pose as a knight?"

Evan's face went pale. By his expression, Ben sensed at once that his hunch about Lyon influencing Evan was spot on.

"It's not like that," said Evan quickly.

"And you agreed to it? Evan, I'm shocked! Why would you agree to fight me?"

"Nothing."

"Nothing, huh? Something must've made you mad enough to want to fight me. What is it?"

"It's Elizabeth, okay?" said Evan, now seemingly exasperated and out of breath. "I wanted–and still desire–to date her. You knew that, and you went after her anyway."

"Evan … I'm sorry. I didn't realize you had feelings for–"

"Save your breath, Ben. I've heard enough out of you," said Evan.

Ben was shock-stricken. Never in his wildest dreams had he guessed Evan had loved Elizabeth in the same way as he himself loved her.

"You don't have to kill me, Evan," said Ben. "You can forget this whole thing and move on with your life."

"No. I can't," said Evan, shaking his head and holding up his jousting lance in Ben's shocked face.

"Why?" asked Ben.

"Because I just don't want to."

"If you're still angry with me because you think I stole Elizabeth away from you–"

"It's not that at all. I mean, I'm still very angry with you about that, but if I don't kill you here now, Lyon will be unhappy with me."

"What does Lyon's loyalty matter to you suddenly? I mean, I risked my life to save you from an evil wizard who kills innocent creatures."

"I know."

"Gosh, Evan, I disobeyed Saint Patrick, who told me to wait to rescue you because he thought it was too risky; he said we'd rescue you as a group," said Ben.

"I know."

"Why do you care so much about Lyon, anyway?"

"I know I made a mistake. I'm sorry. I had to."

"You had to?"

"Yeah, I had to. Lyon was–Lyon is–my real father."

Ben's face went white. "Your ... father?"

"Yes."

"You don't have to listen to Lyon. You can be yourself," said Ben.

"Lyon tricked me into believing that killing you was the only way Elizabeth would pay attention to me. He used my vulnerability to lure me here in this arena to kill you."

"Elizabeth would've paid attention to you, certainly," said Ben. "How could she not?"

"As a friend she would, but not as a potential boyfriend," said Evan, his arm still raised, unmoving. "To be honest, I guess I was half-hoping that killing you here would release some power I never knew I had. I must kill you here."

"Evan ..."

"Ben ... I must."

"Please don't do it. Lyon is only using you; he's using me–everyone ... don't you see? Lyon's promises are only lies to lure his victims to do his bidding. You said it yourself that he is using you to get you to come to this arena to kill me."

"True, but that doesn't matter now. Doing my job matters to me now, and killing you is my job!"

"Does it, Evan? Does it really?"

"Yeah."

"Do you honestly want to throw away our friendship over a silly dispute?" said Ben.

"Silly dispute? Are you kidding me? We had no friendship! It was all lies! Every part of it!" said Evan.

"Do you even remember Weird Veronica?" said Ben, hoping to distract Evan a bit longer.

"Yes. What does that have to do with anything?" said Evan. "Don't distract me. I must kill you here."

"You went to prom with her. You had fun with her, didn't you?"

"Shut up!" said Evan.

"Didn't you?"

"Yeah, I did."

"She was weird. But you didn't care. You danced with her all night, remember?"

"Yeah, I remember."

"Then, after the prom, I believe you went to her parents' house a half mile away, correct?"

"Ben, shut up! This story has no use for me now!" said Evan.

"I believe it does. It does because I think you still have feelings for Veronica even though you told me you didn't. I saw you having fun with Veronica. I saw that you were laughing and smiling. I wouldn't be saying this now if I didn't confidently know you're still in love with her."

"I'm not in love with her. I never was and never will be. Prom ruined my life. Veronica was in love with me. I could see it in her eyes. She was persistent. She'd put her hand on my bottom, and I'd quickly remove it.

"At the time, I was resentful. I asked Veronica because I felt sorry for her. I became the target of ridicule and bullying. Veronica was so invested in me–so much so that she asked me to be her boyfriend."

"And you said yes, didn't you?" said Ben.

"You don't know what it was like being the boyfriend of an outcast. Her parents were the weirdest people I've ever met. Did you know Veronica's dad collected dryer lint? He, Bernie, wanted me to collect dryer lint, too. I told him I wasn't interested. He was horrified—and disgusted, too—that I wasn't as caught up in dryer lint as he was."

"I'm sorry—" said Ben, but he was cut off by Evan.

"Veronica's mom, Sallie, is worse than Bernie, Ben. On the day I arrived at her house after prom, I was swept away by Sallie, who appeared eccentric and batty, and she pushed me up on a wobbly, cracked plastic stool. I was her mannequin. She dressed me up in a frilly blue shirt with a pair of seventies-style bell-bottom pants, high heels, and a large, floppy straw hat with large, embellished circular earrings. I was humiliated, Ben. After I left Veronica's house, she and I had a heated argument. Because of it, I broke up with her."

"Evan … I'm sorry—"

"Ben … enough! I must kill you now."

"Please don't kill me. Elizabeth's here."

"I don't care."

Evan, in a spurt of rage, jumped up and jabbed his jousting lance into Ben's stomach. Ben immediately felt a sharp pain. Stumbling, he fell on his knees. Tears appeared on his face.

Ben had to make a difficult decision. Should he injure his best friend whom he had cared for since childhood, or should he let it go? After all, Ben knew Evan would now not let go over the fact he had dated and was still dating Elizabeth.

Ben knew that if Lyon had not placed the idea of murder in Evan's mind and exploited his vulnerability, he would not have disguised himself as a knight. He knew Evan would not have jabbed him in the chest on his own accord; he loved Ben, and therefore he would not have become injured. All of this, Ben knew, was fueled by his jealousy.

Evan stabbed Ben again.

"Evan, Ben, stop!" Elizabeth cried.

"They must battle it out," said Saint Patrick. "The rules clearly state one must stop on his own accord."

"How can you just sit here and watch this?" Elizabeth asked, gazing into a pair of binoculars from her bag.

"I want to do something," said Saint Patrick, "but I can't. It's against the rules."

Instantly Ben felt an invisible prick in his back. Straining to look, he saw that Evan had managed to grab his jousting lance, which had somehow fallen out of his reach, and was now jabbing it into his rib cage.

"I will not be defeated, Ben, and neither will Lyon," said Evan.

Ben grew limp and stumbled to the grass before Evan's perspiring face. "I forgive you, Evan. You may not be able to forgive yourself, but I forgive you here now," he said.

Then everything went black.

***

A plump old woman suddenly stood before Ben as he lay in the grass moments later. From what Ben could sense through hazy vision, she had gray hair and a kind, sincere smile. On her head she wore a floppy hat.

"You'll be all right, my dear," she said. "You only need to rest for thirty minutes. You took a nasty blow, my child."

Ben, still woozy and disoriented from his confrontation with Evan, managed to ask, "Who's this woman?"

"She's the one who examines those who have been injured in the

Three-Leaf'd Tournament. She also works in your parents' castle as head of its hospital wing."

"I didn't see her as we were coming in," said Elizabeth, gazing first at the woman and then back at Saint Patrick for clarification.

"Oh, where are my manners? This is Mrs. Begbie. She has magical healing properties built into her DNA. I met her on my many travels to and from Ireland. Ben, she'll make you feel better in no time. I trust her with my life."

"Hold still. This may sting a little."

Mrs. Begbie touched Ben's spine with her soft, aged hands.

Ben instantly felt a sharp pain in his stomach and back, and then it was gone. In its place were what seemed to be two small scars, one across his stomach and one across his back.

"Thank you, Mrs. Begbie," said Saint Patrick. "Your kindness is greatly appreciated here."

"You're sincerely welcome, Maewyn," said Mrs. Begbie. She turned to Ben. "Thirty minutes, Hun, and you'll be able to joust safely."

"Mrs. Begbie?"

"Yes?"

"Please call me Saint Patrick. Maewyn is so formal," said Saint Patrick.

"Sure. Will do."

And with a pop, Mrs. Begbie disappeared.

"Where's Evan?" Ben said aloud, looking around.

"He was taken to a tent across the arena," said Saint Patrick.

"Is he all right?"

"All right? Yes, of course he is, but I'm worried about you," said Elizabeth.

"He'll be fine, Elizabeth," said Saint Patrick.

Sweat appeared on Ben's brow as he stood up. The sun was brutal for him now, but he took it in stride. Wiping the sweat from his forehead, he glanced around at his surroundings. Evan was a few tents away, drinking from a water bottle he had received from another contestant. (It was sealed at first, and he had opened it.) For a second, Ben and Evan locked eyes, but they looked away almost at once. It was too painful for Ben to look at Evan right now.

There was a rush of adrenaline in Ben's veins—pulsing, pulsing—as he and Evan were inches from each other, seated on their horses. Evan held his jousting lance aloft, gazing intently at Ben. As Evan pressed his foot against the side of his horse, it trotted forward at a good pace. Evan made the first move, waving his jousting lance high, almost hitting Ben on the side of his face as it sliced the air. Ben was numb. He couldn't move; even lifting his jousting lance was tough. Perhaps it was because of fear—fear of injuring the one person whom he had known all his life.

But it had to be done.

He finally raised his jousting lance, ready to fight back against whatever Evan threw at him. He ignored all the nagging questions that occurred to him and instead focused on the task at hand. Clanks of metal pierced his eardrums as his jousting lance clashed with Evan's. Evan was pushing with all his strength, trying to subdue Ben, but his attempts were unsuccessful. The more Evan pushed, the harder Ben pushed back. As Ben felt Evan grow weaker, he thought about what Saint Patrick had said—that princes who succeed in the Three-Leaf'd Tournament will have the means of protecting Ireland and its citizens. That threat, in this case, was the wizard Lyon. Evan had to get out from under the thumb of Lyon to be much happier. Ben was sure of it.

Evan grew weaker, and then he collapsed to the grass. "You win. I'm exhausted."

***

Lyon stood in the shadow of a tall bush and was disgusted with all he had seen. Evan had failed to kill Ben—a task he had charged him with only hours before. If Evan failed once more, Lyon was sure he'd kill Evan and his friends. The question was, would Evan fail? Sure that his plan would come to pass, Lyon created an evil and powerful wand for Evan. He picked it up from the grass and threw it. It landed at Evan's side.

It surely will entice Evan enough to kill Ben, Lyon thought. *I'm sure of it.*

"Please don't kill me, Evan," said Ben, his eyes not leaving the spot where the wand lay.

"I wasn't going to kill you after all, but my gut now says I must try."

Evan picked up the oak wand and pointed it in Ben's face.

"Please, Evan, don't kill me," Ben begged.

"I don't have a choice. You won't change. You're only going to think of yourself," said Evan.

"I thought you were turning a corner and you weren't going to kill me, after all."

"Well … I lied," said Evan.

"Please, Evan … think about what you'd be giving up if you killed me here," said Ben.

"Giving up? I won't be giving up anything."

Evan held the wand in Ben's face, his eyes unblinking. He flicked it, and before he could register the outcome of what just happened, he felt the energy from the wand's tip explode. Ashes and soot filled the air. When it finally cleared, he heard an agonizing scream.

Ben held his stomach, trying his best to ignore the ever-present pain from his abdomen. He felt blood seep out of him like an ever-flowing fountain of fizzy cola.

"You ..." was all Ben could muster.

Ben's choice was clear. He had to injure Evan. He wasn't going to change his mind. Lyon had corrupted his thoughts.

Ben opened his locket. A white feather wand appeared in his right hand.

"You can still redeem yourself, Evan," he said. "Just forget this little charade of my death, and let's move on with our lives, all right?"

"Uh ... no," said Evan. "You betrayed my trust. You're currently dating Elizabeth after I specifically told you I was in love with her. How can I trust you now? How can we be best friends if trust is not present?"

"Evan ... please ..."

"Ben ... *enough!* If you're going to injure me, just do it already!"

Ben felt his wand's tip burst. Tears flowed down his cheeks as he saw wand sparks flowing ever so closer to Evan, finally knocking him unconscious.

Ben fell to his knees, sobbing. How could he have done this?

Elizabeth screamed, "*No!*"

Saint Patrick was indeed speechless.

Karoline and Raymond remained silent, both in utter shock.

In the distance, Lyon watched the scene unfold in front of him. He smirked and disappeared, knowing he'd have another opportunity to hurt Ben and his friends.

CHAPTER XXV

Hamish Greentines

Leprechaun courthouse, near the village square

S ITTING ON A courtroom bench and bound by magically enhanced handcuffs, a small leprechaun named Hamish kept his head down in shame.

"Hamish, do you know why you're here?" said a voice behind him.

Coronel, a stout lawyer, sat beside him, his eyes gazing into Hamish's light brown ones.

"No, I certainly do not know," said Hamish, his voice low but angry. "I've done nothing wrong. Many creatures accused me of things I have not done. Especially Mr. McGawn. I didn't mean to make him lose his business. I was having fun."

"Hamish, as your lawyer, I advise you to now think about your actions.

I'm not saying you're guilty–oh, on the contrary–but many creatures here today are going to say some things that portray you as a tricky leprechaun," said Coronel. "Is there anything you must tell me now before the proceedings of court start?"

"No."

"Are you sure? Because you won't be able to say anything to me during the trial."

"Yeah, I'm sure."

"Okay. I'll try to defend you the best of my ability, Hamish," Coronel added. "But be forewarned: the judge, Judge Nixon, is a mean one. He's medium-sized in stature, but he has a loud, commanding voice. He's also the judge of the Leaf'd participants and doesn't take kindly to leprechauns who befuddle him."

"Why are you my defense lawyer?" asked Hamish. "If I'm going to lose anyway, then why bother?"

"Because I believe you, Hamish," said Coronel. "I believe that you didn't trick so many creatures as they said you did. Despite your many faults, I believe you can't help yourself."

A female leprechaun dressed in a long shirtdress suddenly entered the courtroom. She was carrying a large suitcase.

As she walked by Coronel, she said, "Long time no see."

Coronel nodded grudgingly. It had been too long indeed since they had spoken to one another, and Coronel wished he could forget their sudden rekindling. Memories of their first date suddenly revisited his mind, and he quickly erased them. That night was horrible, and that was something they both could easily agree on.

"I see you have a new client, Coronel," said the female leprechaun, setting down her large suitcase on a wooden table. "What did you do this time to convince your client to work with you–bribe him?"

"Oh, no, my dear," said Coronel. "I've grown since our last date, Trish."

"Oh, I see you have," said Trish under her breath.

Hamish was confused about the conversation between Coronel and Trish. He gazed around the room, now more nervous than ever. He thought he had a good lawyer, but he wasn't sure. If Coronel had wooed Trish and their date had gone awry, it showed a lot about his character. He was a worse liar than Hamish.

But what other choice did Hamish have?

Trish opened her suitcase and dropped it on the marble floor, trying to draw the attention of Coronel. It worked; he glanced her way and gave her a suspicious look.

Hamish jumped.

The noise from Trish's suitcase was too much for him to bear.

Not paying attention to Hamish's discomfort, Trish proceeded to take out a giant marble typewriter from her bag. It appeared to be stained and scratched from use. Searching through her suitcase again, she found a couple of sheets of parchment paper. She threaded it through the rollers of the typewriter and began typing on it.

Hamish cringed. The noise of the keys made Hamish's arm hair stand up.

"Will you knock it off? Court hasn't begun yet," said a voice behind Hamish and Coronel.

Craning his head, Hamish saw a medium-sized creature in a long black satin robe enter the courtroom. In one hand he held a stack of parchment paper, which Hamish guessed was his case file; in the other hand he held thin spectacles.

Nixon sat in a squishy tall armchair behind a tall wooden desk. He put the pieces of parchment paper he had been holding down on his desk and turned his attention to Hamish and Coronel.

"Now, Mr. McGawn and his lawyer, Deymond Lockman, will be running a few minutes late. Until they arrive, I've decided to review everything about this case to familiarize myself. Sit here in silence if you would please."

The silence was uncomfortable for Hamish. He squirmed on the court bench, making his handcuffs clank.

"Hamish."

He gazed at Nixon, unsure what he'd say.

"Stop making noise. If you continue, I'll have you escorted out of here. Understand?"

"Yes, sir."

"Good."

A loud squeaking noise erupted throughout the courtroom. A tall and stout leprechaun holding several parchment papers appeared alongside a short old man.

"Oh, I see you've arrived," said Nixon, looking up from the parchment papers. "Good. We shall start the trial when everyone is present."

***

When everyone was finally present and the juries of creatures were seated, Nixon gazed into Hamish's nervous face and asked him, "Why do you think you're here?"

"I don't know, Your Honor."

"You don't know?"

"No sir."

"Do you want me to tell you?"

Hamish was silent. He hated trials.

"Yes," Hamish finally said.

"You're here because creatures—past and present—have accused you of crimes that you knowingly and purposely committed. The charges include several counts of theft, kidnapping, and trickery to naive creatures. Explain yourself, Hamish."

"I don't think my client should answer your question, Judge Nixon," Coronel said before Hamish could say anything. "He has a right to remain silent."

"Coronel, hush. Hamish must answer my question because I want to hear his explanation. Is that too much to ask?"

"No," Coronel mumbled. "It does not."

"Now, Hamish, I'll ask you again: what do you have to say for yourself?"

"I didn't mean to hurt anyone here, if that's what they think," said Hamish.

"So you admit it," said Deymond. "You admit to those crimes."

"No … no, I didn't," said Hamish.

"He didn't admit to anything," said Coronel. "He just said he was sorry to whomever he hurt for his supposed crimes. It doesn't mean he committed them."

"Of course he did," said Deymond. "I heard him confess."

"He didn't confess."

"Yes he did."

"No he didn't."

"Hush, you two," said Judge Nixon. "Mr. McGawn?"

"Yes."

"It says here in Hamish's file that you used to own a cart in the village square. You filed for bankruptcy last year. Why?"

"Your Honor, I didn't legally own my cart. I leased it from Queen Kathrynne and King Diamond. They were gracious enough to let me keep it running if I had the coins. For years, Hamish stole my coins. At first I thought his stealing was a joke–that he'd bring them back. When he didn't, I quickly realized that his theft was something to take seriously.

"A few months ago, Queen Kathrynne and King Diamond told me that for me to keep my cart, I needed an updated version of my permit. I paid the fee, received the new permit, and all was good for a while. Then the cost of food went up, and so did my taxes."

"Were you able to pay the high taxes Queen Kathrynne and King Diamond put into effect for the residents?" asked Judge Nixon.

"At first I was able to," said Hert. "Then my finances became scarce. Because of that thief, I had to file for bankruptcy, and ultimately, I had to close my cart. Selling produce was my life; it was my passion. Now I can't show my face in the village square, because I'm afraid of what the other merchants may think of me. They used to respect me, as I was able to persuade customers– young and old alike–to purchase my delicious produce. Now I don't know what to do."

"What else happened after your permit expired? Didn't you start working in soup kitchens?" asked Judge Nixon, examining pieces of parchment paper in front of him.

"Yes, I eventually had to resort to cooking in the village square's soup kitchen for the less fortunate," said Hert.

"And how did that go?" said Judge Nixon. "Did your boss pay you enough to keep your cart up and running?"

"No. I had to sell my cart to keep up with the demand to meet the cost of living."

"What types of jobs did you do at these soup kitchens?" asked Judge Nixon.

"I had to clean dirty tables and deal with rude creatures who came off the street for food."

"Wait a minute," said Coronel. "Let me get this straight. You were poor because of the high cost of living and the taxes Queen Kathrynne and King Diamond implemented a few months ago, correct?"

"No. If it weren't for Hamish, I'd be fine."

"Wrong, sir. You are wrong."

"Are you going to let Coronel question Hert in such an accusatory fashion?" said Deymond, gazing at Coronel, piercing into his soul, making him quiver.

"I'll allow it," said Judge Nixon.

"It turns out that if Hamish hadn't stolen coins from your cart, you'd be worse off in debt. Isn't that right, Hert?"

"No, it isn't."

"I have a hard time believing you, Hert, because I believe you are a savvy businessman who can get out of any hardship that comes your way. I believe you were raised on the principle that money is the cornerstone of a successful business. Correct?"

"Yes, that is correct," said Hert. "However, I don't see what my raising has to do with anything. We're here because Hamish is a liar and a dirty, rotten leprechaun who should be in prison for his appalling crimes."

"True. Indeed we are. We're also here to find out the reason Hamish stole those coins from your cart. To accomplish it, we must first dig into your past, Hert, and find out what makes you tick. You see, Judge Nixon, members of the jury of creatures, the root of Hamish's bad behaviors are a couple of factors. True, Hamish may be a tricky and deceitful leprechaun. There's no denying this fact. But he can also be inquisitive and insightful at times."

Everyone in the courtroom gasped.

"How so?" said Judge Nixon. "Explain."

"We all know leprechauns are natural-born inquisitors. They love to question things. And because leprechauns are curious, Hamish wished to examine Hert's collection of coins."

"Oh, that is foolish," said Hert. "Everyone knows leprechauns are not curious creatures. They are liars and thieves."

"No, they're not, Hert," said Coronel. "They're misunderstood is all. Now Hert, it is my understanding that your parents aided in your venture in the produce business; is that correct?"

"At first, yes."

"And is it true that since you went bankrupt, your parents offered to help you financially? They did help you?"

"No, it's not."

"I believe it is true, sir. What I have here are bank statements addressed to you and signed by Mr. and Mrs. McGawn." Coronel held up two pieces of parchment paper for Nixon and the rest of the court to see. He shook them, and the sound of wrinkled paper filled the silent courtroom. "You see, your parents were happy to help out because they felt it was the least they could do to aid their one and only son. And by doing so, they gave you millions of gold coins, thereby assisting you for years to come."

"Let's not forget that Hamish stole my coins at my cart," said Hert.

"But you quickly replaced them, didn't you, Mr. McGawn?" said Coronel.

"Uh, no, I didn't. I couldn't."

"Don't lie to me, Mr. McGawn. You hated Hamish the moment you met him. Isn't that right?"

"No … well, yes, but that's beside the point," said Hert.

"Then what is the point, Mr. McGawn? You knew you'd talk bad about my client to get him prosecuted and sent to the village's jail because you think Hamish deserves all he gets?" said Coronel.

"No, I just wanted to–" Hert began, but he was interrupted by Deymond, who seemed all too excited to put Coronel in his place and tell Hert's side of the story.

"Hert has built up an excellent reputation setting produce at the village square. Hamish's selfishness and greed ruined it. Hert's father believed he should invest his time and energy in the McGawn family business of selling produce, but on a much larger scale than a cart in a village. My client has expressed to me that he'd rather sell produce on a much smaller scale than his father's dream of building a food empire. Hert, by nature, is stubborn and will not give up on something if he has his mind on it. I noticed that firsthand when I first met Mr. McGawn."

Judge Nixon listened to each story, casually taking in what he had heard. Then he finally asked, "Do you have any witnesses who saw Hamish steal Hert's coins from his cart?"

"I don't have any witnesses to testify against Hert, Your Honor," said Coronel.

"But I have a witness who'd like to testify against Hamish," said Deymond.

"Go ahead," said Judge Nixon, gesturing in Deymond's direction.

An old female creature suddenly stood up. Coronel saw at once she held a cane, propping her upright. He knew at once his so-called witness was not credible. She might not remember anything she may have seen.

"How is she even a witness?" said Coronel. "She's feeble and old."

"Don't make assumptions, Coronel," said Judge Nixon. "Let her speak, and I'll decide if she's credible."

Coronel sighed. "All right, sir."

"Please state your name for the court," said Judge Nixon.

"Why?"

"For the records, ma'am. I keep them in case I may need to ask you further questions after the trial."

"All right. My name is Abergele Greene."

"Please tell me your testimony, Ms. Greene," said Judge Nixon.

"I usually give Hert two gold coins in exchange for the season's produce. Have you tried Hert's produce?"

"Ma'am …" Judge Nixon was about to dismiss Abergele because he thought her testimony was not credible, but he thought better of it. Instead he said, "Yes, I have. Very good. When have you seen Hamish–do you recall?"

"It was a couple of times a week. On one day, Hamish was set on getting some gold. Before I had gone on my usual rounds for produce at Hert's cart, Hamish stopped me on a path a few feet from Hert's cart. He asked me if I had any extra coins."

"And did you find it a bit strange that a leprechaun asked you for some coins?" asked Deymond.

"No, not really. I assumed Hamish needed the coins, so I gave him some."

"And did you happen to hear why he needed the coins?" said Deymond. "Did he give some sob story, saying he was a homeless, desolate leprechaun?"

"In fact, yes. Hamish said his parents perished in a fire and he needed a few coins to get by," said Abergele.

"Thank you, Abergele. You may sit," said Judge Nixon.

She sat.

"Now, let's move on. I'd like to hear from Ben McNealy," added Judge Nixon. "Is he here?"

Ben, who had only slipped into the courtroom to hear his name, gazed at Judge Nixon in confusion.

"Yes, I'm Ben McNealy."

"Come here, my boy," said Judge Nixon.

"Why was I called?" Ben said in Saint Patrick's ear.

"Judge Nixon wants you to testify in Hamish's case," Saint Patrick whispered back. "Go ahead; it's all right." He prodded Ben forward, toward the witness stand.

Saint Patrick and Elizabeth were seated on one of the benches, quietly absorbing the courtroom's setting.

"Please tell me, son, what Hamish has to do with you in correlation with your locket. I believe this locket of yours was your father's before you came into possession of it?"

"Yes sir," said Ben. "Saint Patrick gave it to me, and Hamish stole it."

"Now, I understand that this locket of yours has magical abilities," said Judge Nixon. "Yes?"

"Yes sir."

"This locket of yours is going to help you destroy the wizard Lyon after winning the Three-Leaf'd Tournament and therefore becoming the leaf'd prince. That is your intention, yes?"

"Yes sir."

"I believe your father, Prince William, was on his way to becoming the leaf'd prince himself. Correct?"

"Yes, Your Honor."

"Please tell the court the reason you think Hamish would steal your locket," said Judge Nixon.

"I need the locket as it gives me the ability to fight foes confidently. When Hamish had stolen my locket, I felt weak and vulnerable. I think the reason Hamish stole my locket is that he loves gold. My locket is valuable to anyone who has it in their possession. It is indeed made of gold."

"Thank you, Ben, for your testimony," said Judge Nixon. "You may sit."

Ben sat by Elizabeth and Saint Patrick, watching in earnest.

"Now I have a surprise witness that Saint Patrick brought here to testify against Hamish," added Judge Nixon. "Bailiff, will you get him?"

The tall, beefy leprechaun walked down the aisle of the courtroom and opened the courtroom doors.

A druid entered the courtroom. He was old. A floppy hat barely covered his eyes. Ben wondered how this druid could see. In one hand he carried a large leather-bound book. It had scratches and ink pen marks all over its cover. In the other hand he held a thin, scratched wooden walking stick.

"Oh, Cleary, it's nice to see you," said Judge Nixon.

"Well, you're quite welcome," said Cleary. "You, too."

"Will you tell the court what type of leprechaun Hamish appears to be?" said Judge Nixon. "Your book should give us all a clear picture."

Ben watched in continued earnest. He asked, "Who's that?"

"Cleary, the historian. He studies creatures who have suspicious pasts," whispered Saint Patrick. "He's very wise. He knows just about everything in everybody's lives."

"Does he know anything about me and what I have to do with Lyon?" Ben whispered.

"Yes, of course. I went to him, and he gave me the confidence to train you.

Without him, I don't think I'd have the confidence to train you," murmured Saint Patrick.

Cleary put down the book on the witness stand. For a split second, Ben saw the book's lettering. It read, *Hamish Greentines, A Leprechaun.* He opened the book and began to read for the court.

"Hamish's latest charges are as follows: theft–stealing a golden locket, a priceless heirloom belonging to Benjamin McNealy, handed down by the Rowzand family–and attempted murder–almost killing Elizabeth, Benjamin's girlfriend. Hamish was acting as a co-conspirator in a crime brought on by the wizard Lyon."

"Thank you, Cleary," said Judge Nixon. "Anything else?"

"Yes," said Cleary. He turned several pages of the book made of thick parchment. "Here. Hamish stole a gold bar from King Diamond's study, a gold chain from Queen Kathrynne's jewelry stash, and, most importantly, a golden book sleeve from this book. To this day, I cannot find it."

"I never touched this druid's golden book sleeve. Why would I take it? I have never been on his property," said Hamish. "I never knew this druid existed until today."

"Oh, rubbish. Then why does it say in this book that you stole it?" said Cleary. "After all, this is your book, and it doesn't make mistakes. It updates by magic, based on your whereabouts and actions. In fact, it says you're in this exact courtroom."

Cleary turned the book for everyone in the courtroom to see. A small dot was slowly blinking, with "Hamish Greentines" written below it. "Your Honor, may I say something additional?"

"Go ahead, Cleary."

"Thank you, Your Honor. Now, this book is magically enhanced, as I've said. It updates every time Hamish makes a significant move. In fact, it is updating as we speak."

The continued silence almost made Hamish squirm, but he remained still.

"Is there anything you'd like to say to defend Hamish?" asked Judge Nixon, his gaze toward Coronel.

"Yes, there is. Cleary is just angry with Hamish. Everyone in this room is angry. What Cleary and everyone here needs to realize is that Hamish isn't going to change his ways. Sure, he stole a few things and did some bad things, but should one choose to forget and forgive? It is not Hamish's fault. Stealing is built into him. It takes time to change a leprechaun's ways. It takes dedication and a lot of faith. Thank you, Your Honor, and I hope my defense with help Hamish go free—or, at the very least, get a shorter sentence."

Judge Nixon turned to Deymond and asked him, "What about you— anything to add to counteract Coronel's statements?"

"Yes, if it weren't for Hamish's selfish acts and his repulsive ways, he would not be in the situation he is in now. Mr. McGawn is destitute, and it is all Hamish's fault. He won't be able to recover his reputation as the respected merchant he was in the village square."

"Oh, this is ridiculous," Hamish blurted before Coronel could say anything to stop him. "No creature has gone forward to testify how much of a good-hearted leprechaun I am. What gives?"

"I agree with you, Hamish," said Judge Nixon. "Besides Coronel, no one in this courtroom has been compelled to testify in your favor. I know it is unfair. Sometimes, Hamish, life is unfair. For my court, I don't require witnesses to show up. If they have written statements, it is good enough for me; it so happens Hert had several witnesses testify in his favor, which helps him. I'm sorry, Hamish. But first, I want to hear the jury's decision. Would you please reveal your decision?"

A heavyset creature named Boyd stood up. In a shaky voice, he said, "Guilty on all charges."

"Thank you, Boyd," said Judge Nixon. He turned to Hamish. "Now, before I make my decision, Hamish, there is something I want you to know. I don't take kindly to creatures who steal. Most importantly, I don't take kindly to accused murderers, kidnappers, and repeat thieves. However, I will review your case now, and in thirty minutes, I will reveal my decision. The court is in recess."

***

Because Hamish had helped Lyon, his life hung in the balance. As he waited outside the courtroom, his anxiety had him on edge. In the corner, Hamish heard a low voice. He glanced into the corner, and just behind a column, a figure heretofore familiar to Hamish stepped from beyond the column.

"Hello, Hamish." The figure pulled back its hood, and Hamish saw Lyon's slinky figure and smirk.

"What do you want?" said Hamish.

"Oh, don't get fresh with me, Hamish," said Lyon. "I only want to know how the trial for your life is going. I bet it's going fantastic, isn't it?"

"You are the one who started this, Lyon," said Hamish. "I never wanted any of this–the lying, scheming–everything."

"Oh, what a silly leprechaun you are, Hamish. You brought this on yourself. I didn't force you to scheme, lie, and cheat. You did it on your own accord."

"I'm in a trial because of you. Now my life may be in jeopardy, and I may be sentenced to death. I don't know what to do, and I'm a nervous wreck."

"Oh, silly leprechaun, calm down."

"Calm down? Calm down? Are you nuts?"

A guard who stood outside the courtroom, hearing the conversation, peered around the corner and asked Hamish, "Who's that you're talking to, leprechaun?"

"Can't you see him?" said Hamish.

"See who?"

"The guard can't see me, Hamish," said Lyon.

"You're going to pay for all of your crimes," said Hamish. "Just know I regret telling you about Ben's locket. If I hadn't, maybe none of this would've happened."

"Don't have regrets, Hamish. You dug a hole; now you must lie in it."

"I have responsibilities, and that includes taking responsibility for the crimes I committed and face the creatures I hurt."

"But you'll die if you go back in that courtroom. Don't you want to come with me and escape?"

"With you?"

"Yes."

"I'd rather not."

***

The courtroom remained silent as Hamish was escorted back to his spot on the bench. Moments later, Hamish saw the jury file back in, including the lead juror, Boyd, who had convicted him.

"I've made my decision," said Judge Nixon, after a thirty-minute recess.

He gazed at Hamish, who now looked mesmerized and scared at the same time. "I reviewed all the proceedings in your case, and I have heard the jury's decision, and I have decided that you don't deserve to live. Therefore, as of today, I sentence you to death by the highest court in Ireland. Bailiff, take Hamish away to be put to death."

"No! Don't do it!"

Everyone in the courtroom gasped. Judge Nixon, however, remained calm and gazed around to see who had spoken.

Then he saw him.

Ben, who was now standing, his arms crossed, gazed at Judge Nixon with accusatory eyes and said, "Hamish doesn't deserve to die."

"It is not your decision on whether Hamish should live," said Judge Nixon.

"Just because Hamish has done awful things doesn't mean he should die. We all, at some point in our lives, have done something cringe-worthy," said Ben. "If we were all put on trial for this, we'd all be sentenced to death."

Saint Patrick, who was horrified by this scene, tried his best to prod Ben to sit down, but it didn't work.

"Despite Hamish's faults, I forgive him for taking my father's locket."

"Son, you have given a perfect speech. However, my decision still stands." Judge Nixon turned to Hamish and asked him, "Do you understand these proceedings and your sentencing of death?"

Hamish didn't say a word. Instead he gazed at Judge Nixon, who repeated, "Hamish, do you understand?"

"Yes."

"Fine. Take Hamish away," said Judge Nixon.

The bailiff grabbed Hamish with rough, gnarled hands and took him away on Judge Nixon's orders.

Hamish, looking longingly at Ben as if asking for additional help, disappeared behind tall wooden doors.

"What'll happen to Hamish?" Ben asked, still gazing at the door where Hamish was taken.

"Honestly, Ben, I don't know," said Saint Patrick. "It has been a hundred years since the death of a leprechaun in Ireland."

"Whatever happened to him—the leprechaun?" said Ben.

"The last leprechaun who was put to death was Hamish's grandfather, Brimley—who, like Hamish, had a gold obsession. Leprechauns live a long time, you know. They can live a few hundred years before passing on."

Ben leaned on Elizabeth's shoulder, sobbing.

"Don't worry about Hamish, Ben," Saint Patrick added. "He can take care of himself. Leprechauns, after all, are resourceful. They can get out of sticky situations—even the direst ones, such as escaping death."

CHAPTER XXVI

Ben McNealy

THE SMELL OF ragweed filled Ben's senses as he stepped once again into the thin tent. Participants were already in the tent, showering or talking in hushed voices.

"I see you've made it this far," piped up a prince who immediately saw Ben come into the tent. He sat on one of the cots, his expression was that of intrigue.

"Yeah."

"My father said you're only here because your father died. You want to avenge his name. Is that true?"

Ben didn't recognize the prince. He had a long, flowing robe and a colorful turban. But he took his bubbly personality in stride.

"Yeah," said Ben.

"That must be rough," said the prince.

"Where are you from?"

The prince looked at Ben as if he were crazy.

"I didn't mean to offend you," said Ben. "I just want to know."

"South Africa. My dad pulled some strings to get me here. I heard about this tournament and wanted to give it a try."

"Are you sure you're up to the tournament's challenges?" Ben asked before he could stop himself.

"Yeah, I guess. I mean, sure I am. I made it this far, didn't I?"

"Yes, you did. Hey–what's your name?" said Ben.

"Prince Miguel Japura," said the prince. "And yours?"

"Benjamin McNealy. But people call me Ben for short."

"So it's true."

"What's true?"

"What people have been saying about you," said Prince Miguel. "You're famous around the world. You survived an attack from an evil wizard–Lyon, I believe?"

"Yes, I did. How'd you know?"

"You're famous, as I've said. My dad used to tell me many stories about you," said Prince Miguel. "You're like a hero or something."

"I'm no hero."

"You are–to me. It's a shame we're competing for the title of leaf'd prince, huh?" said Prince Miguel.

"Yeah, it sure is."

"It's time, Miguel. You're next to compete."

Lance had his hand propping the tent open; in the other hand he held a long piece of parchment, from which he was reading names of participants as they were being called.

"Okay," said Miguel. "Thanks."

Prince Miguel stepped forward to go out of the tent, but before he went, he turned to Ben and said, "Wish me luck."

"Good luck, Prince Miguel."

With that Ben saw Prince Miguel leave the tent, letting its flap blow in the light wind.

Ben sat on the cot he'd been assigned, thinking about all he had gone through since meeting Saint Patrick, especially more recently with Evan. He didn't believe he could bear any more surprises.

"Ben, it's your turn. You're on in five minutes."

"Lance, I don't think I'm able to."

"You have to. Creatures expect you to compete."

"I don't know. Between all the chaos and battling my best friend who's gone off the deep end, I don't think I can handle this tournament. I mean, I thought I could, but I don't think that's possible now since my head isn't in the right place," said Ben.

"You can do it," encouraged Lance. "Saint Patrick told me when you first started this tournament you'd be unsure of yourself–that you'd eventually crack and have a meltdown. But I said, 'No, he'll be all right. He's got his father's blood in him. He's a fighter like his dad.'"

"You said that?"

"Yes."

"Still …"

"Ben, you'll be fine."

"And what if I'm not fine, as you say. What then?"

"Don't worry about the what-ifs. Do the best you can with the skills and confidence you have. Saint Patrick taught me that. He's a wise man, you know."

Lance got up from a cot across from Ben and pulled back the tent's flap, but Ben stopped him.

"I know," he said. "Saint Patrick taught me many things, too."

"Two minutes. You ready?" Lance asked.

"As ready as I'd ever been."

"Good."

With the image of Evan still wavering over him, Ben pulled back the tent's flap and walked to the field's arena. Creatures of all different sizes and races filled the bleachers. From the bleachers, Ben saw many creatures' appearances; they had battle scars and were wearing war paint.

Ben couldn't help but visualize what Evan was like now: bruised, hurt, and confused. Saint Patrick had told him hours earlier that Evan had been taken to his castle's hospital wing, where Ms. Begbie had taken him in. That was the last thing he had heard.

"Ah, Ben, glad for you to join us," said Lance, who looked up from his long list made of parchment paper. "Now let me explain the rules for this task." He glanced at the parchment, reciting it aloud: "'A prince must face dangerous tasks of fire, magical objects, and evil gnomes, and, of course, must scale a tower located miles from this spot. Inside it, a damsel, which may be a princess or a foreign dignitary from another land, is waiting patiently to be rescued.'"

Lance looked up from his parchment and said to Ben with a wink, "If you're lucky, you may receive a kiss from one lucky damsel."

"I'm not looking for a kiss, Lance," said Ben. "I'm in love with Elizabeth."

"I know," he said. "But you know how damsels can be. She's locked up in a tower for so long, bored out of her mind. She may still want a kiss from her gallant rescuer; that's all I'm saying."

"Lance, no!"

"Okay, but don't blame me if she plants a big, fat smooch upon your lips."

"All right."

Ben did not want to think of a kiss from some strange damsel he did not know. Pushing it out of his mind, he concentrated on further information from Lance.

"Don't forget this, Ben, as it is important. You will be timed in this task. The judges will be looking at how well you'll be able to reach the end of the maze with your chosen damsel. You are to bring her to the judge's platform over there," said Lance.

Lance pointed to a skinny platform located a few miles from where he and Ben were standing. He added, "You have three hours, thirty minutes. And before you ask, no, you may not have extra time—the judges' rules, not mine. Good luck, Ben."

***

A tall and unmanicured hedge surrounded Ben as he stepped through its entrance. For some reason, Ben felt sick. Being in a magical and unexpecting place was all too real and frightening for him. Even so, Ben took a deep breath and traveled farther into the maze.

Ben felt a small thing fly near his ear; he whisked it away.

Then he heard it—a scream.

Ben looked above him and saw that Mystic, the green pixie, was flying above him; her expression was that of annoyance.

"Don't swat at me, Ben!" she said.

"I'm sorry. I thought you were a fly. What're you doing here?"

"I came to help you."

"You can't help me."

"Why not? No one will know I'm here."

"I can't have help; it's against the rules."

"So what?" said Mystic.

"I care," said Ben. "What if the judges find out you were helping me? I couldn't bear to find out the consequences of you aiding me. No. Leave, Mystic."

Mystic was not listening to Ben. Instead her focus was on telling Ben of the impending danger.

"I can tell you of the approaching danger this maze provides," said Mystic.

"I think that's the point. I'm not supposed to know what's coming," said Ben, walking a little ahead of Mystic in giant strides.

"But you should know. I can help you."

"Mystic, no!"

"No, you listen. I can help you. I can fly high above the maze and warn you of impending danger. I'm small and fast," said Mystic. "Please let me help you."

"Mystic ... I don't think you can help me. This maze is dangerous, according to what Lance had told me. I can't lose you," said Ben.

Mystic's body suddenly became as red as a firecracker. Ben could feel the tense heat of Mystic's body. He stepped back in pain, looking with tears into Mystic's blue eyes.

"Why did you do that?" he said.

"People have said I'm a firecracker when I'm angry," said Mystic. "Now I demand you let me help you."

"All right," said Ben. "You may help me. What do I have to lose?"

"I don't believe you. You have to want my help," said Mystic. "I won't help you at all if you don't mean it. I will hurt you worse than you've ever felt with the heat of a firecracker."

"All right. I genuinely want your help."

"Great. Let's go forth, shall we?"

"We shall."

As the two travelers ventured forth, a thick hedge came upon them. Using her garden magic, Mystic tried to trim down the hedge, but it was useless. The more she used her powers, the thicker the hedge grew.

"What do we do?" Ben asked, looking at the newly-grown hedge and then at Mystic for guidance.

"Hold on a minute," she said. "There must be a way around this hedge."

Mystic flew over the hedge to see if there was a way around it. She had been in the air only minutes when she realized her wings had gotten caught in the hedge's thorns. Unimaginable pain shot through her entire body.

Ben quickly opened his locket. A feather wand appeared. A greenish glow from its tip ignited Ben's surroundings as he flicked it.

Mystic could feel her wings expand; she exhaled. The feeling of being free was a good thing.

"Thank you," said Mystic.

"You're welcome," said Ben.

Farther along, Mystic and Ben encountered a fire pit. The thick smoke and ashy air were too much for them. Ben coughed as he tried to hold his wand, pointing it straight at the flames and thick smoke. With one flick, a spray of water appeared. As it poured over the fire, Ben saw the fire glowing and growing–and growing still–into the ashy air. Then, all at once, it smothered into ashes.

A short distance away from the travelers, a stubby leprechaun appeared within their vision. His toenails were not well kept, and in between his toes were bits of leaves and twigs. A tarp made of dirty cloth, stitched spontaneously, hung loosely on his body.

"What're you doing here, lad?" asked the leprechaun, glaring at Ben.

"I'm here for this tournament." Ben felt offended by the leprechaun's question, but he ignored it for now.

"Don't you know I hear the same answer to that question every time I see people in my neck of the woods," said the leprechaun in a thick Irish accent. "What I mean is, what are you doing here in this maze, competing? You aren't a valuable and trustworthy prince as far as I can tell, and you being here has made me sick to my stomach. Go, go, and be on your merry way."

"I *am not going!*" said Ben.

"Well … you must," said the leprechaun. "You are not a prince to me, and princes, from what I remember, are the only ones allowed to be in this maze."

"But I am a prince–a prince's son."

The leprechaun smiled a curious grin. "Really? Who's that?"

"Prince William of Ireland."

"Oh, I'm sorry. I didn't realize you were the son of a prince," said the leprechaun. His voice was too sarcastic for his own good. "To pass, you must give me gold, or else you'll pay the price of death."

"I don't have any gold with me," Ben said, slightly annoyed by the leprechaun's arrogance.

"Then you *must* die."

He was about to strike Ben dead with a thick and rotten branch that had fallen, but Mystic said, "I have gold for you."

Ben and the leprechaun gazed at Mystic with childlike wonderment. "You do?"

"Yes, I do," she said. "Here."

A golden bar appeared in Mystic's hands. She handed it to the leprechaun, who immediately smelled it. He asked, "Is this gold bar real?"

"Of course it is real. Why would I give you a fake one?"

"To cheat me out of a perfectly good gold bar," said the leprechaun boldly.

"I assure you, leprechaun, this is a real gold bar," said Mystic. "It was given to me by my grandfather. He prided himself on having the finest pieces of gold. He handed it down to me, and now I'm giving it to you."

Hives suddenly appeared on the leprechaun's face and body. He fell to his knees on the grass, coughing and shaking.

"Help me," whispered the leprechaun, his voice low and strained.

Ben was about to reach his arm out to aid the poor creature, but Mystic pulled him back.

"Don't help him," she said. "You must continue; time is of the essence."

Then, gazing down, Ben noticed a brass key by the leprechaun's feet.

"Ben, we must go before he wakes up," urged Mystic, grabbing the key from the grass, flying above him, and dropping it into his open palm.

"Will the leprechaun be all right?" Ben asked.

"He'll be all right; I'm sure," said Mystic.

Stepping over the leprechaun's limp body, Ben was about to reach for the brass doorknob when an arm grabbed his leg and would not let it go.

"Let me go!"

"No, I shall not," said the leprechaun, his voice cracked and muffled.

Ben felt a sharp tingle in his legs and ankles. The leprechaun's nails were digging into his flesh, making red marks. The more Ben tried to free himself, the more profound pain he felt.

"Hold on, Ben," Mystic said. "I'm going to aid you!"

Ben felt a tense heat upon his leg and ankle; then he heard a yelp of pain. Afterward, he felt relief. The leprechaun who once had a tight hold on him suddenly loosened his grip. Ben saw that the leprechaun had sear marks on his arms and neck.

He looked and Mystic and smiled. "You did that for me, didn't you?"

Mystic laughed. "Yes, of course."

"I'll kill you, you pixie," said the leprechaun, who then struggled to get up, finally did, and glared intensely into Mystic's blue eyes.

"You will not kill me," said Mystic boldly. "I have the will to fight, and I'm not afraid of you, leprechaun."

Before the leprechaun could cause damage to Mystic, she snapped her fingers.

They heard a muffled yet clear sound. The tall flower had uprooted itself, ambled over to them, and, with great force, seized the leprechaun with its thin petals.

"Help me!" he begged.

It was too late. The leprechaun's spirit had magically infused itself into the flower, silencing him.

Black shoes and a dirty cloth sat by themselves under the shade of the flower, which had retaken root, and etched into its petals was a single face.

***

"Where did you get the fake gold bar?" Ben asked Mystic as they approached a clearing deep within the maze.

"I received it from the goldsmith from the outskirts of Ireland," said Mystic. "He makes true gold for Queen Kathrynne and King Diamond's private use. As far as I know, it's melted to make tiaras and crowns. He gave me the gold bar in the hope it would help me one day. I only remembered it when we needed it to distract the leprechaun and to escape."

"Would the goldsmith ever make more gold bars for you if you needed them?" Ben asked.

"Of course. It'd have to be fake, however. The real ones are rare. The only people who have that privilege are the monarchy," said Mystic.

In the confines of the maze, Ben and Mystic heard a rustling sound, as if someone was stealthily moving through its tall hedges.

"What's that noise?"

"Gnomes," said Mystic. "I warn you: They can be tricky creatures. Believe me; I should know."

"Why? What happened?"

"It's not important now."

"All right. I will."

The movement became louder and more restless. Ben felt his hair on the back of his neck stand up. Then, coming out of the other side of the clearing, small gnomes approached the travelers without fear.

"Who are you, and why are you here?" said one of the gnomes, his voice low and horrifying.

"We just want past the clearing," said Ben. "We mean no harm to you or your fellow gnomes."

"You shall not pass," said the gnome. "I am the leader of this part of the maze, and you and your pixie friend are trespassing. Leave before it gets ugly."

"I told you, gnome, we can't leave," said Ben. "We must get past this part of the maze; then we'll be out of your hair."

The gnome's eyes narrowed. "I have a hard time believing you," he said. "You will indeed harm us, just like that wizard a few hours before."

Immediately Ben thought of Lyon. He must have ransacked and killed some of the gnomes when he was here. The devastation and the loss of some of the gnomes proved he had been here; it was heart-wrenching to Ben, but he must not think of it; he had to move on.

"I assure you we won't."

But Ben's assurance did not faze the cluster of gnomes at all. One of the gnomes reached into a small bag on his waist and, with one slick movement, threw small particles toward Ben.

"Watch out, Ben! The gnomes' seeds are deadly," said Mystic, stepping back to evade the danger further. "They can be the size of golf balls if these gnomes choose."

The seeds exploded at Ben's feet, momentarily blindsiding him.

Then, as Ben stepped back to dodge further attacks of the gnomes, his movement proved too late; another set of seeds exploded at his feet, plummeting him to the grass.

Stumbling and still conscious, Ben pointed his feather wand toward the gnomes.

"Oh, poor prince. You can't blast me," taunted the leader of the gnomes.

"Leave Ben alone," Mystic said before Ben could retort. "He's a prince to me. You should respect him if nothing else."

The leader of the gnomes rallied his gnomes; his voice echoed, and each gnome held back a handful of seeds, ready to strike.

Pop, pop, pop.

The seeds exploded like firecrackers at Ben's feet and in the grass.

Ben stumbled, falling to his knees.

"You will not hurt Ben any further–not when I'm here."

"What are you going to do to me, pixie?" asked the leader of the gnomes.

"This."

Mystic raised her arms to the sky.

The sky above the maze darkened. Ben looked up. A patch of thick clouds was forming, getting darker as they came together.

Then the rain fell.

After a moment, a cluster of gnomes felt sick–sicker than they've ever felt. They fell to their knees. They exhaled, but they could hardly breathe.

"Help us," said one of the gnomes, his green eyes filling with tears.

"Yes, please," said another gnome, his gaze in the direction of Mystic, who turned her attention away from them to avoid looking at the sad scene before her.

Moments later, thick thorns from the surrounding trees grabbed them; they struggled, but they couldn't get loose.

Finally, drenched, coughing, and covered in prickly thorns, the leader of the gnomes stepped out from his company of gnomes and approached Mystic, stretching out his scratched hand to show his sincerity.

"I'm sorry," he said. "I didn't mean to cause such a scene. It's just that when Lyon approached us, I didn't know what to make of him. He talked about a prince's son and how he was going to bring despair and destruction to us. I didn't know what to do. Then he told us that the only way to avoid this danger was for us to sacrifice the weakest link among the gnomes–that'd be our beloved children. At first I didn't want to believe him. But being a highly respected leader among the gnomes, I believed him anyway. After all, we didn't want our society of gnomes to perish, did we?

"Lyon had promised us gnomes that once this 'son of a prince' was vanquished, we'd be better off and safe from any additional harm from foreign outsiders. He said he'd be glad to sacrifice some of the gnomes himself to accomplish this feat.

"Before I had any second thoughts on the matter, he killed some of our gnome children with his powerful and evil wand. They didn't even have a chance. We mourned for weeks for our fellow gnomes' children."

"That's what Lyon does. He takes and takes without a second thought," said Ben. "If there's one thing I've learned from Saint Patrick, it is this: Evil wizards are evil. They'll always be evil. They lie and cheat other creatures out of their livelihood and possessions one scheme at a time. That is why it is important that I continue. I will defeat Lyon once and for all, and Ireland will be peaceful once again."

"You know Saint Patrick?" said the leader of the gnomes.

"Yes, he's my trainer and mentor in this tournament."

"Okay. That's nice."

"Oh, do you know where a tower may be located? I'm supposed to find it within this maze," said Ben, who turned from walking away with Mystic, looking at the gnomes.

"Beyond that tall hedge over there," said the leader of the gnomes, smiling.

"Thank you," said Ben. "You've been a great help to us."

"You're welcome."

***

A tower rose out of the distance. Its stone walls were too far from where

Ben and Mystic were now standing, but as they moved closer, the more extravagant and ornate details became vibrant. It was clear to Ben that this was no ordinary tower. It had a spell upon it, and someone was there.

"Now I must tell you, I won't be able to assist you any further," said Mystic, looking at the scale of the tower, aghast.

"Why? You wanted to assist me this whole time, and now you're breaking a promise. What gives?"

"My powers are helpful to me only to a certain altitude. This tower is too high for me. My magic would not work even if I were to attempt a spell."

"Oh, don't be disappointed," Mystic added, seeing the disappointed expression on Ben's face. "I'll still assist you; I'll just assist you from a different altitude than the tower's; that's all."

"All right. I guess that'll be okay."

Ben leaned on the tower's side wall. A spark of electricity suddenly shot through his body, singeing him. He stepped back, slightly confused at what had just occurred to him. He gazed up at the tower's long and ornate window, and while he was looking, a rope ladder made of twine appeared. It seemed sturdy, but Ben was unsure.

Ben stepped upon the twine ladder; a feeling of excitement and dread filled his consciousness. Who or what was at the top? Was it safe?

Ben inhaled, continuing, confident that he had made the right decision.

The inside of the tower was dark and dimly lit. Candles provided little light as Ben surveyed his surroundings—a small room. At the other side, a bed was visible in the dull candlelight; its colorful quilt only just showing its pure brilliance.

Then Ben heard it: "Prince William, is that you?"

Ben recognized the voice. "Princess Lexis, is that you?"

"Yes. Have you come to rescue me?"

"Yes, but you might be confused about the person doing the rescue. I'm Ben McNealy, Prince William's son."

"Where is he, then?" Princess Lexis asked. Her voice was strained and hoarse from crying.

Ben got closer to Princess Lexis, and within the murky darkness of the tower room, he saw that she had been crying and that her dress was old and tattered. She lay against the bed's frame, her face buried in the confines of her dress.

"He's not here right now. But I'm here." Ben held out a reassuring hand, but Princess Lexis did not look up.

"Leave me alone," she said, her voice low but commanding.

"No, I was told to rescue you. You must go with me to be safe."

"I refuse to go with you."

"Please go with me," said Ben, reaching out another arm, attempting to prod her up.

But she didn't move; she didn't look at him.

"I told you I'm not moving," she said.

"Please go with me," said Ben. "I'm trying to be nice, but you're not making it easy for me."

"I'm sorry it's so difficult for you, but I made up my mind: I'm not leaving, and that's it."

Ben pulled out his feather wand and pointed it in Princess Lexis's direction. "Get up, Princess."

Princess Lexis looked up. Wiping her damp eyes with a corner of her dress, she saw Ben's determined but frightened face.

"I can't go," she said. "If Lyon saw that I was gone–"

"You mean he was here in this tower?"

"Yes. Lyon put a spell on me and this tower so whoever attempted to rescue me would not be able to. He said they'd be dead if they tried."

"Well, Lyon doesn't scare me, and your safety is all I care about, so let's get out of here," said Ben.

With the tip of his feather wand acting as a flashlight, Ben guided Princess Lexis to the tower's window.

"I don't know about this," she said.

"Please go," said Ben, continuing to prod Princess Lexis out the window with the tip of his feather wand.

A bloodcurdling screech pierced Ben's eardrums. A second screech echoed throughout the tower's enclosed space. It was louder than the first. Ben felt a tingle of dread run down his spine.

Then, as his nerves died down, he was able to understand the scene. In the boundaries of the room, a great outline sashayed and slithered about. Ben felt sick as he realized what the winged creature was—a dragon.

Despite this, and ignoring the situation at hand, Ben continued to prod Princess Lexis out of the tower's window.

"I can't balance on this ledge; it's too tiny," said Princess Lexis, who stepped one leg out of the window and then the other, moving onto the tower's ledge.

"You're going to have to," Ben called out as the dragon's large presence moved further inside the tower's room.

Ben and Princess Lexis could suddenly feel the breath of the dragon; she held her breath, and Ben stepped back toward the open window to avoid its breath of smoke.

"Hurry! I don't think I can physically stand on this ledge much longer," said Princess Lexis.

With precision and trust in himself, Ben flicked his wand. Light from the wand's tip engulfed the whole room, momentarily blinding the winged creature. It moved and flailed blindly across the room, hitting everything in sight.

Wham!

The force of the dragon's tail hit the tower's window, breaking it into chunks of stone and debris.

Ben's stomach lurched.

He heard a terrifying scream of pain and fright, and then he heard silence.

Sauntering to the window, Ben gazed out. His eyes widened at the sight below him. Amid debris and broken pieces of stone, he saw the dragon's shadow on the grass below. A few inches above it, a barely conscious princess was hanging by the collar of her dress.

"Hold on, Princess Lexis," he called. "I'm going to save you."

Instinctively, and with caution, Ben flicked his feather wand out of the window's open frame. A glow shone around Princess Lexis's unconscious body, pulling her upward. As she reached the window's open frame, Ben, in a quick motion, reached and grabbed the hem of her dress, pulling her in and hugging her.

She collapsed on the weight of his body.

"You okay?" he whispered.

Princess Lexis heaved out a long, drawn-out breath and cough.

"Yes, I am now," she said, immediately seeing Ben's dark brown eyes through hazy vision. "What happened?"

"You fell when the dragon smashed the tower's window; I saved you."

"Oh."

Then, as her vision was restored and the haziness left her, Princess Lexis could see Ben's terrified but concerned expression.

"We need to get out of here," he urged.

He opened his locket. The grappling hook he had used to escape the fiery clutches of a dragon appeared.

"Don't be worried, Princess," said Ben, who recognized the sense of panic in her expression. "It'll be all right. We're getting out of this tower, and hopefully, if I have done it right, we'll be safe on the ground in no time."

Ben searched the dim room. In his peripheral vision, he saw the bed he had found Princess Lexis lying against. It had long wooden bedposts that looked as if they had rotted with age, but still sturdy. Or at the very least, he hoped they were.

Wrapping the grappling hook around the closest bedpost near the open window, Ben said to Princess Lexis, "Hold on to my waist. We're going to go down this tower's wall."

Princess Lexis was unsure about scaling down such a high tower, especially since Lyon would scorn her for escaping his clutches, but she felt she had no choice. She was hoping to be rescued, and Ben was her only chance at freedom at this present time.

"Yes, I guess."

Princess Lexis held her breath. The feeling of sliding down a grappling hook with uneven knots wasn't her idea of a rescue.

"How much longer?" Princess Lexis asked, not even looking below her.

"Not too much longer," said Ben. "A few more feet."

With a sigh of relief, Princess Lexis dipped her feet into a nearby stream. It felt good to be out of a stuffy and dusty tower.

"Thank you," said Princess Lexis.

"You're welcome," said Ben.

"Is that dragon dead?" Mystic asked, gazing from a tree, flying out of it, and hovering over it.

"Yes, I assume it is," said Ben.

"I saw it fall out of the window. I would have helped you and Princess Lexis escape, but I didn't want to get hurt," said Mystic.

"Let's go," said Ben. "Lyon will soon come after us if we dawdle."

**

Soon Ben and his friends were moving through the maze at a quick pace. Sounds of birds and insects filled the air.

Growl.

Ben and his friends stopped.

"Lyon's wolves," Ben whispered into Mystic's and Princess Lexis's ears. "Lyon must be close."

He took out his feather wand and pointed it in front of him, waiting for Lyon's wolves to attack. They continued to walk, looking alert.

Growl, growl.

"C'mon, you wolves. I'm ready for you," said Ben.

Bursts of light suddenly blindsided the travelers. Mystic fell out of the sky; Princess Lexis screamed and fell to the grass. Ben stepped back, stumbling in response to the unknown bursts of light.

A second burst of light entered the air and headed toward the travelers. Ben continued to stumble toward the light. He raised his shaking wand arm and said, "Come out, you coward."

Out of the rustling bushes, several wolves appeared, their eyes glowing. They circled the travelers, their mouths foaming.

One yipped.

The sound proved too much for Princess Lexis's ears, and she covered them.

A rush of adrenaline filled Ben's subconscious. He did not want his newly-formed friendships to die out because of hungry wolves. He boldly and confidently flicked his wand, and without too much struggle or more yipping, the wolves were silenced.

They were still hungry. Ben managed to silence them but not subdue them.

They moved closer to Ben and his companions.

"Ah!"

Ben, in a panic, craned his head in the direction of the person who had screamed, his wand still raised. Not too far from him, Ben saw that Princess Lexis had managed to get herself up against one of the maze's tall bushes. One of the wolves was pressing up against her, its mouth salivating. She tried to push the creature away forcefully with her palms, but it was no use. It was still insisting on making a meal out of Princess Lexis, one way or another, and she knew it.

Ben carefully moved toward Princess Lexis, all the while keeping his wand aloft.

"Be still," he said. "Any movement and you're wolf chow."

Princess Lexis obeyed.

Wham!

A yelp sounded.

The wolf fell to the grass. One of the tall hedges had snapped and had dropped convincingly at the right time, suggesting someone had made it happen. Ben guessed it was Mystic who had done the rescuing, because he hadn't made the hedge fall.

But Ben and his friends didn't have any time to process the incident, because more wolves appeared.

The travelers ran, hoping the distance between them would be enough.

***

In the shadows, a figure watched from a distance. Its cloaked hood only just covered its face. Foliage and high hedges covered some of its body. Ben noticed something was amiss; he sensed a familiar figure, but he didn't know who it might have been. As Ben and his friends continued, the rustling of undergrowth continued.

"Who's there?" Ben whispered, holding his wand out in front of him to ready himself for unforeseen threats.

No one answered.

"Stay close," Ben added, ushering his friends down a winding dirt path within the maze. "No telling what's out there."

Everyone obeyed.

"Fancy meeting you here, Ben."

Ben turned, his wand raised, pointing it in the direction of the unknown figure who had spoken.

Mystic landed; she was petrified by fear.

Princess Lexis gasped.

"Who's there?" Ben said.

"You don't remember me, do you?" said the figure. "It is such a pity you don't remember me. I thought we had come to know each other well."

"Lyon?"

The figure took off its hood. Its long cloak dropped to the grass. "Now do you remember me?"

Ben couldn't forget Lyon. He had the unique smell of bad ragweed and strong perfume about him. Around his neck, a necklace with a cursive *L* lay on his chest, underneath his old and stained shirt.

Ben raised his wand, holding its tip inches from Lyon's face.

"You're bold, aren't you, Ben?" said Lyon, and he raised his own wand, its tip inches from Ben's face.

Then light entered the air; Ben felt a pinch. He looked down on his chest and saw just a drop of blood drip to the grass near his feet. He felt woozy, but he stood firm.

Despite being injured, Ben held his wand, shakily, toward Lyon's direction; his expression was as menacing as those of members of an evil cult in the woods.

With a flick of his wrist, Lyon effortlessly ignited his wand again in Ben's direction.

Then there was another blast.

And another.

Ben felt as if he'd had the wind sucked out of him. He lay barely conscious, barely breathing.

Lyon leaned toward Ben, whose feet were behind him, his knees barely touching the bloodstained grass. In a loud voice, he said, "You are certainly a worthy foe. I'm sure your father would be proud to know you fought to the very end."

Weak but still conscious, Ben said, "Shut up, you coward!"

"I'm going to let your comment go—for now. I almost feel remorse for doing this very next thing: I must kill you, Ben; I must murder you. You obviously won't give me the chance to become the leaf'd prince, so I must do what I think is best."

"It was my birthright," said Ben in a frail voice. "My father–"

"Your father was a fool," said Lyon. "He gave up his life to save you. Only fools will do that."

Ben shook his head. "No, my father wasn't a fool."

"Yes, he was. The sooner you realize this fact, the better. He was a fool for giving up his life in exchange for yours. He was a fool to refuse my willingness to be leaf'd prince on his own accord, and you are for doing the like."

Ben was about to open his mouth to retort, but Lyon said, "I'll drop this whole notion of killing you if you, yourself withdraw from this sacred tournament."

"I can't. I must compete."

Lyon waved his wand in the air.

Suddenly Ben felt a coldness and despair seep all around him like an invisible mist. He was quickly fading in and out of consciousness, and just as he started to make sense of what was happening to him, he heard a noise so terrifying it made him jump.

Only then did Ben gaze around himself and find the source of the noise. The maze's hedges had been flattened, as if a large rolling pin had pressed their foliage. Mystic and Princess Lexis, who had once been there with him, were now gone. Among the clouds, images of Elizabeth and Evan were etched so carefully and craftily that they were as clear as day, even though it appeared to be dark and gloomy.

"What did you do to my friends?" he asked. He was conscious, but only just.

"Calm down! I haven't done anything to them yet," said Lyon.

"And you won't."

In the distance, a figure heretofore unknown to Ben and Lyon appeared. It was wearing a long, flowing robe, and in its hand was a walking stick of some sort. Its tip glowed, and it pointed directly upward, making lightning bolts streak across the sky.

"Saint Patrick?" said Ben.

Lyon turned, and just beyond the downed hedges, a figure stood near him now, its hood opening directly at Lyon.

"Don't hurt Ben," it said.

"You know I must," said Lyon in a commanding tone to the unknown figure.

"I say to you again: don't hurt Ben."

The figure pointed the stick in the direction of Lyon, unfazed by Lyon's threat, its tip inches from his perspiring forehead. Then, without warning, the figure flicked the stick. Light immediately shot from it, and Lyon fell to the grass, nearly unconscious.

Two other people were now with the figure. One was a teenager, possibly seventeen or so; the other was a middle-aged woman. Their eyes were locked to the scene before them, and they could not look away.

The woman, Suzette, stepped toward Lyon, and without any hesitation, she grabbed Lyon's wand from inside his cloak pocket and pointed it in his face.

"You have ruined my life," she said.

"Don't blast me, Suzette. Please don't."

"Why should I let you live? You don't deserve to live."

Suzette was about to flick the wand, but Saint Patrick said, "Don't do it,

Suzette. He may have, as you said, 'ruined your life,' but you will ruin yours if you flick your wrist."

Suzette hesitated, but she still held Lyon's wand for protection.

Lyon, sweaty and disoriented from the blast, struggled to get up. When he finally did, he was able to seize another wand from inside his cloak, and he pointed it at Suzette.

"You said I ruined your life? What about Evan, our son? Wasn't his life ruined when you selfishly took him away from me?"

"Lyon, I had to–for his protection and mine. You were getting out of control. Your selfishness got in the way of what truly matters: love."

"Love? You never loved me?" said Lyon. "You left me stranded on our first date at the carnival, remember?"

"Lyon, you killed a child. A child who only wanted to find her mother. How can I forgive you for that?"

Light burst from the two wands, making a noise like thunder.

Saint Patrick and Elizabeth stepped back, their eyes glued to the scene unfolding in front of them. He tapped his cane on the grass, and an invisible shield appeared to protect them from any harm coming their way.

Ben, meanwhile, had awoken and wondered what was happening. He stumbled toward Saint Patrick and Elizabeth, his gaze toward the scene.

All calm was temporarily restored.

Suzette held the wand shakily in her palm, her gaze fixed upon Lyon, and she did not look away.

"Go ahead, blast me and see what happens," Lyon taunted.

Suzette didn't move.

"Go ahead, I said!"

Suzette, in a moment of heroism, flicked the wand. Instead of hitting Lyon (as she fully expected it would), the wand's stream missed him by inches.

"Ah, is that all you can do?" Lyon glared into Suzette's eyes. "You may be my son's mother, but you were nobody to me." And with a flick of his wrist, Lyon magically grabbed the other wand with a free hand.

Suzette ran toward the invisible shield where Ben, Elizabeth, and Saint Patrick were, on the hillside of the maze. Just as she reached the invisible shield, a blast of fire from a wand came near her, but it missed her entirely. In the crossfire, it hit Saint Patrick's cloak, setting it ablaze.

"Ah! Look at what you've done!" he said.

Desperate to put the blaze out, Saint Patrick tried to use his magic, but it was hopeless. It rose higher and higher, darkening the sky. Saint Patrick couldn't help but breathe it in. He could feel his lungs grow smaller and shrivel up.

"Please help me!" he cried out.

"I'll help you," said Mystic, who saw Saint Patrick's desperate need for aid.

Flying over to him, she tried helping him by casting a water spell, but the hot smoke proved too strong.

Seeing that Saint Patrick needed further help, and on impulse, Ben launched at Lyon, bypassing Saint Patrick's shield of protection. In response, Saint Patrick, despite his injuries, tried to prod him back, but Ben was not listening to him. Instead his mind was on something else. He waved his feather wand. The spell had unfortunately done only little to Lyon, not injuring him.

Ben tried with all his might to pull Lyon's wand out of his hand, but his fingers held on with a tight grip like super glue.

"Ben, let it go! It's not worth fighting with Lyon now. You must finish and win the tournament first," said Saint Patrick.

"He's not listening to you. What shall we do?" said Elizabeth desperately. "Ben, stop resisting Lyon! In time we shall defeat him!"

But Saint Patrick's second plea did not convince Ben to let go of Lyon's wand. It only made him try harder, which in turn made Lyon resist him.

Finally, after some struggle, Lyon clutched Ben by his shirttail. They each played a game of tug-of-war, pulling to and fro until finally it ended. Lyon was able to get his wand from Ben by digging his dirty, gross fingernails into his bare arm.

Ben reared back in pain. The feeling of being scratched is not all fun for anyone to bear. He fell to the grass, massaging his arm.

During the chaos, Lyon appeared exhausted; however, he wasn't too exhausted to fight. Not by a long shot.

Lyon laughed a menacing laugh.

"Ben, you know it is impossible for you to defeat me, right?" he sneered, his eyes on Ben. "You can't win. If I live, you will be beaten down time and again."

"Don't listen to him!" said Elizabeth, beyond Saint Patrick's invisible shield. "He's trying to get inside your head. You can defeat him; I believe in you!"

"Ben, no girl is going to tell you the truth. You are weak. You are not going to defeat me, as I am stronger than you. I killed your parents, and I will kill you."

"Don't listen to him, I beg of you!" said Elizabeth.

Ben was pulled in too many directions. His worst thought had come to pass. Maybe, just maybe, Saint Patrick had made a grave mistake in recruiting him to take part in defeating an evil wizard. Perhaps he wasn't cut out to defeat Lyon.

Just then, he thought about all the amazing things he had done and the people he had met. Without putting thought into action, and without Saint Patrick's encouragement, he wouldn't have met Queen Kathrynne, his grandmother–who, he knew, loved him even though she did not fully understand him as her son, Prince William. He would not have met King Diamond, who, he presumed, displayed kingly qualities to a people who needed it in times of chaos and uncertainty.

Despite his uncertainty about it all, Ben knew he was given instruction and guidance by Saint Patrick to finish and win the Three-Leaf'd Tournament; and in doing so, he would be able to defeat Lyon.

The Irish people needed a hero. Ben knew he was their hero. Elizabeth believed him, and why should he not believe in himself?

Ben acted on instinct and ran toward Lyon. Despite Saint Patrick's previous warning on confronting Lyon, he raised his feather wand, and with a flick, a jet of light entered the air, moving toward Lyon in a fluid motion. Lyon reacted, and with a flick of his own wand, an invisible barrier appeared around Lyon, much like Saint Patrick's, blocking Ben's attack. In response, Ben fell backward onto the grass beside Lyon, who smiled a devilish grin.

"I told you, you silly prince, you won't be able to defeat me," he said. "I'm more cunning than you know."

Bruised and left with a few scratches here and there, Ben struggled to get on his feet. When he did, he saw out of the corner of his eye the barrier glowing in the sun, which now appeared among the clouds as if an evil witch had put an enticing spell on it. He raised his wand, ready to strike again, but as powerful as his wand was, Ben knew it was folly. Lyon would counteract his spell, making it useless, lest he get another one–one more powerful than this.

But even so, he had to try. Ben flicked the wand; its streams rebounded on the impact of the invisible barrier, causing Ben to this time lose consciousness.

The only thing he remembered was Lyon's sneer and Saint Patrick's rough hands catching him.

***

White noise filled Ben's ears as he slowly opened his eyes. Around him he saw that Elizabeth, Mystic, Princess Lexis, and Saint Patrick were all near him.

"What happened?"

"You were struck by the spell of your own wand," said Saint Patrick. "Luckily I was there to catch you."

"And Lyon?" said Ben. "Where's he?"

Saint Patrick didn't say anything. He didn't have to.

"How much longer are you going to be around this poor prince?"

"Shut up, Lyon. He's in this position because of you."

"Oh, Saint Patrick, I don't take kindly to a person who blames other people. It's indeed a shame that once you die, all the poor boy's going to remember of you is how much of a selfish person you truly are."

"Enough games," said Saint Patrick. "If you want to blast me, just do it."

Lyon stared into Saint Patrick's eyes, his wand unmoving.

"Do it, I say! Blast me!"

The noise was like thunder. Ben watched from a distance as Lyon and Saint Patrick were inches apart, each wand lit, sparks flying in every direction.

"Why don't you let the prince's son finish me off, huh? Is that what your training sessions were for—to learn how to finish me off?"

"Shut up."

"I'll do it. I'll finish you off."

"Ben, *no!*"

Elizabeth stepped in front of Ben, her arm lightly pushing him back. "You don't know the outcome of this," she said.

"I must do this. I must finish what my father couldn't."

Ben lightly pushed Elizabeth aside. He walked closer to Lyon. He smelled of bad ragweed and strong perfume—something familiar to him.

Without looking into Lyon's eyes, Ben opened his locket.

A jeweled box suddenly appeared. Engraved on its surface was an image of a four-leaved clover. It was shiny and dazzling, covered in green sequins. It looked as if a prince would have treasured it for years and as if it would have been the most valuable item in his possession.

Lyon gasped, for he knew what the box contained. He gazed first at the box, and then at Ben, and said, "Give me the box."

"Don't listen to him, Ben. You hear me? Don't listen to him."

"Do as I say. Don't listen to Saint Patrick. He's only a fool, after all."

"No, he isn't. He taught me many things, but he's certainly not a fool. You, Lyon, are the fool."

Just as Lyon reached for the box, it rose in the air, hovering above their heads.

Ben and Lyon's eyes were fixed on the box. They tried to get the box with their wand currents, but they counteracted each other, like magnets. A rumbling exploded and hissed.

The box hovered near Lyon; Ben struggled to keep his wand's current in the air as it continued to go toward Lyon.

Ben's stomach lurched.

Would he lose?

Ben's wand stream suddenly became stronger. The box reversed its course and floated near Ben.

"That's it, Ben … lower the box," Ben could hear Saint Patrick say.

Saint Patrick pointed his own wand at the box; it floated near him.

When this happened, Lyon felt weak; his wand's current was slowly becoming weaker.

Lyon collapsed. "No!" he cried.

The box landed near Saint Patrick's invisible shield and it exploded, causing bursts of light and noises to erupt.

***

When the silence prevailed, Ben looked at the box. It appeared intact, as though the previous wand fight had not happened at all. The gold lettering was just as striking as it always had been.

"Ah! I can't believe you two!" shouted Lyon.

In a fit of rage, Lyon blasted his wand toward Saint Patrick. Saint Patrick, in turn, shot toward Lyon.

Lyon fell to the grass. Feeling his chest, Lyon realized he had become injured by Saint Patrick's wand sparks. He tasted blood. Then, as he looked for his wand, he realized it was not near him. It must have fallen when he was injured.

There, among the hedges, a single wand lay by itself, its tip pointing at Ben.

With only seconds to spare, and against Saint Patrick's wishes, Ben ran toward the wand, his adrenaline pumping. He was just a few feet away when he saw the wand's tip light up. He reared back, for he was afraid it would backfire on him. He gazed at the wand, mesmerized by its mystifying glow.

Then, as Lyon waved his wand hand close to the grass, his wand slid toward him; he grabbed it.

Still weak, but conscious, Lyon flicked his wrist. The wand's tip ignited, sending a stream cascading toward Ben.

Elizabeth screamed.

Saint Patrick, however, remained calm. He pushed Ben out of the way, and the stream bypassed Ben.

"Thank you," breathed Ben. "You saved my life."

"Sure," said Saint Patrick.

"This seems like a sincere moment, but I'm not touched," said Lyon. He flicked his wand, and more streams cascaded toward Ben and Saint Patrick.

Saint Patrick tapped his cane on the grass; Lyon's wand stream instantly became ice and fell to the grass.

"You will no longer have dominion here," said Saint Patrick. "Your days of wreaking havoc are long gone. Ben will be the leaf'd prince and banish you, never to return."

Saint Patrick then turned to Ben and said, "Open the box."

"Here?"

"Yes, here."

Ben went over to the box and picked it up. "There's no way to open it," he said.

"Wave your hand over the box; it should open."

Ben waved his palm over the box. It shook and glowed, and with a pop, its golden lock opened. A jeweled cane–like Saint Patrick's–appeared.

"What's this?" Ben asked.

"Every leaf'd prince gets one of these canes as a sign of loyalty to the Irish people they are called to protect," said Saint Patrick. "I was once a protector of Ireland, as you know already. Your mother wanted me to give this to you as a sign of good faith."

"Thank you," said Ben. "I appreciate it."

"Sure."

"You aren't going to take Saint Patrick seriously, are you?" said Lyon, his voice weak and frail.

Ben gazed at Lyon, who was still on the grass. He was nothing like an evil wizard at all. His powers and life appeared to have been sucked out of him.

"You're the last wizard I'd like advice from," said Ben. "After all I've gone through, Saint Patrick is still the kind of person you're not–a loyal friend."

Before Lyon could say anything else, Ben, trusting his powers, tapped his cane on the grass. Bright colors entered the sky, and the wind started to push Lyon's weak body toward the box. He resisted, but it was no use. With a snap, Ben heard the box close and lock, trapping Lyon's spirit and his magical wolf spirits inside.

"Now you are a true protector of Ireland," said Saint Patrick. "I'm proud of you."

"Me, too," said a voice behind them.

Ben turned and saw Nixon Magpie standing there in a burgundy robe. Ben recognized him as the judge of Hamish's trial several weeks earlier.

"What are you doing here?" Ben said.

"I'm one of the judges of the Three-Leaf'd Tournament."

Ben smiled nervously. "Hi. Sorry I was rude. I didn't know."

"It's all right, Ben," said Nixon. "I came to give you this."

He handed Ben an old piece of parchment much like the one Lance had used in the Tournament. "Open it," he said.

Without question, Ben unraveled the parchment. Inside he saw green cursive writing. It said,

Congratulations to the winner of the Three-Leaf'd Tournament. You are indeed a protector in the eyes of the Irish people.

Signed,

Nixon Magpie, Executive and Judge of the Three-Leaf'd Tournament

"Ben, your grandmother would like to talk with you."

Lance stood at the edge of the maze's entrance, where Ben, Elizabeth, Mystic, Suzette, and Saint Patrick were standing. Ben held the box tightly to his chest.

"All right. Tell her I'm coming."

CHAPTER XXVII

Ben McNealy

"HI, YOUR MAJESTY, Ben is here."

"Send him in."

"Of course, Your Majesty."

Lance propped open the door, and Ben was greeted with the most heavenly smells imaginable—smells of lilac and citrus.

"Come in, Ben."

Ben stepped further into the room. The smell of perfume seemed stronger now. A circular bed located in the center of the room filled the back wall. Tall, ornate shutters and curtains covered the tall windows.

Queen Kathrynne got up from her chair near a mirror and sat on the circular bed. "Now Ben, I hear that you defeated Lyon," she said at once before Ben had time to say anything. "I'm certainly proud of you."

"Thank you," said Ben awkwardly.

"You know, this was your father's room when he was alive," said Queen Kathrynne. "Of course, he was hardly in this room; he still loved gazing out of these windows."

"Really?"

"Yes. Why don't you sit down on this circular bed?"

"Uh, no thanks, I'm fine."

Queen Kathrynne raised her eyebrows. "You sure?"

"Yeah, I'm sure."

"May I show you at least one thing?" said Queen Kathrynne, getting up from the circular bed and walking over to another door in the room.

"Okay."

Queen Kathrynne opened the door and grabbed something inside of it, and she closed the door. "This," she said, "was your father's."

Queen Kathrynne opened a wooden box. Inside it was something that smelled wonderful.

"A flower," she added. "Your father loved this flower." She sighed. "I sincerely don't know why. He didn't much care for flowers. He would kill them, as he'd forget to water them. They'd sit in this room all day while he was out doing ..."

Queen Kathrynne trailed off. Remembering her son was hard for her. For a mother, it was especially tricky.

"Oh. Did my father say why he loved this flower so much?" Ben asked. He finally sat on the circular bed, letting the softness sink into his body.

"I'm not sure he did. One thing is for certain, though; he hated me, and he hated his life as a royal."

"I'm sure he didn't hate you," reassured Ben.

"Yes, I suppose you're right," said Queen Kathrynne.

"Queen Kathrynne?"

"Yes, Lance?"

"Ben is requested at the castle's hospital wing by Evan."

"All right. Ben is on his way."

Ben got up from the circular bed and followed Lance to the bedroom door. Before he went out of the room, he said to Queen Kathrynne, "My father was a good man. He didn't deserve to die. Oh–I like his flower, too."

Queen Kathrynne grinned. "Thank you, Ben."

He smiled back and closed the door behind him.

***

"Ben?"

"Yes?"

"Is that you?"

Mrs. Begbie turned to Ben and Elizabeth, who entered the room. "Evan's still a bit sedated. He needs rest, so keep it brief."

"All right Mrs. Begbie, we understand," said Elizabeth.

Mrs. Begbie left the room, cracking the hospital room door to suggest no secrets could be exchanged between them.

"So how are you feeling? Better?"

Evan gazed up at Elizabeth in his bed and smiled slightly. "Yeah."

"It seems weird that we ended up here, huh, Evan?" said Ben, trying to break the silence that was developing between them.

Elizabeth gave Ben a disapproving look.

"What I mean to say is, I'm sorry about your dad."

"It's okay. You didn't know he was the way he was." There was a silence between them that was broken when Evan added, "I'm sorry I deceived you about being a knight. Mrs. Begbie filled me in about Lyon. Thank you."

He turned to Elizabeth, who momentarily looked up and said, "Lyon blackmailed me. I desired to go on a date with you, and he used it to his advantage." He turned to Ben. "Sorry, Ben."

"Oh, don't worry about it. Lyon used all of us. The important thing is, we're all safe. And you're welcome about getting rid of him."

"So Mrs. Begbie says you'll be out of the castle's hospital wing in a few days," said Elizabeth, after an awkward silence. "That's exciting."

"Yeah, it is." Evan coughed. "Saint Patrick visited me earlier."

"Yeah? What did he say?" said Ben.

"He said how proud he is of you. He says you're going to be a great protector of Ireland."

"He said that?"

"Don't be modest. What you did was incredible," said Elizabeth. "I'm proud of you too."

"How's our patient doing?"

Ben turned and saw that Saint Patrick was standing at the hospital door's arch, holding his cane to prop him up.

Mrs. Begbie had by this time returned to the room. She held a plate of food and a syringe.

"It's time for Evan to take his medicine, by the orders of Queen and King Rowzand," she said.

She placed the food on the side table and, with a long needle, pricked Evan's free arm.

"Is Evan going to be all right?" asked Elizabeth, her eyes filling with tears.

"The truth is, I don't really know," said Mrs. Begbie. "He may or may not.

Lyon roughed him up. I guess we'll have to wait and see. I think it's time for you two to leave. Evan needs his rest. You may visit him in the morning."

"All right. Come on, Elizabeth."

Ben was about to assist Elizabeth out of the castle's hospital wing when she pushed Ben's arm off hers.

"I'm staying," she said. "Evan needs me."

"Elizabeth, did you hear what Mrs. Begbie said? Evan needs his rest," said Ben.

Seeing the sense of urgency in Elizabeth's demeanor, Saint Patrick asked, "Is it all right if Elizabeth stays in the room with Evan just until he wakes up? I see that he has fallen asleep."

Mrs. Begbie sighed. "I guess so. The medicine must have already taken effect." She picked up Evan's food tray and set it aside. "Let me know if Evan wakes up. I should then give him another dose of medicine." She then left the room, leaving the door propped open.

"I will," Elizabeth called out in the hallway. She did not know whether Mrs. Begbie had heard her, but she had guessed.

Elizabeth sat on the chair closest to Evan and closed her eyes.

"Let's go. Elizabeth will be fine. Besides, I have a few things to tell you–things that are important," said Saint Patrick.

With some hesitation, Ben walked with Saint Patrick out of Evan's room, out of the hospital's wing, and upstairs to a bedroom where they could have a private chat.

CHAPTER XXVIII

Saint Patrick

"YOU KNOW, IN my years as a bishop, I ministered to the Irish citizens, bringing them to the beloved Creator," Saint Patrick said after he and Ben were settled in two oak chairs in a large, round tower room a few corridors down from Evan's room.

"Yes, Elizabeth told me once before."

"I have a confession to make."

Ben felt his throat constrict. "What is it?"

"A week after you were born, a figure took you in the confines of a basket to keep you safe from harm. That figure was me. I took you to the twenty-first century because I thought it was the best place for you."

"Oh."

Saint Patrick could sense Ben's confusion, so he continued. "Lyon was going to kill you. Your mother and father had asked me if I'd be your guardian if anything were to happen to them, and I said that I would."

"Okay. So why did you become an ordained bishop?" Ben asked to break the silence that was developing between them.

"My becoming an ordained bishop mattered because it enlightened those who were lost and helped those who were still struggling with life's difficult decisions about a higher power or divine being," he said. "If it weren't for a divine being influencing me, I wouldn't have successfully helped people become closer to the Creator. Because of that influence, I impacted many lives and made them better. I have dealt with all types of people, including several kings. Because of my strong attraction in their lives, I successfully converted them to Christianity. I taught many wealthy women. Because of my influence on them as a teacher and bishop, many of those women became nuns."

"Okay. What else?" said Ben, wanting to hear more.

"Well, do you remember Cleary, the druid at Hamish's sentencing trial?"

"Not really, but what about him?"

"Well, I visited him. I might've told you earlier, but I don't remember if I did or not. It has been a few weeks since Hamish's trial."

"Why did you?"

"To get some guidance on finding you. I took you as a baby in the cover of the night to safety, as you know. Now that you are seventeen, I needed you and your friends to help me to fight Lyon," said Saint Patrick, getting up from the chair to stretch his legs.

"Wait. I'm still confused. So why did you need us in the first place? You could have defeated Lyon and been done with it, right?" said Ben. "You didn't need us."

"That's where you are wrong. I did need you and your friends. I'm too old and feeble to fight on my own; I couldn't do it. It was your father's dying wish that I train you to become the leaf'd prince, the protector of Ireland."

"Oh," said Ben.

"Here."

Saint Patrick dug in his cloak and found a torn and stained piece of parchment paper. He handed it to Ben, who immediately took it. It said,

> My dearest Saint Patrick,
>
> Would you be so kind as to train my firstborn son, Sir Benjamin Henry Rowzand, for the Three-Leaf'd Tournament when he comes of age at seventeen? (That is the age required—and beyond—to compete.) If you train Ben, I'm sure he'll get the stuff you're showing him. He's a smart guy.
>
> I'm afraid I won't be able to compete for the tournament this year, as I must go into hiding with Bridgette. Lyon has already demolished most of the villages here in the town square, and I'm afraid that if he finds Ben, he'd kill him.
>
> If Lyon happens to find us, please remember and honor your promise of being Ben's guardian.
>
> Thank you again!
>
> Sincerely,
>
> Sir Prince William Dagwood Rowzand, Prince of Ireland

Ben's eyes watered as he finished reading his father's letter. He folded it up again and placed it in his pocket. "May I keep this letter?"

"Sure, of course you may. May I continue?"

"You may. Sorry I interrupted you."

"It's no big deal. So where was I? Oh—right. I had gone to Cleary's to get some guidance on finding you. Upon entry of his house, I sensed he knew I was coming and why I was there in the first place. Good old Cleary! I could always count on him to help me center myself, bringing me back to the reason I wanted to find you.

"First he praised me for how great I was with the sons of kings, teaching them and finally converting them to Christianity.

"Second, Cleary asked me why I had baptized people and ordained priests to lead the new Christian communities and helped wealthy women to become nuns. I told him it was my calling. If it weren't for Cleary having full confidence in me, I wouldn't have had the self-belief to find you or the patience to train you.

"And there's one more thing: your father made a will."

Ben's mouth became dry. "What? You mean this letter you gave me isn't it?"

"Oh, no. Yes, the letter was something your father wanted me to give you when I thought it was the right time, but no, the letter's not his will."

"Then where is it? Am I mentioned?" Ben asked eagerly.

"Unfortunately, I don't know where your father's will is located at the moment." Saint Patrick sat back down in his oak chair. "Queen Kathrynne has it stashed away somewhere. And yes, you are mentioned."

"Well, do you think she'll let me see it if I ask?" said Ben, getting up and glancing out the window, seeing the rolling hills and houses around his grandmother's castle. He needed a distraction from what Saint Patrick was telling him, as it was all too confusing now.

"I don't know if she will. And if she does give it to you, I don't think it's a good idea for you to see it right now."

"But why?"

"Because you are too overwhelmed by Evan being in the castle's hospital wing, and you are heated by what I'm telling you."

"I'm not heated at all. All I want is to see my father's will. Is that too much to ask?"

"All right … Ben … I'll ask Queen Kathrynne if you can see your father's will the next time I see her," said Saint Patrick. "I'm not guaranteeing she'll say yes to it, though."

"I'm fine with that."

"Good."

"So you must know I was there at the time of your mother's and father's deaths," Saint Patrick added, his voice cracked and frail.

"Why didn't you save them?" Ben instantly wanted to know. He sat back down on his oak chair, listening intently.

"I would've saved them, but I couldn't. Your father and mother didn't want me to."

"Why?" Ben asked to break another silence.

"Your father told me that he didn't want me to be held as a hero in the eyes of the Irish people," said Saint Patrick. "He wanted you to be held as that inspiring hero. He was done with all the stigmas of heroism."

"What about my mother? Didn't she have a say in this at all?"

"She agreed with everything your father laid out in his will–the training, the tournament–everything."

"Then why did my father choose me? Why not someone else?" said Ben.

"Why do you think?"

"Because ... he believed in me ... because he knew I had the strength to conquer what I choose to do at the moment."

"Exactly," said Saint Patrick. "Don't dwell on the past. Look toward the future. Your father was a brilliant man–even though he chose to keep that notion to himself. Now let's go. I'm sure Queen Kathrynne has dinner prepared for us. I'm starving."

"Okay. May I first visit Evan in the castle's hospital wing? I'm sure he wants to see me."

"Sure. But be quick. Oh, before I forget, here's some soda bread for you and Elizabeth to share. Don't let Queen Kathrynne know I have it. She'd kill me if she found out."

"Where'd you get this?"

"The castle's galley. It's not as good as mine."

Ben laughed. "Thanks."

"You're welcome," said Saint Patrick.

As Ben and Saint Patrick left the tower room, Ben pondered about all Saint Patrick had told him, in silence, as he continued down the hallway to the castle's hospital wing, the soda bread Saint Patrick had given him safely concealed inside his pocket.

CHAPTER XXIX

Ben McNealy

"**B**EN, IS THAT you?"
Elizabeth was still sitting in the chair beside Evan's bed, her arms folded in her lap. She looked up only when she sensed someone else was in the room.

"Yeah, it's me. Have you've been here this whole time?"

"Yes. Where else would I go?"

"I don't know. Maybe to get some food?"

Ben reached into his pocket and pulled out something wrapped in parchment paper. "Want a snack? It's the castle's soda bread; I don't know if it's any good. Saint Patrick seems to think so, because why else would he take some? He told me to give it to you, as you might want it."

"I don't want it."

"We can share it."

Elizabeth gave Ben a dirty look. "Ben …"

"Okay. How's Evan?"

"No change," said Elizabeth.

"Do you think he'll wake up soon?" Ben asked, taking the soda bread out of the parchment paper, breaking off a chunk, and eating it.

"Mrs. Begbie seems to think so," said Elizabeth. "The only question is when."

"Has he woken up since I left to talk with Saint Patrick?"

"No."

Mrs. Begbie came into the room holding a long needle and a syringe. In it, Ben guessed, was the same medicine Evan had received earlier when he had visited him. "It's time for Evan's second round of medicine," she said. Carefully holding the needle, Mrs. Begbie pricked Evan's free arm. Once done, she said to Ben and Elizabeth, "The castle's hospital wing is closing for the evening. No guests are allowed past ten o'clock."

"Okay," said Elizabeth. "Ben and I are leaving. 'Night, Mrs. Begbie."

"Good night."

Elizabeth linked arms with Ben, and as they were making their way to the door, something caught Ben's eye—movement.

"Look," said Ben. "It's Evan. He's responding. I saw his hand move."

"I didn't see anything," said Elizabeth.

"No, really, I saw Evan's hand move."

"Son, I see Evan every few hours now, and never once have I seen his hand move," said Mrs. Begbie. "While it's true that he was once awake and alert, that doesn't mean now that he'll return to his original state—at least for the time being."

"Was Suzette, Evan's mother, here in the hospital wing? Maybe she can get him to respond more. Is she out in the lobby?" said Ben.

"Yes, she stopped by to see Evan for a few minutes; however, I don't think having her in now makes any sense," said Mrs. Begbie.

"But look, I'm not crazy. I saw Evan's hand move."

"No one is denying you saw Evan's hand move," said Elizabeth.

"Ben? Elizabeth? Is that you?"

Mrs. Begbie spun around from leaving the room. She had tears in her eyes.

"Yes, it is us, bud," said Ben. "You doing okay? You gave us quite a scare."

"I'm fine," said Evan, his voice cracking and tired sounding.

"I'm glad you're doing fine," said Elizabeth. She turned to Mrs. Begbie. "May we have a minute?"

"I'm afraid you may not. Evan needs to rest. You two may come back in the morning. But don't worry; Evan's going to be all right." Mrs. Begbie rushed Ben and Elizabeth out of Evan's hospital wing and closed Evan's door, and she walked down the hall, disappearing.

Right then, Queen Kathrynne appeared. She was holding what seemed at first glance to be a long piece of crushed-up parchment, but on closer inspection, it was plainly just a fancy piece of paper.

"Saint Patrick said you wanted to see your father's will," she said.

"Yes, I do," said Ben.

"Be careful, Ben. The truth is sometimes hard to swallow." Queen Kathrynne handed the piece of parchment to Ben. He immediately unfolded it and read its contents:

The Last Will and Testament of Sir Prince William Dagwood Rowzand:

I, Prince William Dagwood Rowzand, of sound body and mind, leave my fortune to my son, Sir Benjamin Rowzand– future protector of the Irish people. He also will receive all my magical abilities, encased in a gold locket I have had specially made for him by the goldsmith in the hope he will have the strength to fight magical foes who deem a threat to the Irish people.

He will be instructed and spiritually guided by his guardian, Maewyn Succat (Saint Patrick) until such time he is able to be known as the leaf'd prince in my absence.

When Lyon is at last defeated, I declare Ben's companions–whether they be boys or girls–be guides to him as he prepares to take on the role of leaf'd prince. And if Ben chooses so, I declare that if he has a significant other, they are crowned as rulers when he becomes king of Ireland, in succession behind King Diamond and Queen Kathrynne, of course.

Signed,
Sir Prince William Dagwood Rowzand

"What does this mean?" said Ben, as he reread his father's will.

"Your father has desired for you to rule Ireland in succession of your reign," said Queen Kathrynne. "Of course, you don't need to make a decision now. Focus on the tasks you were given as the leaf'd prince for the time being."

"Okay."

Saint Patrick approached Ben, Elizabeth, and Queen Kathrynne. He addressed Ben, asking, "How's Evan?"

"He's doing much better," said Ben.

"That's wonderful," said Saint Patrick. "And how are you doing? Any questions regarding your father's will?"

"Yes, I'm fine. I have many questions, but Queen Kathrynne … sorry … my grandmother has encouraged me to take it one step at a time."

"She's a wise woman."

Ben smiled. "I agree." He turned to Queen Kathrynne. "I will carry out my duty as leaf'd prince if that's okay with you."

"Of course."

"And what about Elizabeth?"

"What about me?" Elizabeth asked.

Ben turned to Elizabeth. "Will you join me as a companion to help me as the leaf'd prince?"

"Yes, I'm honored to help you," said Elizabeth.

"Great."

***

Ben, Saint Patrick, and Elizabeth walked down a narrow hallway to another room, led by Queen Kathrynne. As she opened the door with a key from her dress pocket, they were greeted by the smell of delicious food. They stepped inside.

"What's all this?" Ben asked, looking at a spread of food on a long, narrow table.

"I don't know whether Saint Patrick told you, but this is called the Leaf'd

Prince Affricating Dinner. It is honoring you and all you've done for Ireland and its citizens."

"Oh, this is amazing."

"Oh–before I forget–next week you'll be knighted as the leaf'd prince and officially start your duties," said Queen Kathrynne.

"Okay."

"Don't be disheartened, though; you'll be fine," said Saint Patrick, who sensed the sudden fear in Ben's eyes. "Queen Kathrynne believes in you, and so do I."

"And I believe in you also," said Elizabeth.

"I only wish Evan were here to celebrate with me," said Ben.

"This food smells delicious."

Ben immediately turned and saw a familiar face he longed to see. "Evan!"

"Hi, Ben."

"You're … all right."

"I'm a little weary from the medicine, but Mrs. Begbie says I'm going to make a full recovery soon."

Ben smiled. "Good."

"Shall we start the Affricating Dinner?" said Queen Kathrynne.

"We shall," concurred Ben, Elizabeth, and Evan together.

***

By the time eight o'clock rolled around, everyone was stuffed and ready for bed.

"Thank you for dinner, Your Majesty," said Elizabeth, who curtsied and left, walking to her room she was assigned, down a narrow hallway, to rest.

"Thank you for everything. You helped me beyond measure," said Saint Patrick.

"You're welcome. My pleasure."

"I don't know if this is any of my business, but should Ben go back to the twenty-first century?" said Lance, who had come in to hear the conversation between Ben and Queen Kathrynne and who broke a moment of silence and reflection.

"I never thought about that. Elizabeth, Evan, and I must go back and take my finals for high school," said Ben.

"Well, you must stay here in this era to begin your duties as leaf'd prince. After all, you earned it," said Queen Kathrynne.

"Here's a thought: Maybe we can bring Ben and his friends' tests here," said Lance. "It'll be a stretch, but I think it can be done."

"I'd like that," said Ben. "Of course, I'll have to tell Elizabeth about it."

"Sure," said Queen Kathrynne. "What can be done to aid you and your friends is fine by me."

"I agree with Ben," said Evan.

Saint Patrick had been listening to everyone's conversations and finally addressed Ben. "May I have a private word?"

"Okay. What's up?"

"Since you're being ordained as the new leaf'd prince soon, there's something I must tell you."

"What?"

"In addition to being your guardian in the medieval era, I'm your great-great-great-grandfather."

CHAPTER XXX

Saint Patrick

B EN'S STOMACH CONSTRICTED.
"You're serious?"

"Yes."

"Your mother and father thought it'd be best for me to tell you now, before you venture into your duties as protector of the Irish people."

"Why didn't you tell me ahead of time? Why now?" Ben asked.

"I didn't want you to be distracted by what you knew in advance," said Saint Patrick. "I wanted you to be focused on the task at hand–the task of defeating Lyon–and you did that, and I'm proud of you."

"Did my parents know that you were family?" Ben asked. "And there's something else I want to know."

"Yes?"

"Were you the one who made the hedge fall?" said Ben.

"Yes, I was. I wanted to save Princess Lexis from Lyon's wolves," said Saint Patrick. "That is a part of the reason your parents wanted me to be your guardian—because I was already family in some form. That is one of the reasons I wanted to talk to you."

"What's the other reason?"

Saint Patrick pulled Ben aside and reached into his pocket, pulling out a necklace. "Here. Take it."

Ben took the necklace. It was gold plated, and at first glance, it appeared old, as if it had been given to Saint Patrick by a wise traveler many years ago.

"How did you get this?" was all Ben could muster.

"It was given to me on my many travels by a peddler who said to have magical abilities. I kept it in the hope you would have some use for it."

Ben held up the necklace and examined it. At the end of its chain was a three-leaved clover. It shone with brilliance despite its age.

"What do you want me to do with it, then?" Ben finally asked.

"Well, according to the peddler, you place a three-leaved clover on the charm of the necklace and blow on it. It's supposed to bring you luck, come the new year," said Saint Patrick.

"Oh. Thank you."

"Sure."

EPILOGUE

Ben McNealy

T HE MORNING SUNLIGHT streamed into the windows of Ben's room as he awoke. He soon reflected on all that had happened since Lyon's demise. He thought about how much Elizabeth, Evan, and Saint Patrick had sacrificed to get where he was now.

He thought about Mystic and how it was Lyon's ultimate act of selfishness that had caused her only home to burn up in smoke. Ben supposed that Mystic must have been heartbroken about it. She had lived there for years, celebrating milestones and grieving losses. He assumed that because of Lyon's wolves and Lyon himself, she would have to leave Ireland and find safety elsewhere. At best, that was the impression he had from overhearing other creatures' conversations in the castle.

Queen Kathrynne, filled with empathy for Mystic, said she'd order the finest builders and crafters in all of Ireland to rebuild her tree house home—at least that was what Ben heard as he was eating lunch out on the patio with Elizabeth, Evan, and Saint Patrick. Upon hearing what Queen Kathrynne had done for her, she was filled with joy at the prospect she'd get to see her tree house standing again, and she humbly accepted the offer.

Lance had been given the task of burying the box that Lyon's evil spirit was residing in by Queen Kathrynne, and he took it seriously. He threw it into a river near the castle's outer boundaries and watched it drift away like an abandoned boat wandering in a sea.

Builders and crafters got to work on rebuilding Mystic's tree house, on the orders and guidance of the queen.

Karoline, meantime, had ventured beyond Ireland's boundaries to see what the world had to offer her. It was Ben's understanding that the reason she wanted to travel was that, since she respected her father's wishes of not rebuilding the Green Leprechaun, she'd go across the boundaries of Ireland instead—to keep her mind free of the awful memories of what had happened here in Ireland.

***

In a month, Karoline lost her father to an illness that plagued the kingdom. Ben was unsure how it had started or who had it, but he had compassion for Karoline nonetheless. Karoline had mentioned to Ben once that she'd always cherish the fondest memories of working for her father, and he was glad he had bonded with her at that moment as a friend.

Ben was told later that the peasant Jeremy had left Ireland to cope with the tragic death of his wife because it was fresh in his memory. Despite this,

Ben understood. He couldn't have dealt with such a tragedy as his own wife passing before his very eyes; it'd be heart-wrenching.

Notwithstanding his victory of winning against Hamish in a trial for Hamish's life, Hert McGawn ultimately decided to leave Ireland, as it was too expensive to keep up with the demands of running a cart. He left without notice or explanation, leaving a note behind that read, "Sorry, I must go."

Aside from what had happened to him and the people he had met–some of whom left Ireland or got killed by Lyon.

Ben smiled. He was, at long last, glad it was over.

Saint Patrick stayed in Ireland, as he wanted to support Ben in his newfound venture as leaf'd prince, and Ben was grateful for the support.

Taking the three-leaved clover out of his pocket, he placed it on the necklace's charm Saint Patrick had given him, upon a table, and blew. Some dust and green sparkles flew into the air and out of an open window.

Ben grinned. Everything indeed was going to be all right.

CPSIA information can be obtained
at www.ICGtesting.com
Printed in the USA
LVHW111137041119
636249LV00001B/112/P